The Forgotten

M. STRINGFIELD

ISBN 978-0-9984378-1-1

Coverless Books

coverlessbooks.com

DEDICATIONS

This book would never have been completed without the love and encouragement from my husband, my children, and the friends I hold most dear.

For Jonathan, Gabriel, Isaac, Brandy, Saira, and Nicole. It would have been impossible to get this far without your support and guidance.

A special thank you to anyone who has taken the time to pick up this book.

CHAPTER ONE
Evelyn Moore

I walk with my head down, a cigarette pressed between my lips. I only look up to acknowledge the murmurs of congratulations from those who have stopped to watch. I give them a slight wave, or a quick nod as I move past. I don't have time to stop and talk. I am going to The Chasm. Today is the day I am reunited with my daughter.

The wind stings my face, pressing against me as I march forward. The sun hangs low in the sky. Its golden rays shine down from behind patches of thin, white clouds. It's not much, but it helps illuminate my path as I leave the bright lights of the city behind me. The snow is falling hard. Those thick, white flakes are beautiful as they catch the rays of the sun, each one glistening in the air before fluttering to the ground.

Felicity is a wonder during winter. I think about turning around to catch one more glimpse of its tall buildings, and thin, winding streets, but I can't stop until I reach The Chasm. In only a few short moments I will be surrounded by desolation. It won't be long now. The air pressure is beginning to drop, and the closer I get to The Chasm the worse it will become.

I take another long drag of my cigarette. The smoke blends into the fog closing in around me. I pat the pocket of my coat, reassuring myself that my breather is there in case the weather takes a sudden turn. It can happen in a matter of seconds. The oxygen will thin, my lungs will ache, and I will suffocate. I wonder if I would still be able to hear the sirens wailing from this far out.

I smile to myself at the thought of those sirens. While most residents hear a warning when they sound, I hear my daughter. Those sirens. They remind me of the night Char was born. She was kicking and screaming while the sirens blared beyond the hospital walls. It wasn't safe to go outside. The wind whistled as it arched through the cracks between buildings, the dust rattled against the walls, but that wouldn't stop the patrols from taking her away.

I had only minutes with my daughter, but I will always remember the head of blonde hair that covered her pink scalp. I remember her eyes being the color of a clear midnight sky: deep blue. They were filled with life, with hope.

I was forbidden from touching her, but I ran a finger over her cheek while the doctor had his back turned. It was soft, softer than I had expected. That's when I knew I loved her. Even though I wasn't supposed to, I loved her from the moment she was born. That was the last time I saw her.

"Evelyn! Hey, wait up!"

I hear the sound of feet pounding snow, and labored breathing beside me. I don't have to look up to know who it is. There is only one person that would work so hard to catch up with me on a day like today.

"Patricia, " I say, the cigarette bobbing in my lips.

"I'm sick of this winter shit," Patricia says, breathless. "Thought they would have at least loaned you a car, let you drive all the way to The Chasm. I don't care what anyone says. The freezing wind is as bad as the dust storms."

I nod in response. I'm in no mood for small talk. The closer I get to The Chasm, the bigger the knot in my stomach grows. It won't be long now.

"You do know that once you get there, you will have to walk back, right? This isn't a one way trip," Patricia says. "Giving you a car is the least they could do."

"They offered." I take one last drag from my cigarette, and let it fall to the ground at my feet. It sizzles as it hits the snow. "I refused. I wanted to walk."

"Coldest day of the year, and Evelyn wants to walk. Fine. You like to torture yourself. I get it. But you could have at least gotten the car for me," Patricia says with a laugh. "You made sure she was coming, right?"

"Char will be there," I say. "She's qualified. I found out three weeks ago."

"Have you thought about what you'll say when you see her?"

I shield the wind with my hand, and turn my face to Patricia. Her black curly hair flays out from beneath the cap she wears. It's made of silver spun cotton as soft as silk, pulled down tight. Her ears are studded with diamonds, three on each lobe. They create a beautiful contrast against her dark, smooth skin. She is an attractive woman, even with the thick creases around her eyes.

"No. I don't know what I'll say yet. I figured I would know when I saw her."

"That's right. There is no real way to prepare for something like that."

I look at my friend and strain a smile. She moves a little closer, enough to make our shoulders touch, and then she nudges me softly in the side.

"Everything will be okay, Evelyn. You'll see. Char is very brave for choosing to become a patrol. Don't you ever forget that. Our cities need as many of them as we can get."

"I'll only get her for three years." I swallow, fighting off the lump in my throat. "I've waited all this time, Patricia. All this time and she will die in three years. Then she will be gone again. Just like that."

I've never understood how anyone could choose to take a job that ended in certain death. Yet, we have enough patrols to keep us safe from worry. Now my own daughter has chosen the same path that many before her have. She will patrol our lands for three years, and then her term will end. She will end. Those are the rules.

"And after those three years it will be Alexander's turn to cross over. The probability of both of your children becoming a patrol is low, Evelyn. You know that. So, when it's all said and done, at least you'll have Alexander. Besides, you've let go of Char once. It won't be hard to do it again."

I stop walking long enough to pull the pack of smokes from my jacket pocket. I take one out, place it between my lips, and then motion for Patricia to come close. She cups her hands around mine, blocking the wind as I light the end.

"I'm sorry," Patricia says, quietly. "That was insensitive."

"It's fine," I tell her. "You're right. It'll be easier once her brother is here."

Patricia and I don't say much more as we continue our walk toward The Chasm. The further we move from the city, the darker our path gets. The sun is beginning to set, and the shadows of decaying trees hover over us. They are an interesting contrast to the trees that surround the border of the city. Those are big, and lush, thick enough to act as a fence around the perimeter. Those trees are full of life. There is no life around The Chasm. Almost everything here has been destroyed, decayed, or abandoned. Even the white snow has turned brown.

From here I can see the bridge that crosses over the center of The Chasm. It arches high into the air, surrounded by thick patches of fog swirling with the wind. It serves as the only pathway between Char's world and mine. Around this bridge is a large chain-link fence that shimmers red with the hue of the setting sun. I can see the faint silhouette of the guard growing into focus, standing and waiting right outside the gate.

Only a few more feet to go, and I will get to see her. I will never again have to walk this path without knowing what my daughter looks like, what she smells like, or the curve of her lip as she smiles. Eighteen years, and I have known nothing more than her name.

"It's depressing here," Patricia finally says. She rubs her mittens together for warmth. "No life, no lights, nothing to look at. I don't know how those patrols can stand it."

"It's their job. I'm sure they get used to it."

The Chasm is nothing but dying earth. The land here is decomposed, and disintegrated. The ground is mossy in the spring, and cracked in the summer. No grass grows here, not anymore. Even the trees are brown and brittle. I imagine them shattering at the slightest touch. Most of the homes that were once here have since collapsed, leaving nothing but empty, broken shells where they once stood.

The land here is a strange juxtaposition to the city jutting into the sky behind me, filled with life. That's why the only people who travel this far out are the ones that are required to: doctors and nurses, truck drivers with food rations, or the coroner to inspect the dead.

"Name, please," the guard states as we approach. He stands in front of the gate, his back almost touching the metal. The black color of his uniform creates a stark contrast against the silver of the fence.

"Evelyn Moore. I'm here for Char Moore," I tell him. I flick the ash from my cigarette, while Patricia rubs my back through the thickness of my coat.

"One moment," he says. He flips through a few pages on his clipboard. "I'm sorry. I don't see anyone by that name. Can you spell it?"

"Char. That's C-H-A-R. It's short for Charlee, with an L-E-E at the end. I'm not sure if she uses her full name or not, but I had given her the nickname Char before she left. I was told she would be crossing over."

"She, as in a female? Named Charlee?"

"Yes, my daughter," I say. "She was named after her father. Do you need the entire backstory, or can we move on?"

The guard gives me a look, one eyebrow raised. Then he slowly tilts his head down before flipping back through his clipboard. "Ah yes. Here it is. Charlee Moore. Female," he says, smirking. "I'll let them know you're here."

"Good," I say.

"She's coming! Can you believe it? She's almost here!" Patricia exclaims, tugging on my arm. "I'm going to ask her about my boy. You don't think she'll mind, do you? She might not know him, but I bet she does. If he's got a loud mouth like his momma everyone will know him."

"I'm sure it's fine, Patricia. I'm sure she won't mind."

Patricia has been my friend for years. She was there for me when Char was born, waiting right outside the room. She was the first person to console me after the nurse whisked the baby away; the first one to hold my hand, the first one to tell me I was being ridiculous for crying.

Just as Patricia was with me when my babies were born, I was with her when her son came into the world. Only ten minutes old, and he was placed into the arms of a patrol and sent out over the bridge. He was off to Calloway, like all of the other children. When it was all said and done, Patricia straightened herself up in bed, flattened out the blanket with her hand and said, "Damn. I think I have some milk about to spoil in my fridge."

All these years, and this is the first time I've heard her speak of her son. Thinking of him makes her eyes light up, highlighting the golden rings around her pupils. I had always assumed that Patricia considered our children to be an afterthought: something that comes to mind on nights when you can't seem to sleep, or when you've had a little too much to drink. I always figured she didn't care about them much. Not like I do. But I suppose no matter how hard we try to forget, there are some things that will haunt us forever.

The guard mumbles into his hand radio, and the gate begins to rattle.

CHAPTER TWO
Alexander Moore

I place the worn wrench down on the pile of snow beside me, and spin the front wheel of my bike. My fingers hurt. They've been numbed from the cold. I look out to my left, at the row of small houses lining the streets. Everyone else is indoors. Some of the homes have broken windows, some have front doors that no longer shut, but they still provide some solace from this harsh winter. I can't remember the last time it snowed this hard.

As the tire continues to whirr in front of me, I hold up my hands and examine the tips of my fingers. They've turned a strange shade of red, almost purple. I shove them beneath my armpits to warm them back up, and turn my attention back to my bike. The tire must be misaligned. It jumps to the left at every full rotation.

"What are you going to do with a bike in this weather, huh? Go skiing down The Chasm?"

"No, Harry. I'll be giving you the middle finger when I ride by your slow ass trudging through all this snow," I say. "That's what I'll do with it."

I place my hand on the spinning tire, and it jolts to a stop. I wiggle my fingers, trying to warm them back up again. Then I press soft fists into my spine, and arch my back. It feels good to finally stretch.

"Oh yeah? I think it'll be you face down on the ice, and me giving the finger, thank you very much," Harry says. His dimples stand out against his dark skin as he laughs. He's quite the charming ass. Not like me: tall, gangly, and awkward. "Besides, it'll probably get stolen like the last one."

"And the one before that?" I smile. "Third time's the charm, right? Anyway, I'm not worried about it. They were probably dismantled and sold for food, which means whoever took the damn things probably needed them more than I did. But I'll keep this one locked up so no one can get it. It'll be fine."

"Whatever you say," Harry says, shaking his head.

"Look. It's starting to come together nicely, isn't it? I got the front wheel I was looking for. Found it over in Hoffman's Dump. It took me three hours of rooting through trash, but I found it. The rim's a little bent though."

"Alex, it's a tire," Harry says. "You could have strapped a brick on the front, and I wouldn't know the difference."

"That's because you're stupid."

Harry punches my arm, hard. I barely feel it beneath all the layers I wear: two shirts, a thick sweater, and a coat so large I could tuck another human beneath it.

"Look. I brought you a hat," Harry says. He holds up an oversized knitted cap. "Found it by The Chasm. Figure some kid went there, got spooked, and dropped it while running away."

I snatch the hat away from him and put it on, making sure it's pulled down enough to cover my ears. I let out an exaggerated sigh, and pat the top of my head. When I shaved my hair off last week I forgot to think about how cold it would get when the weather turned. I wanted something different. A fresh start, I guess. I was tired of looking young and vulnerable. Unfortunately, the short hair only draws more attention to my oversized ears.

"Wow! Thanks, Harry," I say. "Let someone else freeze tonight. I haven't had a hat in years. You didn't happen to find any gloves with it, did you?"

Harry shrugs, and shakes his head. He crosses his arms over his chest, and leans back against the tall metal pole next to him. It reaches up about twenty or so feet in the air, and at the very top sits a speaker shaped like a horn. There are dozens of these speakers placed sporadically throughout Calloway. Their purpose is to announce the safety levels of the city every morning, along with the expected weather for that day. That's why most people are indoors right now: Not only because the threat level is elevated, but because we received a frostbite warning early this morning.

"Sorry. You know gloves are hard to come by," Harry says.

"I know, I know." I shove my hands into my coat pockets. "Wishful thinking."

11

"Hey, Alex," I hear a small voice say. "Nice hat! Where'd you get it?"

I turn around and see Mara stumbling towards us. The wind pushes against her, and she keeps her head tilted down to shield her face from the falling snow. Mara is like a shadow, following Harry and I around wherever we go. I don't know if she has other friends, and I don't bother asking her. There's something to be said about having a friend that will come to your house in the middle of a dust storm, while the sky is black as night and the sirens wail, simply because she likes the company. Mara is a loyal friend, and loyalty is hard to come by.

"Harry found it for me," I say, smiling. "Pretty nice, right?"

Mara stands next to me now, ankle deep in snow. I don't know how she stands it. I can tell she doesn't wear socks beneath her shoes, because her jeans are about two sizes too small. She reaches a red, chapped hand up to wipe the bit of snot dripping from her nose. Then she uses that same hand to shove a strand of messy blonde hair from her eyes.

"Yeah, it's great," Mara answers. She shifts her weight from one foot to the other, and tugs the front of her thin coat closed. It has no zipper, only a faint bit of worn metal where one used to be. "What's with the bike? It's too cold to ride."

I shrug. "I'll get to where I'm going faster, so the cold won't matter much."

"I guess that's kind of smart," Mara says. She pulls her coat a little tighter. "Where's Char? Have you talked to her today?"

I look down at my feet, and nudge a bit of snow with the tip of my shoe. "Talked to her a little bit this morning."

"Today's her day, right?"

"Yeah, it's today."

"You'll be alright," Mara says with a smile. "My brother left last year. It wasn't so bad."

"Your brother isn't a patrol." Harry spits into the snow, and wipes his mouth on his sleeve. "Totally different situations. He doesn't have an expiration date."

"Don't say it like that," I say quietly.

"Well, it's true isn't it? Besides, it's not like you don't have other family waiting for you when you cross over. Sure, you won't have your sister anymore, but you'll have parents, right?"

I take a step closer to Harry. "Stop it. Please."

Mara wedges herself in front of me, and puts her hands in the air. "Both of you need to stop. Char's your sister too, Harry. Maybe not by blood, but she's still family."

"Not in the way it counts," Harry says, his voice soft. "I don't have anyone waiting for me on the other side. Not like you two do. They wouldn't let me cross over even if I wanted to."

Mara walks to Harry, and puts her head on his shoulder. Harry never found out who his real family was, which means that by Felicity's standards he does not have one. Char and I have been the only family he's ever known, but like Harry said, not in the way it counts. I will never forget the day I caught him in our backyard, thin and starved. He was grabbing handfuls of gravel, and sucking off bits of dirt to fill his bloated, empty stomach. I can still remember those bony ribs protruding from his skin, and the way his eyes sunk deep into his skull.

Char was eight, and I was only five, but we had been on our own for a while by then, and we knew how to care for ourselves. That's why we decided to take Harry in. We fed him what food we had left, gave him some of my old, worn clothes to wear, and let him sleep on one of our extra blankets. He has been with us ever since.

"Don't worry, Harry," Mara says. "Char can find something out once she's in Felicity. She'll find out about where you belong."

"I don't want to talk about it anymore," Harry snaps.

Before I get the chance to argue, the speaker above Harry rattles to life. It belts out static, and an ear-piercing screech. Harry stumbles forward, and throws his hands over his ears. Mara topples back into the snow with a gasp.

"Attention residents of Calloway," the speaker blares. The words make my teeth rattle. "Charlee Moore, please report to The Chasm. I repeat: Charlee Moore, please report to The Chasm. We thank you for your cooperation, and wish you the best of luck with your patrols."

"It's time," Mara says, brushing the snow off her pants.

The front door of the house creeks open, and Char steps out. It's the first time I've seen her in her patrol uniform, and the sight of those dark green clothes makes my throat tighten.

"I'm here, I'm here. I lost track of time." Char stumbles on the tilted concrete steps. She straightens herself up, then runs her hand over her short, cropped hair. "You guys coming or not?"

"Yeah." I clear my throat. "We're coming."

Char walks over to me and pats the top of my head. "Hey, nice hat."

"I found it for him," Harry says. "Over by The Chasm."

"Nice find," Char says, smiling. "Time to get going. Don't want them to think I've changed my mind."

Mara tucks a strand of knotted hair behind her ear. "Is it okay if you guys go on without me? I'd like to stay here. I can keep an eye on your place now that everyone knows you're leaving. Make sure no one tries to break in."

The Chasm sucks the life from everything that surrounds it. The air is thick, the clouds are low, and the wind never stops blowing. Like most the people here, Mara is afraid of The Chasm. We all have that same fear lingering in the back of our minds: That we will fall down into that black abyss, and no one would ever hear from us again.

"Don't worry about it, Mara. You don't have to come," Char says.

"Great." Mara's eyes light up, and her lips curl into a slight smile. "Have a wonderful first day. Please come back and visit as soon as you can."

"Of course," Char says. "Thanks for watching the house for us. The boys should be back in a couple of hours."

Mara stands on her tiptoes and waves goodbye. The sun has begun to set, casting a red hue over everything it touches. Only a few more hours left before the sky is black, and we have no light left to illuminate our path. I wonder, briefly, if it would be worth it to stall, to think of some way to keep Char from crossing over, but I know in the end it won't matter. Today is her day to cross, whether I like it or not. Instead, I keep my mouth shut, and the three of us slog through the deep snow as we head toward The Chasm. We don't say much of anything as we walk.

We know we've gotten closer to The Chasm when the houses begin to fade behind us. They've become nothing but blotches of brown, and gray, and black. Calloway looks best from a distance, when the people and homes are nothing but a blur. But as the town is at its best, the edge of The Chasm is at its worst. Most houses left here have all been destroyed. From what, I'm not sure. Now they lay in piles around the muddy snow, collapsed and decaying. The few left standing look ready to crumble into nothing at the slightest breeze. The Chasm sucks the life from everything it touches. Even the trees here are dying.

"Did you remember your paperwork?" I ask Char.

"I remembered," she says.

I try to keep focused as Harry and I walk Char to the end of our city, but my heart begins racing the closer we get. I can already see the bridge jutting out from behind patches of thick, white fog where the center rises high into the sky. The bridge sits in the center of The Chasm, surrounded by a rusted metal fence. A single guard stands in front of the gate.

Once Char begins to cross, our lives will change forever. No matter what happens next, things will never be the same. My sister will become a patrol. It will be her job to keep our cities safe. Then in three years she will be gone, just like that: An afterthought to everyone except for me.

The guard straightens himself out as we approach, adjusting his belt, and fidgeting with the buttons on his shirt. His hair is slicked back, and his cheeks are chapped from the cold.

"Charlee Moore?" The guard steps forward. He is now holding a radio transmitter in one hand, and he keeps his other hand resting on the gun clipped to his belt.

"That's me," Char replies.

"I'll need to see your transfer papers, and your identification," the guard says.

Char reaches into her back pocket. She pulls out a wrinkled piece of paper, and her plastic identification card, and then hands them over to the guard. He squints as he examines them, holding them up into the light to get a better angle. The guard looks at Char, then back down at the papers, reads them over again, and then looks at Char one last time.

"Welcome to the patrols," the guard states with a grin. "Your mother is waiting for you on the other side." He presses a button on his radio, and brings it to his lips. "All clear. You can open it."

The guard steps to the side as the gate creaks, and swings open. Char takes one step forward and pauses, looking down at her feet. I shove my hand inside of hers, and look out over the bridge. Even this close I can't see the other side. The center of the long, thin bridge rises up so high that the other end is impossible to see. In my mind I imagine Char's body disappearing through the low, thick clouds as she crosses that centerline. I droop my head, and nudge the snow with my toes.

From behind me I hear the sound of heavy footsteps approaching. They are frantic, and fast. My sister tightens her grip on my hand, squeezing hard enough to make me wince. Something must be wrong. I try to turn around to see what's happening, but Char's hand slides up my arm. She grips my elbow tight and twists, making it impossible for me to move.

I glance at Harry who is biting his bottom lip, and staring at The Chasm. He wipes his nose on the back of his coat sleeve, oblivious to the footsteps approaching. I turn back to Char to ask her what's going on, but before my lips can even part the guard draws his gun. I watch as Char's paperwork flies up into the air, and drifts away with the wind.

"Step aside," the guard commands.

I stare down the barrel of the gun with the guard's words repeating in my mind. Step aside. I could hear him say it, but I haven't any idea what it means. Should I shuffle a bit to the left? Maybe I should run as fast as I can in the opposite direction. I could duck, and cover my ears. All of those things I know I should be doing, and I can't seem to do any of them. Instead, I cannot stop thinking how cold the metal of the gun must be in this weather. I focus on the bit of rust that encircles the muzzle. There are scratches on the right side of the barrel. The hammer looks off, tilted a bit too far to one side.

"I said move!"

Before my brain can send the signal to my feet and tell them to run, Char barrels into my side. The two of us crash to the ground with such force that my head whips to the left, bashing against the snow. My ears are ringing. I can hear Harry's voice shouting, but I can't make out his words. All I know is that the three of us are lying on the ground now. The snow is soaking through the fabric of my pants.

That's when I hear the gunshots. The sound pounds through my skull like fireworks. Between the gunshots I can hear the sound of young voices shouting. They are yelling at the guard, at each other, but the only words I can make out are over and bridge. The guard's deep, strong voice screams for backup. The next few seconds feel like hours as the noises begin to fade. They are replaced by the sounds of bodies as they hit the snow.

Thump, thump, thump.

"I have to do something," Char pants in my ear. "I need to help."

"You can't," I whisper. "I won't let you."

"Everything will be fine. Just don't move, and whatever you do, don't look."

I look the moment Char pushes herself to her feet. I can't help it. I don't move, but I sure as hell look. My eyes are drawn to the blood as it soaks through the white of the snow, turning it a strange shade of pink. It looks like candy as it spreads.

"Holy shit. Holy shit," Harry sputters.

Three kids are dead, at least from what I can see. They look angelic as they lay in the snow, their arms and legs bent at strange angles. Not a single one of them look older than ten. I think I recognize the boy closest to The Chasm, but it's hard to tell with all the blood gurgling from his lips.

My eyes pan over to the guard lying motionless in the snow. Blood oozes from the wounds in his stomach. His mouth is opened wide, and his eyes are glazed over. The gun is still in his hand, pointed straight out in front of him. When I look around us I notice there are patrols in the distance. They run towards the chaos, but are too far away for it to matter.

Char is crouched down next to the guard. She pries the gun from his rigid fingers, and raises it in the air while she hurries to her feet. In front of her stands the only person still alive: A girl, shot in the arm. Without hesitation Char aims the gun at her chest and pulls the trigger. The gun clicks. The girl flinches. Nothing happens.

"You don't have any bullets left." The girl's voice is shaking. Her lips are quivering. Tears stream down her cheeks. "Just let me go. I... I have to get over the bridge. I promise I'll come back. Please."

The girl's voice fades as she repeats the word please over and over again. Then she stands there, silent and shaking, eyes darting back and forth between the open gate, and my sister. The girl wants to cross over. She wants to be in Felicity, the same as the others now dead in the snow. It's a craving they have. They are willing to die if it means getting a quick glance at the other side.

"Don't do it," I whisper.

The girl begins to run with her eyes focused on the bridge. The other patrols begin to run, too. They draw their guns, and aim at the girl. They shout at her, demanding for her to stop. The girl pays no attention to them. Those patrols are still too far away. Right now, the only thing standing in the girl's path to freedom is my sister.

I close my eyes and brace for the roar of the patrol's guns. I wait for the cadence of their bullets drumming the air, and the spray of blood across my face. Char's blood, because she will get caught in the crossfire. I'm sure the others wouldn't mind killing one of their own so long as the girl is dead before she reaches the other side.

My muscles tighten, and my heart races. I throw my arms over my head, and wait for the storm to pass. But as I lay there, motionless, the only sound I hear is the wind whipping through the hole in the ground.

"She got her," I hear Harry whisper. Then he laughs. "Holy shit."

I sit up, and look back over at my sister. "She got her?"

Char has the girl by the front of her coat. Her grip is so tight that her knuckles have turned white. The girl's eyes are red, and swollen with tears. She begs for Char to let her go. The girl is pleading for her life now, screaming about the other side, about how she has to cross over, but it doesn't matter anymore. Char is a patrol. No one is allowed to cross that bridge.

It happens so fast that I could hardly register it: Char, dragging the girl to The Chasm. The girl's feet making deep lines in the snow. The word no is sputtered so many times that it begins to lose meaning. Then I hear her scream. It's a loud, ear-piercing scream that fades the farther she falls.

The girl is gone, way down deep in the belly of The Chasm.

CHAPTER THREE
Char Moore

I stand at the mirror hanging from the wall, and stare at my image inside the cracked glass. My eyes are red. There are dark bags under each one of them. I use a finger to pull down the bottom of my lower eyelids, and try to blink away the tired look in my face. I don't think I slept at all last night.

I turn around and look over the rest of the room. It feels empty. Though nothing has moved, and I can't take any of it with me, my bedroom doesn't feel as full as it once did.

"Stop it. Everything will be fine," I say aloud.

I stand up and walk to the center of the room. I put my head down, close my eyes, and wait for the announcement. It'll come any moment now. My windows will rattle, my heart will flutter, and my feet will shuffle me away.

"Attention residents of Calloway. Charlee Moore, please report to The Chasm. I repeat: Charlee Moore, please report to The Chasm. We thank you for your cooperation, and wish you the best of luck with your patrols."

There it is. I straighten out my coat, and head for the door. Every step is harder to take than the one before it.

"It's time," I hear Mara say as I walk out the front door.

"I'm here. I'm here. I lost track of time," I say as I stumble down the stairs. "You guys coming or not?"

"Yeah." Alex clears his throat. "We're coming."

I bite my lip, and try to smile as three of us say our goodbyes to Mara. The sun is beginning to fade, and the temperature has started its steady decline. We have to hurry if we're going to make it before it gets too dangerous. The boys aren't dressed for this kind of weather. Not like I am. They don't make anything quite the way they make gear for the patrols. My boots are thick, and lined with fur. They've even given me a matching olive-colored jacket, lined with wool. The only thing I feel is the ground crunching beneath my feet, and the mandatory breather bobbing up and down in my pocket.

The Chasm isn't too far now. The bridge is drawing near, and I'm able to see the center rising up in the dark sky. The rusted fence that surrounds it glistens with the red of the sun as it sets. My heart races at the sight of it. Only a few more minutes, and I'll be standing in front of that gate, waiting to cross.

"Did you remember your paperwork?" Alex asks.

"I remembered," I say.

I steal a quick glance at Alex, and notice him wiping his eyes with the back of his sleeve. When he pulls his arm away, the blue of his coat glistens with moisture. I clear my throat and turn my attention back to the gate, and the guard standing right in front of it. His eyes dart back and forth across the land behind me, and his right hand rests on the gun clipped to his belt. He stands up tall as I approach, his young face stern.

"Charlee Moore?" he asks.

"That's me," I tell him.

He asks for my paperwork, and I hand it over still wadded into a tight little ball. He flattens it out in his hands, and checks the picture on my I.D. The main job for any guard is to make sure the correct person leaves. It takes a lot of work and skill to forge a new patrol's documents, but it's been done once or twice in the past. Those who make it to the other side of the bridge can barely touch their feet to the soil before they're caught. Then it's down into The Chasm they go. Those few moments of freedom aren't worth death, in my opinion.

"Welcome to the patrols. Your mother is waiting for you on the other side." He brings the radio to his lips and says, "All clear. You can open it."

The gate creaks and begins to swing open. My heart is pounding the inside of my ribs, and I have to swallow hard to keep my nerves from lumping in my throat. I take one step forward, and then I stop. Alex shoves his hand into mine. I look at the guard to make sure I have the time to say goodbye, but he isn't watching me anymore. His eyes are locked on something behind me. Suddenly I am aware of the footsteps closing in on us. They are heavy, almost desperate sounding. The guard's hand drops down to his gun. Alex turns to look behind us, but I grip him tight, keeping him still. I know what is about to happen.

The guard whips out his weapon with trembling fingers. He points it at Alex, screaming at him to move, but Alex is frozen. I don't give him time to react. I tackle him to the ground, grabbing Harry by the coat sleeve as we fall. I wrap my arms around both of them, and pull them in close. I steal a quick glance over my shoulder and see four kids approaching The Chasm with guns clasped in their fists.

Before I know it the guns are going off. I don't know who fires first, the kids or the guard, but the sound of gunfire riddles the air. Blood litters the ground, splattering in every direction. The guard takes his first bullet to the stomach. Then he takes another, and another. He falls to his knees, and is able to fire two more shots before he collapses.

"I have to do something," I tell Alex. "I need to help."

"You can't," he whispers. "I won't let you."

"Everything will be fine." I say. "Just don't move, and whatever you do, don't look."

I push myself off the ground and run to the guard's side. I don't have time to stop and check for a pulse, and I don't need to. His eyes are empty, void of life. His mouth is hanging open with blood trailing down his chin. I crouch down beside him and pry the gun from his rigid fingers. I scan the area, looking for any survivors. There is only one person left. She's been shot in the arm. Blood drips down her fingertips, splattering to the snow at her feet. I aim the gun out in front of me and pull the trigger. It clicks, but nothing happens.

"You don't have any bullets left," the girl says. Her eyes are red, and swollen with tears. Her voice quivers as she speaks. " Just let me go. I... I have to get over the bridge. I promise I'll come back. Please."

I throw the gun to the side and look around me. More patrols are making their way toward us. They are running fast, but not fast enough. There is no way they'll get here in time. I stare at the girl as she stands before me, shaking. Her eyes flicker between me, and the open gate behind me. I know what she is thinking. She can run and risk getting caught, which means a trip into The Chasm, or she can stay here and get The Chasm just the same. I know she will run. I would run too, if our roles were reversed.

The girl bolts toward the gate. I take a deep breath and lunge forward. My hands hook on the front of her coat, and we both topple to the ground. I make sure to keep my grip tight as I scramble to my feet, and then I yank the girl up with me. She slaps at my hands, begging for me to let go. She kicks at my legs, and claws at my face, screaming words I can't understand. The girl is sobbing. Snot is dripping down her face. It makes me sick when it strings over her gaping mouth.

I stare into her panic-filled eyes and think about how easy it would be to let her go. Today is my only day of true freedom. In the few remaining hours, after the darkness blankets the sky and the sun begins to rise, I will belong to Felicity. I could let this poor girl go, and no one would think twice about it. I could blame it on nerves, on clumsiness. I could tell them that she simply got away. Let someone else track her down. Let someone else deal out her punishment.

But I am a patrol now. It is my job to make sure no one crosses that bridge. I tighten my grip around the front of her coat, and lift her up into the air. My arms jerk forward, and I let her coat slide out from beneath my fingers.

The girl screams as she falls into The Chasm. I stand with my toes close to the edge, watching her body fade into the black abyss.

"Hey," I hear someone say. "What the hell happened here?"

I turn my back on The Chasm, and see an older patrol standing a few feet away. He is close to the end of his term by the looks of it. His steel blue eyes are framed in dark circles, with thick lines around the edges. I look over his shoulder and see five more patrols behind him, inspecting the scene. One of them nudges the dead guard with his foot.

"An attempted escape," I tell him. "Four kids. They shot the guard."

"Fuck," he mumbles. He pulls the green cap off his head, and tucks in his coat pocket. He runs his fingers through his curly brown hair, and shakes his head. "When will these kids learn? There is nothing for them on the other side."

"One girl survived, but she tried to run," I say. "I threw her into The Chasm."

"I caught that. Good work. Name?"

I hold out my hand. "Moore. Char Moore."

"Archer Evans," the patrol says. He grabs my hand and gives it a good shake. "You're the new recruit. I heard you were crossing today. Welcome to the patrols."

"Not a great way to start," I say. "Do you happen to know why there wasn't more security around the gate? There was only one guard. No other patrols. That sounds like a big oversight."

Archer frowns. "I couldn't tell you. As far as I know there were no real threats that we were aware of. That kind of news travels fast. I'll look into it, though. Regardless of the threat levels there should be at least two other patrols at The Chasm. I'm not sure what went wrong."

"It could have been much worse." I look out over the bridge. "Am I alright to go? I was supposed to be over the bridge ten minutes ago."

"Go. Get yourself to Felicity. I'll clean this mess up." Archer points to Alex and Harry, still clutching each other in the snow. "Who are those two?"

They looked. Dammit, they looked.

"That's my brother Alex, and his friend, Harry. They came to see me off. Can you make sure they get back okay? It's getting dark."

"No problem," Archer says. "Get yourself over the bridge. Get some rest. You've earned it."

I give him a nod, and straighten out my coat. I run my fingers through my hair, cut right below my chin, and pluck my bangs back in place across my forehead. I take a deep breath as I turn my back on Calloway, and start my walk over the bridge.

CHAPTER FOUR
Evelyn Moore

Ten minutes. My head is humming; my pulse is rising. Ten minutes and Char is not yet over that bridge. I can't even see her silhouette against the darkening red sky where the bridge curves up at the center. It shouldn't take this long for me to spot her. There must have been some sort of error. Maybe there was an issue with her paperwork. They should have notified me if something had gone wrong. It's been ten minutes, and my daughter isn't even halfway over the bridge.

"This is taking too long," I tell the guard. He checks his watch. "Where is my daughter? She should have been here by now."

The guard shrugs. He holds his radio in one hand, and turns the antenna with the other. He looks out over the bridge, back at his watch, back at his radio. Then we stand in uncomfortable silence, the smoke of my cigarette billowing between us. I take one last drag and throw it down in to the snow.

I pull my phone from my back pocket and check the screen. It glows blue in my palm. No missed calls, but now it's been fifteen minutes and she still isn't halfway over the bridge. The guard fidgets with his radio, but it's good for nothing but static. No matter how many buttons he presses, nothing changes. The damn thing must be broken.

I cross my arms over my chest, and then drop them to my sides. "Someone needs to tell me what the hell is going on."

"Calm down Evelyn," Patty says. She puts a hand on my shoulder. "Maybe she was running late. They're waiting for her to arrive. That's all."

"No, I heard it," I tell her. "I heard them confirm she was on her way over. You heard it, too. We all heard it. So where is she? Hey!" I poke the guard in the chest with my finger. "Where the hell is my daughter?"

"Your friend's right. You need to calm down," the guard states. "Something happened, I'm waiting to hear back. We have people on the other side working on it."

The static of the radio disappears and the line falls silent. Suddenly a voice comes through: "Code Seventeen. I repeat, Code Seventeen!"

Within seconds four patrols emerge from behind us. They nearly knock me down as they walk toward the bridge with their weapons drawn. They begin to line up, shoulder to shoulder, at the base of the bridge. Their guns point forward.

"What the hell is going? What are they doing here?"

"Give me a damn second lady," the guard states. There are more voices shouting through the radio, giving orders I don't understand. I try to get a word in, but the guard holds up a finger and gives me a look. He presses the button on his radio, and pulls it to his lips. "I need a status on Charlee Moore."

I grab the pack of cigarettes from my pocket. My fingers tremble as I try to light another one. Goddamn nerves. Goddamn useless guard. Even Patty stands silent next to me, wringing her mittens together as we wait. I can't keep still, taking a drag every second, pushing my hair from my eyes, kicking the snow with my feet. Then a few moments later: "Charlee Moore. New recruit. She is heading over the bridge now. Patrols are sweeping the area. All subjects have been apprehended."

I slump my shoulders and sigh. She's fine. My daughter is fine. She is heading over the bridge, and on her way to me.

"Like I said," Patty says with a smile. "She's on her way."

My daughter is finally headed home. I should be relieved, but I have an uneasy feeling resting at the pit of my stomach. Something happened. There was a code seventeen, and I have no idea what that means. Was Char shot? Was she attacked? Is my son okay? The subjects have been apprehended. The thought makes me sick. Was there a murder? A robbery?

I will never find out what happened. Whatever caused the delay will be withheld from me. No one will tell me what that code seventeen meant. Not the guard, not a patrol, and especially not Char. All information regarding Calloway must never leave Calloway, good or bad. It is the same for Felicity. The two sides must always remain separate.

Patty taps my shoulder. "There she is."

"Finally," I mutter.

I see a figure in the distance walking swiftly over the bridge. She isn't limping. She isn't clutching her chest, or her arm. She has no visible wounds that I can see. I throw my cigarette down into the snow, and straighten out my jacket. I comb my long brown hair with jittery fingers and tuck any loose strands behind my ears. My heart is racing with every step my daughter takes.

She's here. She's finally here.

I want nothing more than to run up to her, wrap my arms around her, and tell her how much I've missed her. But instead, I decide to let Char come to me. She straightens out the front of her jacket, and fixes her short hair back into place. Her mouth curls into a timid smile, and before I know it she is standing in front of me.

All I can do is stare.

"Char," I finally say. The words pinch my throat. I take a slow breath, trying my best to keep it together. "You're blonde. Dark blonde. Like your father."

I reach my hand up, and lightly run my fingers over her hair. She pulls her head back a tiny bit, but never asks for me to stop. I had imagined my daughter would look like me, but I can see now that only her eyes are mine. They are dark green, almost hazel, with flecks of gold around the pupils. Stern eyes, hardened, like she has seen more than her soul could bear. She is thin, but not as thin as I am. Instead she is strong, built like her father. If it weren't for her eyes, I never would have guessed she were mine.

"Evelyn," Char says. "It's nice to finally meet you."

"Please, call me mom," I say, and then I drop my voice to a whisper. "If you want to, that is."

"Mom," she says.

I grab ahold of my daughter's hands, and rub my fingers over her palms. They are thick with callouses, lined with creases as deep as a river. She stiffens as I study her. Her eyes narrow, and I can see the muscles in her jaw grow rigid. I let her hands fall to her sides, and I take a small step back. Before I get the chance to apologize her arms are around my neck. She pulls me tight against her. I bury my face into her hair, and breathe in deep.

My daughter is home, and I am holding her for the first time.

I pull myself away and wipe my eyes with my coat sleeve. "I'm very happy to see you."

"I'm Patricia," Patty says, holding out her hand. Char accepts it with a nod. "It's nice to finally meet you, but if we don't get going soon it's going to get dark out. I brought food, and I don't want it to spoil. I bet you're hungry anyway."

"I could eat," Char says, her voice quiet.

I give her shoulder a squeeze. "Let's go then."

We walk into the city, toward the glow of the buildings that stretch into the reddened night sky: tall white slabs of stone as high as the gray clouds. Some stretch so far that they disappear into the sky, their tops nothing but a faded blur. The lights of the city can be seen even from here. I always imagined them as a beacon of hope for those crossing over the bridge.

Patricia walks in front, guiding us into Felicity. I keep Char close as we walk. I can't stop touching her, worried that if I can't feel her she will somehow disappear. Gone again. I keep a hand touching her arm, sometimes moving it to the small of her back or the top of her shoulder. They are light touches, never too hard or too desperate for the feel of her. Sometimes I look at her and smile, but she never notices. Most of the time she is staring at the ground. Other times she stares off into the distance, looking at nothing.

By the time we reach Felicity the sun is gone, and the sky is black and empty. The lights from the city are bright enough to illuminate the streets as we walk. We navigate through the narrow roads: the perfect size for walking, but too small for most cars. No one drives much around here anyway. Everything we need is provided for us, and all the stores we might want to visit are on every corner — Doctor's offices, clothing boutiques, furniture stores, grocery shops. Anything and everything we need is within a short walking distance from our homes.

The only exception is the library. It sits at the center of the city surrounded by a field of white roses, and paths made of stone. The library is the most beautiful building in Felicity. The roof is dome-shaped, and made with a pattern of glass prisms etched in gold. Every evening when the sun begins to set, the light bounces off those prisms and projects small rainbow patterns onto the surrounding buildings. They slowly rise into the sky as the sun falls.

Before long we reach the building I call home, at nine Willow Court. It's a white high rise with blue lights cascading down the front corners. The colors change depending on the weather. I thought that was a nice touch when I picked the place. The windows here are large and round, and you can see inside almost every unit perfectly: All of the furniture, the people, even the tiny knick-knacks sitting on their coffee tables.

I enter my code at the front of the building, and the glass doors slide open at the center. Our feet echo against the empty corridor as we walk to the elevator. Char is the first to step inside. She waits with her arms crossed, and her back leaning against the wall. When the elevator doors open, she is the first to step out.

"There's me," I say, pointing to the door with 4220 etched into the steel. After I unlock it, Char pushes the door open and walks inside. The heat of the room flows out into the hallway. It smells of lilac and fresh baked bread, my own custom scent. Every place has one.

"Make yourself comfortable," I say.

She smiles, and walks into the open living room. I can see her eyes drinking in her surroundings: the white walls and metal trim, the large leather couch, and the empty side tables made of hammered steel. Patricia spares no time getting started in the kitchen. She is waltzing about, pressing buttons and smiling every time they beep. I wait in silence, letting Char get settled in.

Patricia declares dinner ready, and the three of us sit around the large, round dining table. The food is lined up across the center: sliced ham, mashed potatoes, a bowl of buttered corn, a plate of rolls, and another bowl filled with chocolate pudding. Char takes a single slice of ham and plops it onto her plate. She takes one bite, and sets her fork down.

"Don't be shy, Char," Patty says. "There's plenty of food for all of us. You've got to be hungry. Take whatever you want."

"It all looks great." Char grabs a roll, and sets it down on her plate without taking a bite. "I don't mean to be rude, but it's been a long day. I'm not hungry."

I place my hand on her forearm and give her a smile. "It's okay. You don't have to eat."

"Well, I'm taking another slice of ham then," Patty says. There's a dollop of pudding resting on her chin. "Hey, Char? I have a question for you."

Char clears her throat and sits up straight. "Yes?"

"Do you know my boy?"

"What's his name?"

"Harold," Patty says, biting into her ham. "Harold Davenport. I think they call him Harry."

CHAPTER FIVE
Char Moore

I take another bite of ham to keep myself from speaking. Patricia waits, her eyes watching my every move. Her son's name is Harold Davenport. Harry. I should have known. They have the same dimples. Same smile. Same eyes. Harry Davenport. I have known him since he was two: Little Harry with his fists full of rocks, mud dribbling from his chin. As his mother shovels food into her mouth, he is huddled in the corner of his room sleeping with his coat on because it's too damn cold not to.

Patricia will never know the things her baby Harold had been through. She does not care that her son has her eyes, or that he sometimes walks to the edge of The Chasm late at night so he can see the lights of Felicity glowing over the horizon. Lights so bright that even stars can't shine there. All he ever wanted was to be over that bridge.

"No. Sorry. I don't know him," I say. "Calloway's pretty big."

I try to stomach another bite of food, but eating makes me sick. Everything here makes me sick, and the closer we got to this damn city the worse I felt. It's nothing like I thought it would be. The excitement I had to be crossing over faded as the lights of Felicity grew brighter. And I knew they would be bright. I knew because I would stare at them, too.

I could feed half of Calloway with the food on this table alone. Sure, we get rations. We get crates of near-expired milk, powdered protein we mix with oats, and drops of vitamins we add to rusty water. The rest we have to buy at the only general store in the center of the city. Buying one loaf of bread could take three weeks worth of work because the prices there are too damn high. One summer it took ten of us putting our money together to buy one whole turkey to bake, and we made sure it lasted a week. There was one small slice for each person. We ate it sitting on the floor.

Patricia waves her wrist haphazardly in the air, and takes a large bite of roll, half of it gone at once. "Well, never mind then."

I clear my throat. "Does he have any brothers or sisters? Anyone else I might know?"

"Unfortunately not. I know we're all supposed to have two, but I only had one." She leans in close and whispers, "Complications," and then smiles.

I look over at my mother. Her eyes are closed and she is rubbing her temples.

"I'm sorry to hear that," I tell Patricia.

In order to ensure a hearty population in Felicity, it is required of every couple to have at least two children. I like to think of them as recycled humans. Have two, and maybe one will survive long enough to make it over into Felicity.

"It's fine," Patricia says. She plops a spoon full of corn down on my plate. "You should eat some more."

"You're not worried about him?"

I immediately feel my face grow flush. I stare at the pile of corn, and push it around with my fork, hoping that no one else heard me. Why would I ask such a thing? What was I thinking?

"Worried? Honey, you've got to be joking," Patricia says with a flick of her wrist. "You know it's not safe for the children to grow up here. They're better off in Calloway."

Evelyn places a hand on my shoulder. Her voice is weak. "How about another glass of wine? Some water?"

"No. I'm fine," I tell her. "I'm sorry. I didn't mean to imply anything."

Patricia wipes her mouth with a napkin, and straightens herself up in her chair. "That's not what it sounds like. You questioned whether or not I was worried about my son. That sounds like implication to me."

Evelyn clears her throat. She scoots her chair back hard enough for it to loudly scratch against the tile floor. "Are you sure you don't want another drink? Anything at all?"

My heart races. I feel my ears growing hot. Patricia spoons another bite of pudding into her mouth while she stares at me, waiting for my response. I should have kept my stupid mouth shut, but the words slipped out. You're not worried about him? The thought makes me sick. I try to think of a way to turn the situation around, but there's nothing I can say to fix this

"If you ask me, it sounds like you think they're not safe over in Calloway," Patricia says. "As a patrol, I question whether or not you can fully understand your duties while being so misinformed."

Evelyn heads into the kitchen with an empty wine glass in her hand. "She is not misinformed, Patricia." I hear her pour more wine into her cup, and moments later she's back at the table. "Right, Char?"

I nod, and shovel another bite of food into my mouth. When I was younger one of the older residents explained to me why things were the way they were. He told me stories of a long, and terrifying war. How the border of trees were there to keep the others out, and to make sure we didn't wander where we shouldn't be. He tried to explain to me why I would never be able to see my mother, and to him it seemed to all make sense. But deep down inside I still felt betrayed. There is no reason good enough to torture the children the way they have.

Maybe it's true that the soil became tainted with radiation. They say the children began to die off, their bones too brittle, and their bodies too frail to survive. Maybe it's true that the ones that were lucky enough to survive were kidnapped and sold off; the more healthy children brought in the most money. Maybe that is why they built the bridge, and why they sent the children to the other side to live alone. The adults stayed in Felicity to rebuild, believing that both sides would be safer if they stayed separate. Maybe that is why the patrols were formed, why it's their job to maintain order.

Or, maybe it's all a lie.

Felicity was built to the sky while Calloway crumbed to ruins. I have a hard time believing that a society that claims to have the children's best interest in mind can be so quick to dismiss us. Saying, or even implying, that you think in such a way could be punished by death.

The silence in the room breaks me. I have to say something.

"You misunderstood what I was saying." I look at Evelyn. She is sitting rigid in her chair with her hand on the stem of her glass. Her eyes stare at nothing. "Look, I wasn't implying that the children aren't safe in Calloway, okay? Worrying about someone you love is natural, especially if we know they're alone. I used to worry about my mother because I knew she lived here by herself when my father died. That doesn't mean she's in danger, or that Felicity isn't safe. It's natural for us to worry. That's all I meant."

Patricia leans back into her chair, and uses her fingernails to pry a piece of ham from between her front teeth. Once it's been released, she smacks her lips together and smiles. "My apologies, dear."

Evelyn exhales a loud gust of air. She drops her arms to her sides, and hangs her head for a second before perking back up. She grabs her wineglass off the table, and takes a giant swig.

"I suppose it's time for me to head out," Patricia says. "You two should spend some time together, one on one. Eighteen years. Can you believe it? That's a lot of catching up to do. Char, it was nice meeting you."

"Same," I say.

Evelyn walks her friend to the door. They hover there for a moment, talking to each other under their breath, probably about me. I shove a roll in my pocket while their backs are turned.

Patricia steps through the doorway and into the hall. She turns to me one last time, and smiles. "Make sure you get plenty of rest tonight, Char. Tomorrow's a big day."

"I'm sure she'll be fine," Evelyn says as she pushes the door shut. "You take care." Once she's sure Patricia is gone, she turns to me. "I'm glad she's gone. Patricia can take some getting used to. I told her not to come today, but she insisted."

I walk myself into the living room, and sit on the edge of the couch. It's softer than I had imagined. Uncomfortable. "It's fine. Really."

Evelyn shrugs. " Do you want a drink? I have more wine, or there's whiskey. I have coffee, too."

"No, that's okay. I'm not thirsty."

"Just for me then."

I watch as Evelyn heads into the kitchen, and rummages through cabinets. She pulls out a small square glass, and adds some ice cubes. Then she reaches into another cabinet and grabs a bottle labeled Whiskey. After she removes the top, she waves it beneath her nose before pouring it into her glass. When she's done, she walks back into the living room and sits next to me on the couch.

"Do you mind?" she asks, pulling a pack of cigarettes from the side table drawer. I shake my head. "Bad habits die hard."

I wave a hand in the air as she lights the cigarette. The smell is stronger than I imagined it would be. Not many residents of

Calloway smoke, because it's too expensive to pick up the habit. I scrunch my nose, and try to hold my breath as the smoke fills the air.

"I'm sorry," Evelyn says.

"It's fine," I say. "So, what do you do here? Do you have a job?"

"Most of us work." Evelyn takes another drag of her cigarette, and lets the smoke drift through her lips as she speaks. "I like to paint. I have a few portraits down in the library, and some in shops around town. Nothing serious. I mostly do it for fun."

I never would have guessed she was an artist. Probably because everything in her place is monotone: white couch, steel cabinets, and gray walls. Black, white, or black mixed with white. I wonder if her paintings are the same: white canvases with splotches of black, and some swishes of silver.

"They pay you for that?"

"Of course. Not much, but enough to buy little odds and ends for myself. Most of our stuff is provided for us, like the furniture, this condo, the food. It's easy for us to get by here, not like it is in Calloway."

I sit up straight. "What do you mean? Why did you say that?"

Evelyn squeezes her eyes shut, and rubs her temples in slow circles. "Do you hear that?"

"Hear what?"

"The music. It's soft and quiet. I can't tell where it's coming from."

I stop and listen for a moment. "I'm sorry. I don't hear anything. Are you okay? You look a little pale."

Evelyn opens her eyes, and clears her throat. She smiles at me, but her face looks pained, like it hurts her to keep her eyes opened. "Yes, I'm fine. I didn't get much sleep last night."

"You said you knew things weren't as easy for us in Calloway. Why did you say that?"

"Did I say that?"

"A few second ago."

"Oh. Well, I didn't mean anything by it." Evelyn finishes off the rest of her glass, and heads into the kitchen to pour herself another. When she returns, her glass is more full than last time. She has to balance it funny in her hands as she sits. "It's a gut feeling."

I chew on my bottom lip. The hairs on the back of my neck stand on edge. "Don't you remember your time in Calloway? You came over that bridge the same as I did. Everyone here does."

Evelyn takes another swig of whiskey, and a long drag from her cigarette. "You're right. I came over that bridge once, many years ago. Much too long ago. My mind doesn't remember things like it used to. Old age." She flicks her cigarette into a glass bowl beside her. "But enough of that. Tell me about your brother. What does he look like?"

I clear my throat, trying to forget my last memory of him, sitting in the snow at The Chasm, surrounded by dead children. I told him not to look. "He's a good kid. He likes to be called Alex. He looks a lot like you. Same face. His eyes are blue though. A real light blue."

Evelyn smiles. "Blue eyes!" She takes another drink. "Just like his father. Is he tall?"

"He's tall for his age. He's about my height now, and I think he still has a few good years of growing in him. He'll probably be real tall when it's all said and done. Skinny as a pole though."

"Skinny as a pole," she repeats with a laugh. "Just—"

"Like his father?"

"Yep! Just like his father. He was tall, and skinny. Blonde like you, but with the brightest blue eyes you'd ever seen. He was wonderful. Smartest man I've ever met."

She leans back into the couch, melting into the cushion, with a smile lighting up her face. It's hard to feel emotion for a person you've never met, but as I sit next to her, watching her smile as she thinks of her family, I think I can grow to love her.

"Tell me about my father," I say. "What did he do?"

"Charles was a wonderful man. Best man I'd ever met," Evelyn says. She looks up at the ceiling and stares at no place in particular, like her memories of him are trapped between the steel beams. Then her face falls. "Are you sure you don't hear that music?"

"No," I say, shaking my head. "Maybe you should get some rest."

"Nonsense," Evelyn says, waving a hand in the air. She takes another big gulp of whiskey, draining the last of it from the glass. "We were talking about your father. He was brilliant. You were named after him. Did you know that? We thought you were going to be a boy until the moment you popped out."

45

I laugh. "Of course. No one names their daughter Charlee without reason."

"I think it fits you." Evelyn smiles. "You remind me so much of him."

"I wish I could have met him. I think I was nine years old when a patrol told me he had died. They never told me what happened though."

Evelyn takes a deep breath and closes her eyes. "Your father did a lot of great things for this city. A lot of great things."

Her head bobs to the side, nestling into the cushion. The cigarette threatens to fall from her lips. I pluck it carefully from her mouth, and put it out in the bowl beside her. Then I take the glass from her hand, and put it on the coffee table.

"Mom? What happened to my father?" Evelyn doesn't say anything. Her chest heaves up and down, and soft snores bubble from her lips. I clear my throat, and nudge her in the side. "Evelyn! Tell me how my father died."

She takes a deep breath, and looks at me with bloodshot eyes. "The Chasm, dear. He got thrown into The Chasm."

CHAPTER SIX
Alexander Moore

"Hey! Wake up."

I turn over in bed; a groan escapes my lips. My head is throbbing. I don't think I've been asleep for very long.

"I said wake up, asshole."

"Leave me alone."

"Alex, I'm not playing around. You need to get your ass up. This is important!"

"Fine, fine." I let out an audible yawn. "I'm getting up."

I sit up in bed and rub my swollen eyes with cold fists. I throw the blanket to the ground, my eyes still half closed, and struggle to get to my feet. After a few blinks I can make out Harry's silhouette standing in front of me, arms crossed.

"What the hell is going on? What time is it?"

"I don't know. I didn't look," Harry says. His eyes are bloodshot, and lines cover one side of his face. I can see his pajama top peeking out from beneath his dark brown coat. "Someone's at the door."

"What? Right now?"

"Yes, right now. They've knocked at least a dozen times."

"Shit," I mutter. I adjust my coat, pulling it back down around my hips. I stumble toward the window, and take a quick glance outside. Still dark. Everything is quiet. I turn back to Harry. "Did you check who it was?"

"Someone is knocking in the middle of the night. I'm not going anywhere near that door. Don't be an idiot."

"So you want me to do it?"

Harry shrugs. "Figured we both could."

"Maybe it's Char," I say.

"If it were Char, she'd walk right in."

"Then who the hell is it?"

Harry shakes his head, and then rubs his nose on the back of his coat sleeve, wiping away the dripping snot. It's cold. Not as cold as it has been, but it's still pretty damn cold. I can see my breath fading into the air in front of me every time I exhale. I can't imagine what anyone would want at this hour, in this weather. Three hard knocks pound the front door. The force makes the walls rattle. The sound makes my stomach turn.

"Okay." I take a deep breath, and run a hand over my shaved hair. "Maybe grab a broom, or a kitchen knife or something. Just in case."

"What are you going to do? Open the door and stab them? What if it's a patrol? Shit. Alex, what if something's wrong with Char?"

"Fuck," I mutter.

I dash out of the bedroom, with Harry following close behind. Three more knocks ring out before I can reach the front door. I fumble with the locks before throwing the door open.

Outside the snow is falling hard. A teenage boy dressed in short sleeves and dark jeans stands before me. His shoulders are hunched, his hair is soaked, and his body shivers. He holds something square and black clasped to his chest.

"Who the hell are you?" I ask.

"Are you Alex Moore?" His brown eyes are wide with desperation. They lock on mine, and he takes a step forward. "They said you lived here. They said you'd help me."

I lean forward and look out onto the street behind him, first left, and then right. The road is empty. The street lamps have faded to a strange deep-orange hue. It's the only bit of light I see. Everything else is black.

"Who the hell is they?" Harry asks. He stands shoulder to shoulder with me, blocking off the entry.

"Please. I'm looking for Alex Moore. The one who fixes the television sets. He fixed one for a friend once." He takes another step forward. "He needs to fix this for me."

"I'm Alex," I say. It's true that I've fixed a few sets for people in the past, but never in the middle of the night. Never like this. "I don't know who you are, and I was sleeping, so—"

"My name is Adam."

"Sorry, Adam," Harry says, stepping back. He tugs my coat and says, "Come on, leave this lunatic be. I'm tired."

"You can come back in the morning," I say, my hand readied on the doorknob. "It can wait until then."

"Wait," Adam says.

I turn my back on him and shake my head. When I try to push the door closed it bounces back open. Adam has shoved his big, black boot in the way. I keep a firm grip on the door, refusing to let it open any further. "Look, I'm sorry, but—"

"This is a radio," Adam says, placing the black box down on the step beneath him. "I need you to fix it."

"We're not doing shit," Harry yells from over my shoulder. "Get your crazy ass home and don't come back. Find someone else!"

I laugh at Harry, and shake my head again. "Look, you're going to—"

Adam reaches behind his back, his eyes never leaving mine. With shaking hands he pulls out a gun, and points it at my chest. I throw my arms up and take a step back, letting the door creak open. Somewhere behind me I hear Harry dive to the floor, but I don't take my sights off Adam. His eyes are wild, glazed over. His bottom lip trembles.

"Okay. Okay, I'll fix it," I tell him, trying my best to keep my voice steady.

Adam nods and licks his lips. "Good," he says. "You have five days."

"Five days," I repeat. "Not a problem."

Adam doesn't move. He keeps his gun up, with one eye squinted to keep out the falling snow. I hold my hands in the air, my only movement the rapid rise and fall of my chest. After a few moments of silence, he turns his back and runs. I wait until the darkness swallows him before I grab the radio, and carry it into the house.

Harry runs to the door, slams it shut, and locks it tight. He presses himself against the wood, and slides down until he's seated. He presses his palms into his forehead, and shakes his head from side to side. "What the fuck. What are we going to do now?"

I shrug. "We're going to fix his radio."

"Are you crazy? Alex, he pulled a gun on you! We need to get to The Chasm. We should find a patrol and tell them what happened. I'm sure they can track him down, and—"

"No one's going to The Chasm," I say. I crouch down in front of the radio and turn it over in my hands, inspecting each side. "Did you see him? Did you really see him, Harry? Because I did." I let my hands fall to my sides. My shoulders slump forward. "Something was wrong. I don't know what it is, but he wouldn't have threatened to shoot unless he was desperate. I have to fix it for him."

"I think you've lost your damn mind. Can we at least get some sleep first? We can talk about it some more in the morning."

"Fine. I don't think I can do much with this right now anyway. The power cord is missing, and who knows what's wrong with the inside. We should head out to Hoffman's dump in the morning. See what we can find."

"So you think you can fix it? Like dead serious, for sure fix it?"

"It's not in bad shape, all things considered. I can fix it."

"I still think we should tell Char," Harry says.

"Yeah, maybe," I say with a shrug.

"Hey, Alex?"

"Yeah?"

"Have you ever even fixed a radio before?"

I push myself to my feet, taking the radio with me. I walk it into the kitchen, Harry right behind me, and place it on the small blue counter.

"I'm serious," Harry says, grabbing my coat sleeve. "You've fixed a few televisions before, the fridge, old bicycles, but I've never seen you with a radio."

I grab him by the sides of his face, and use my right hand to pat his cheek. "Chill out, Harry. I'll get it done."

"And if you can't?"

I think to myself for a moment. "Then I suppose we're in trouble."

CHAPTER SEVEN
Char Moore

I can't sleep. I've been tossing and turning for hours. Evelyn had a nice bedroom waiting for me: A large room with a double-sized bed, and it's own attached bathroom. Marble floors. Steel trim. White everything, except the walls. Those are gray. The soft, cushiony bed pisses me off. The lavender smelling soap in my private bathroom pisses me off. I have five pillows on my bed, four of which I have already tossed onto the floor. I want nothing more than to scream.

I scoot myself deeper into my bed, and cover my head with the blanket. The damn lights have been shining outside my window all night, saturating the darkness, making it impossible to settle in. The window takes up an entire wall, letting every ounce of brightness shine inside. The snow is so white it nearly glows, even at forty-two stories up. I throw the blanket off my head and stomp over to the window.

There is a small red button right next to it. I've been eyeing it all night. I press it down with my thumb and the shade falls down, drowning out the light. The room falls black.

"Of course," I mumble.

I press the button again and let the shade fly up and blind me, because I shouldn't have it this easy. No one in Felicity should have it this easy. It's damn unfair. I sit back down on the edge of my bed, and put my head in my hands. I miss my brother. I wonder what he is doing on the other side of the crack. I wonder if he's having a hard time sleeping like I am, worried about the days ahead, or if he's fast asleep in the room he once shared with Harry because he was too afraid to sleep alone.

I hold my stomach and groan. Harry. Harold Davenport. I've wanted to know his name since the moment I took him in. He understands that if he doesn't find out who his family is, he will not be allowed to cross over. There would be no one on the other side to help him transition. I wonder what would be a worse fate: Living with the woman I met last night, or ending his life down in The Chasm.

I stand up and begin to pace the room. I walk to the window and press the button. The shade flies down. I press it again, and it goes back up. Down. Up. Down. Up. I walk to the bedside table, and pick up a small ornamental turtle sitting on top. It's hideous, made of some sort of heavy metal. Silver in color, of course. I'm starting to think Evelyn might be colorblind. Her home looks sterile, untouched. It's like she is too ashamed to live in it.

I like to think that is the case; that she isn't oblivious to what is really going on. She lost her husband to The Chasm. He was thrown down into the hole, like so many others. I tossed a girl to her death yesterday, and I would do it again if I had to. The thought makes me sick. I wonder if the ones who lived here when the lands were first divided would be ashamed of what we have become. We are a world divided, with skeletons filling the crack.

I look at the clock. Any minute now my first official day as a patrol will begin, and I haven't slept a single moment. I rub my eyes, and yawn. There is a knock at the door.

"Yeah?"

"Char, it's Mom. There's a gentleman at the door for you."

"I'll be right there."

My muscles are aching from tension. My eyes burn from exhaustion. Today is going to be a long day. I grab my pants from the floor and slide them on, then pull my jacket off the back of the couch. The roll I stole at dinner is still sitting in the front pocket. I pull it out and take a bite. I run my fingers through my hair, combing it back into place.

The patrol I met yesterday is standing in the kitchen with my mother. He is holding a cup of steaming coffee in his hands. Evelyn slouches next to him. She has dark rings beneath her eyes. Her hair is knotted at the back of her head, and she has a silk robe pulled tight around her waist.

"Archer," I say. "What brings you here?"

"Someone has to fetch the new recruit," Archer says. "You look like shit. Have some coffee. Your mom made some for us. It's decent."

"I have travel cups," Evelyn croaks. "So you're not delayed."

"Yeah, sure. Coffee sounds good."

I lean against a kitchen cabinet while Evelyn pours some coffee, adds some cream and sugar, stirs. When I could get my hands on coffee I would always drink it black. I won't mention that now. She's probably making it the way she likes it; the way she thought I would like it too.

"Here," she says, holding out the Styrofoam cup.

"Perfect, thanks." I take a sip of the coffee, and try not to cringe.

Archer walks to the door and readies his hand on the knob. "You ready, Char?"

"Yeah. I'm ready."

"Will you be back soon? You can stop by any time you'd like," Evelyn says.

"As soon as I can."

After some quick goodbyes, Archer and I are out on the streets with the sun rising into the sky. I walk beside him, fidgeting with my cup of coffee, taking short sips to keep the cream from coating my tongue. I can't live the last three years of my life drinking this shit.

The streets are empty. Our feet echo on the pavement because there is no snow on the streets. That's something new. Mounds and mounds of white snow, parted in the center, creating neat little paths for us to walk on.

We turn the corner, and I spot another person — a bug-eyed woman with rainbow feathers in her hair. She is sitting on the bench outside of a flower shop, talking to herself, waiving her hands, and frowning. She screeches something that could be considered laughter, and then mutters incoherently under her breath. A strong gust of wind carries her scent to us. It reeks of stale cigarettes and mildew, like she was dampened and left in a dark room to rot.

"We had a meeting last week about her," Archer says, his voice low. "She's bringing down the morale of the city. Lots of complaints from the residents. She'll probably end up in The Chasm soon."

I look over my shoulder at her one last time. Her face is buried in her hands and her shoulders shake. I think I hear another shrill cry before Archer and I turn the corner. We walk down the street labeled Royal Lane. I pay attention to the street names so I can learn my way around. Otherwise, everything thing looks the same. I stare up at the tall buildings and shake my head. When I look back down I'm nearly run over by a large, round man with shoulder-length hair.

"Excuse me," he mutters while shuffling past.

I stop in my tracks, and turn to get a better look. That face is familiar. "Jeremy?"

The man looks around, confused. "Yeah?"

"I thought I recognized you! You crossed over a couple of years ago. How's your sister? She came to Felicity earlier this year, right? Back in May, I think."

"I'm sorry, but do I know you?"

"I was a friend of Lana's. Char Moore. You don't remember me?"

"No, I'm sorry," he says. "I've got to go. Sorry."

I watch him turn the corner, my cheeks red with embarrassment.

"Well. That was awkward," Archer laughs.

"It was weird is what it was. Do you know him?"

"Nope. Never seen him before in my life," Archer says. "But that doesn't mean anything. I don't pay much attention to the people around here."

I feel uneasy as we continue our walk. I look up at the city jutting into the sky to keep my mind off of what happened, looking for anything different. All white buildings, or shades of gray so pale it looks like white. Perhaps one building has round windows and another has square, or one has a door made of glass instead of steel, but the similarities are eerie. They are reproductions of perfection. Rows and rows of the same.

I clear my throat. "Where are we headed?"

"We have a meeting the beginning of each week," Archer says. He takes a long sip of coffee and smacks his lips. "We always meet in the library at the center of the city. We'll be briefed about anything that might have happened the week before, what things we need to work on, that kind of stuff. You'll get your official patrol schedule telling you when and where you work. It changes quite often, so don't get used to one place in particular. It can also mean that sometimes you work in Felicity for a month straight, without ever stepping foot in Calloway. Or vice versa."

"So it could be weeks before I see my brother again?"

"It's rare, but it's possible," Archer says. "I've been helping out the new recruits for awhile now. They usually take it easy on you guys. I wouldn't worry, but you should be prepared for anything."

"How long have you been a patrol?"

"My term ends in about six months," Archer says.

"Have you decided which way you'll go yet?"

My heart falls the moment the words escape my lips. Blame it on lack of sleep, or nerves, or even my own stupidity. Either way I regret it. I feel my face growing hot. I asked a man how he plans to die in six months time. A man I've met twice.

Archer laughs, and shakes his head. "Haven't thought about it."

"Sorry," I say. "It was a stupid question."

"It's fine. You're a newbie. Always thinking about the end when you're only at the beginning. I thought about it a lot my first week too, and then after that you don't think about it anymore. It's just the way it is."

"Just the way it is," I repeat.

"Most people choose a bullet to the head," Archer continues. He puts a finger to his temple, and makes a clicking sound with his tongue. "Quick. Painless. Whatever. But," he lowers his voice, "aren't you the least bit curious about what's down there? In The Chasm?"

"What's in The Chasm is death, Archer," I say with a laugh. "That's the point."

"I know. I was joking. There," he says, pointing. "The library."

The library is a large, square building with a round roof shaped like a dome. It juts out into the sky like a cluster of diamonds shimmering beneath the sun. The building itself is white, no surprise there, but everything is trimmed in gold: the doors, the windows, even the sharp creases of the roof. The library sits in the center of an open field in what I can only assume to be bright green grass in the summer time. Now it's covered in snow, but even that looks beautiful, untouched. There are thin paths cleared from each corner of the lot to the front of the building, with marble benches placed every couple of feet. The air here smells fresh, like rose petals, even though no flowers bloom in the winter.

The wind picks up and ruffles my hair, sending a shiver down my spine. I retreat into my coat, pulling the collar up around my ears, shielding myself from the cold. Only a few more days of winter, and the weather will warm back up. I can't wait.

Archer laughs, and pats me on the back. "Come on, turtle. Let's get you inside before your shell freezes."

The inside of the library is as breathtaking as the outside. The prismatic ceiling projects a rainbow arch at the center of the room, and the sun warms everything it touches. Books cover the walls from bottom to top, with golden shelves in between. I look around for Evelyn's paintings, but the walls are only covered in books.

Lined along the center of the room are four long tables, set up in pairs. Dozens of patrols are sitting around them. Archer and I sneak into the meeting, and stand off to the side.

A man with cropped blonde hair and tanned skin stands at the front. He presses his eyebrows together in the middle, and his forehead folds into three thick creases. He scans over the crowd, and then his brown eyes lock on mine. When he smiles, the rest of the room turns around to stare. My cheeks grow flush. I tuck my hair behind my ear and clear my throat. Archer rams an elbow into my side.

"I'm Charlee Moore," I say. "You can call me Char."

"Welcome to the patrols," the man at the front states.

"Welcome to the patrols," the others repeat.

"You can call me Tyler," the man says. "We are happy to have you on board."

"Thank you," I mutter.

"Char will be shadowing Archer for the week," Tyler announces to the room. "Everyone else will go about their patrols as usual, as per their envelopes. Char, your information will be in with Archer's. Any questions?"

"No, sir," I answer.

"Good. On to business." He clears his throat. "We had a bit of a disturbance last night where several residents of Calloway tried to force their way over the bridge. It ended in death for the guard, Gordon James, and the four residents of Calloway."

I can still see the guard lying in the snow, his mouth wide, and his eyes open and staring. I remember the way his blood bubbled from the wounds. He had a name. I'm sure someone out there misses him.

"For those of you who have yet to read the report, Char here witnessed the entire incident," Tyler continues. I feel my cheeks growing hot again. "I am pleased to announce that although she was not yet officially on duty, she handled the situation with great poise. Thanks to her, the only surviving escapee has been thrown into The Chasm."

I can hear frantic whispers among the patrols, but I keep my eyes straight ahead.

Tyler raises his voice to cover the noise. "While we commend our new recruit for doing justice in this situation, the rest of you need to pay closer attention while on duty. If any of you hear or see anything, and I mean anything, that might be considered threatening to our way of life, it must be reported, and appropriate action must be taken. I don't ever want to see that kind of shit again. We've had this conversation one too many times."

A small woman with brown hair braided down her back stands up. She raises a hand in the air. "But sir, we've been doing what we can. We can't be blamed when something like this happens."

"A guard is dead," Tyler says. "Four residents of Calloway are dead. If it is your job to keep our land protected, to keep the people safe, and yet five people die, the only conclusion is that you have failed to do your job. Every single one of you can be held accountable for what happened last night. If you don't agree, I'm perfectly fine with finding someone else to take your position. You can do all the complaining you want while you're sitting at the bottom of The Chasm. Is that in any way unclear?"

"No, sir," she says as she huffs back into her seat. "Sorry, sir."

"Archer, you start the line," Tyler says. "Let Char follow your lead. Everyone else line up behind them. Let's get this day started."

I follow Archer as he walks between the rows of tables. Everyone is staring at us. We stop in front of Tyler, who stands next to a large plastic bin. It's filled with envelopes lined up one after the other. He thumbs through them, and pulls out the one marked ARCHER/CHARLEE.

"Well done yesterday, newbie," Tyler says. "The patrols can use more competent people like you. It's rare these days." He reaches under the table and pulls out an olive-colored backpack. "This is yours. Inside you'll find everything you might need - food, water, additional breathers, stuff like that. Your gun is in there too, I expect you to have it clipped to your belt at all times."

"Thank you," I say. I grab the backpack, and sling it over my shoulder.

Tyler turns to Archer. "Take care of this one. I can already tell she'll be great."

"Yes, sir," Archer says, smiling.

He snatches the envelope away from Tyler, and I follow him to the other end of the library. He sits on the ground in front of a long row of shelves marked HISTORY. I slide myself down next to him, and immediately begin rummaging through my backpack. I find the gun, check the safety, and then strap it inside of the holster on my belt.

"You're very popular today, Char," Archer says. "Quite a way to start."

"Well, it made me uncomfortable."

He laughs. "Of course it did. Now, let's see where we're stationed." He rips open the top of the envelope and pulls out a letter. He reads it silently to himself, mouthing the words, before carefully tucking it back inside the envelope. "We're going to be out by the edge of The Chasm today, on the Felicity side. They're ramping up security around the bridges. We don't want a repeat of what happened yesterday. Tyler's already pissed at us enough."

"It must be happening a lot then if he's that angry about it."

"It's happening more often than we'd like. If the population dwindles in Calloway, it will begin to thin out over in Felicity too. To sustain life on both sides, we need to keep incidents like this to a minimum."

"Huh. Interesting." I look out over the library. Most of the other patrols have gathered their things and started leaving, heading out to their duties.

Archer nudges my shoulder with his hand. "Spit it out."

"Seems funny, that's all. The whole cycle. We've been conditioned to throw people down into The Chasm, which most of them deserve, but then we're also supposed to make sure they are enough people crossing over. I never realized how counter-productive it all is."

"The system isn't perfect," Archer says with a shrug. "It's a learning process. Back ten, fifteen years ago things were different. From what I've been told, they used to let the assholes go, believe it or not. They'd do something wrong, and they'd get locked away. That's it. They'd let them stew in their own shit in some dump at the back of town, chained to a radiator or something. Then the asshole would get a stern warning, and be let go. And every single one of them did it again. They had that itch. And once they get that itch in them, they can't get rid of it. They did it again, and again, and again. Each time more worse than the last."

"People are idiots," I say.

"Nah. People are blinded by greed and desire. The thought of attaining something they've been otherwise forbidden from makes their mouths water. You keep something they desperately want right out of their reach, and they'll find a way to get it. Sooner or later."

"If only they knew," I say, quietly.

Archer folds his arms in front of him. "Knew what?"

"Everyone thinks Felicity is supposed to be better than Calloway. It's supposed to solve all of our problems, right? But, then I crossed that bridge, and..."

"And you hated it?"

"It wasn't what I thought it would be," I say.

"It's not only you. We all feel the same way. When you're conditioned to one way of life for eighteen years, it's difficult to accept anything else. I think it's harder for us patrols because our job is supposed to be about justice."

I lower my eyes to the ground, and pluck a piece of fuzz from my pant leg.

"I know what you're thinking," Archer says. "That our cities have a strange definition of justice. This isn't the kind of shit you signed up for. But let me ask you a question — after witnessing both sides of that bridge, would you have done anything differently? Knowing what you do now, would you have still signed up?"

"Of course I would have. I didn't sign up for me, Archer."

"None of us do," he replies.

"Then what brought you here?"

Archer looks down at the envelope in his hands, and traces a finger over the torn edge. "For my sister," he says, his voice soft. "She was eleven when she was killed. Chased down like a dog in the streets. Robbed for the shoes she wore, then strangled because she refused to hand them over."

"Archer..."

"Look, we all have our reasons for joining the patrols, and those reasons don't change the moment we cross over." Archer grunts as he pulls himself to his feet. He reaches his hand down, and gestures for me to grab hold. "Remember that when you see those bright lights in Felicity, and you want nothing more than to watch the city burn."

"Three years, and I won't have to worry about it. Three years and I'll be gone," I say. I grab ahold of his hand, and let him help me to my feet. "It's strange to say it out loud. It doesn't feel real."

"That's because the shock is still settling in," Archer says. "But trust me: after two, you'll be begging for the bullet."

CHAPTER EIGHT
Alexander Moore

I've been standing in the kitchen staring at the radio for the past hour. I wasn't able to get to sleep after what happened last night. I tried for a while before calling it quits. I only have five days to get the stupid thing fixed. It's taken me weeks to find the parts I needed to fix my bike, and even longer to put the pieces together. I'm starting to have my doubts.

I fish through the cabinet looking for my screwdriver. When I finally find it, hidden in the back behind a few glass jars, I use it to start taking everything apart. The screws are old. Not a good sign. It takes a lot of muscle to get the first one out. I place it on the counter and begin taking out a second screw when I hear Harry walk up behind me.

"How's it going?"

"Fine for now. I haven't done much yet. Just now starting to take the thing apart, so I can get a good look at the inside. So far I've only been staring at it, like somehow it will tell me what's wrong."

Harry laughs. "Well, did it?"

I shake my head, smiling. "Nope. Nothing."

"That's too bad. What's the plan?"

"Gotta get this thing open first before I know." I pluck another screw out, and place it on the counter with the others. "Almost there."

Harry pulls a bowl from the cabinet, and dumps a pile of dry oatmeal inside. He opens his mouth in a giant yawn as he walks to the sink, turns it on, and lets the brown water run for a few seconds. Once it clears up enough, still slightly rust-colored, he adds some to his bowl. He stirs the oatmeal around a bit, then opens the cabinet to his left and frowns.

"Seen the vita-drops?"

"Over there," I say, nodding towards the drawer next to the fridge.

Harry pulls out the bottle, unscrews the dropper, and adds three small drops to his bowl. He swishes it around with a spoon, and digs in.

"We need some fucking milk," he says with his mouth full.

"You're supposed to wait five minutes for the oats to soften."

"Too hungry to care."

I chuckle at the sight of Harry chomping away at his oats, and the way he shovels them into his mouth so fast that some has splattered on the floor by his feet. I finish removing the final screw from the radio, and gently wiggle the back casing off. I can tell how thick the plastic is once I'm holding the pieces in my hand. At first glance, it seems the inside is in relatively good condition.

Harry stands beside me, peeking over my shoulder. "How's it look?"

"Actually looks good," I tell him. "Which is surprising. I think the heavy plastic casing around these components made the radio relatively weatherproof."

"I have no idea what you just said."

I sigh, and roll my eyes. "The outside was thick enough that the inside didn't get ruined."

"Why the hell didn't you say that?"

"I did. You're just stupid."

"Have you ever thought about being less smart?"

"Sometimes," I say, laughing. I turn the radio over, and shimmy off the front. I turn the side nobs, and watch the red lines for the tuner move side to side. It sticks a little, but otherwise seems to work fine. The inside of the speaker seems fine too. A little bent, but nothing I can't fix. I put the pieces back down on the counter, and shrug my shoulders. "I don't know what Adam wants me to do. It looks fine to me."

"Have you tried turning it on? Maybe they forgot that part."

"It wouldn't matter because it doesn't have batteries. Get dressed and we can head down to Hoffman's Dump. I might be able to pull some batteries out of something else. It's the only way to really see what's wrong with it."

We stop at Mara's house on the way to the dump. Her place is set directly between our house, and the back of Calloway where the dump resides. She accompanies us without question, and it doesn't take long for us to fill her in on what happened last night. Now we've only got another mile or so to go before we reach Hoffman's dump.

"My brother had a radio once," Mara says. "His caretaker gave it to him. It was more symbolic than functional, because the thing only forecasted the same announcements we heard from the speakers outside. Things like the weather, and safety reports. It did it at this strange, three-second delay, like an echo. Only with these horrible high-pitched screeches between."

"One time I fixed this television set for Char's friend, and the whole time it was nothing but static," I say. "The screen was white, with these black lines, sometimes colored dots. All the sets were like that. But then I dropped my screwdriver on the top of it and all of a sudden I saw a picture of The Chasm. It flashed in real quick, and then disappeared. After that I couldn't stop picturing Char's friend sitting in front of the television, smacking the top, and watching The Chasm flicker in and out. It all seemed pointless."

Mara pulls her coat a little tighter around her chest. It's cold, but not as cold as yesterday. "Doesn't matter. Everyone wants electronics. My brother actually cried when I broke his radio. I knocked it off the table and it shattered. Pieces were everywhere."

"I never understood it," Harry says. "Why would anyone want something that never worked? What's the point?"

"Because they're rare," I tell him. "How many televisions have I fixed now? Three? And there are thousands of people in this city. Char used to tell me that having a television, or radio, or even my bike, is more dangerous than anything else."

"Yeah, I think that point was made very clear last night," Harry says.

We don't say much more as we walk down the path that takes us to the dump, each of us lost in our own thoughts. I can see the mound in the distance. The bits of metal piled on top glisten under the light of the sun. The sign out front is hard to miss. Its large white letters spell the word: Hoffman. Small white bulbs line each letter, always lit, even though it seems no electricity runs to them.

"What are we looking for?" Mara asks.

"Batteries," I say. "It would be great if we could find an antenna, or another radio we could salvage for parts if we need to."

"Alright," Mara says. "I'll take left then."

"I'll be on the other side," Harry states.

I wait for them to leave before I begin rooting through the junk in front of me. The trick with Hoffman's is realizing the outer crust of the mound has already been picked through. Most people want a quick grab, something valuable right on top that they can sell for food. They don't want to spend time digging to the good stuff underneath. Every so often I have to stop and warm my hands back up, but it doesn't take long for me to break through the layer of junk on top.

"I found boots!" I hear Mara squeal. "I can't believe it!"

I peek my head around the corner. Mara sits on a lump of plastic, pulling the soaked shoes off her feet. She shakes the snow off a pair of bright yellow boots, and slides her feet inside of them. A smile lights up her face.

"They're so warm." She jumps up and down. "Can you believe it? They fit! They really fit."

"Nice find," I hear Harry shout.

"Yeah, that's awesome," I say.

I turn my attention back to the spot I've dug out for myself, pulling out pieces of twisted metal or splintered wood, and tossing them to the side. I go to grab another fistful of junk when something strange catches my eye. A square corner, smooth and brown, juts out from the mound. It looks clean, untouched, despite being buried under a foot of snow and garbage. I'm still staring at it when Harry and Mara walk up.

"I found three batteries," Harry says. "It took a lot of work prying them out. There was a fourth one but it was oozing something brown, so I left it. The batteries look like the ones I saw in the radio when you took it apart this morning."

"I didn't find any batteries," Mara says. "But I found this short silver thing that looks kind of like an antenna." She holds up a small metal rod, and smiles. "Hey, what are you looking at? Your face is funny."

"I found this weird thing." I point at the brown corner jutting out of the mound. "It looks out of place, doesn't it? It's in good shape, whatever it is. Help me get it out."

Mara drops to her knees beside me. She starts digging with her hands, scooping up whatever she can and tossing it to the side. Harry hesitates, standing with his arms crossed, looking down at me with rigid jaw.

"I don't like it," he says. "It doesn't feel right."

I stop what I'm doing, and look up at Harry. "What do you mean?"

"I think we're in deep enough shit right now. You don't know what that is, or what it's doing there. After last night I don't trust anything anymore. We have the batteries. I think we should go."

"Harry, how long have I been coming down here?"

"I don't know, a year at least."

"Almost three years. And how often have I been able to find something like this? It's not electronic. It's not rusted metal, or melted plastic. It's different. It's…"

"It's got a handle," Mara says. "I think it's a case. Look, there's a lock here in the center. My brother packed one like this with some clothes when he crossed over. Wonder what it's doing here."

I start pulling on the handle, trying to get the case loose, when Harry taps on my shoulder. "Alex, we—"

I wave one hand in the air, shushing him.

"No, Alex—"

"Hold on. I almost got it."

"Look up!" Harry shouts, shoving the side of my head.

I tilt my face up, still holding the case by the handle. The sky has turned the color of rust. Gray clouds roll over the horizon, darkening the land as they move. I'm still staring at the sky when the sirens begin to wail.

"We have to run!" Mara shouts, but I can hardly hear her.

I look back down at my hand, gripping the handle. I can't leave without the case. I begin pulling as hard as I can, ignoring the screech of the sirens, ignoring the cries of my friends.

"Let it go!" Mara shouts, tugging on my coat.

Harry throws his arms around my waist, and tries to pull me away. I shove my foot into the mound, and use as much strength as I can muster to loosen the case. Harry might want me to let it go, but I use his momentum to help me pull. The case breaks free, and we both tumble backward. I stumble to my feet, helping Harry up as I stand. He brushes himself off, and then shoves me in my back. I'll apologize to him later. Right now we have to go.

The wind picks up. It howls through the lining of trees, drowning out the wail of the sirens. Mara is the first of us to run. By the time we reach the road, my legs are shaking and my heart is pounding. Still I run faster, even though my muscles burn and my lungs ache. I count the steps in my head, letting the rhythm guide me: one, two, three, four, one, two, three, four.

"We're not going to make it," Harry pants.

"Trees," Mara says, breathless. "Get to the trees."

We make a hard right, and head toward the thick patch of trees at the edge of the city. There isn't much cover, but it'll have to do. Mara's house is still too far. Once we weave between the thick trunks, and under the low branches, the three of us collapse. We huddle together in the dirt.

The trees begin to shake. All I can taste is dust. It coats my tongue, and burns my lungs. Mara puts her arm around me, and pulls herself a little closer. She shoves her face into my coat and coughs. I use the case to shield our faces from the storm.

That's when I see the bullet hole. One small hole puncturing the center of the case, with thick, dried blood caked around the edge. I squeeze my eyes shut, and wait for the storm to pass.

CHAPTER NINE
Evelyn Moore

I press my hand against the windowpane, feeling the chill from the glass spread through my palm. The wailing scream of the siren pierces the air. The dark clouds roll swiftly over the horizon, swallowing The Chasm as it moves. From this height I can see everything: the vast stretch of orange sky streaked with darkened clouds, the dust rolling over the land like a hurricane, and the people scrambling for cover.

"Here, tea," Patricia says.

"Thanks," I say, keeping my eyes on the horizon. "Put it on the table for me."

I hear the clink of the glass hitting the steel side table. Patricia puts a hand on my shoulder, and gives it a gentle squeeze. "You look worried. It's only a dust storm, Evelyn. We've had hundreds of them."

"No, that's not it."

"Are you worried about Char? The patrols have means to keep themselves safe. There are plenty of buildings, and they have those tents—"

"It's not that."

Patricia's footsteps fade as she walks into the kitchen. I know she is making herself a cup of tea because I can hear the distinct sound of clanking glasses, and water being poured into a cup. A few moments later she is back at my side, holding a steaming cup of tea.

Patricia takes a small sip, and smacks her lips together. "Well, are you going to tell me?"

"Tell you what?"

"Don't give me that tell-you-what crap."

I clear my throat. "It's nothing important. I had a strange dream last night. It's still bothering me."

Patricia takes another loud sip of her tea, and looks out the window. "Not another dream, Evelyn. You know you shouldn't be letting them bother you."

I sigh, and turn myself away from the window. I lean my back into the cold glass, and cross my arms over my chest. "I know. Believe me, I know. But this one was different. Anyway, like I said, it's not important."

"Well, if it was important enough to bother you, then it's important enough to talk about. Come on then. Tell me what this one was about."

I muster a smile, and turn my attention back to the storm raging outside. It's closing in on us fast. I can hear the faint roar of the wind growing louder. It won't be long before the sirens become pointless, the rush of the storm overpowering. I take a deep breath, and push a strand of hair behind my ear.

"I dreamt of Felicity. At least, I think it was Felicity. The entire city was destroyed. I'm not sure from what. It was nothing but a pile of rust, and ruin. Everyone else was dead or gone, I don't know. It bothered me."

"Oh, Evelyn," Patricia says as she places her tea on the side table. "As your doctor, I am required to tell you that there are a lot of reasons you'd have a dream like that. You know you're a worrier."

"This time it felt different, like it was about more than our city. Everything around me was destroyed. I was lying in a pile of dust somewhere. Maybe on a pile of rubble." I steal a quick glance at Patricia, who watches me intently as I speak. "I tried to run, but my legs wouldn't move. I was paralyzed." I look back out the window, and watch as the first plume of dust crosses into Felicity. "When I opened my mouth to scream, the sand poured in. I could feel it, hot and gritty, inside of my lungs. It burrowed into my eyes. It tunneled through every inch of my body until I became nothing but sand myself. Then, before I knew it, I was gone. Just like that."

Silence. Patricia doesn't say a word. I keep my eyes focused on the storm as it rages forward. I don't want to see the look on Patricia's face. I can feel her eyes staring at me, silently judging me. She must think I've lost my mind.

"It was only a dream, Evelyn."

"I know. I said it wasn't anything important."

There was something more to the dream, something that Patricia doesn't need to know. Beyond the destruction of our world, through the agonizing death that I endured, there was something much more unnerving: the music. It was a quiet melody, calm, never ending. It was as though someone left a music box opened, and it sang for the rest of eternity. It was playing while the city crumbled. It was playing while fire rained down from the skies. It was playing while the sand devoured my body. Even now I think I can hear it, quiet, resting at the back of my mind.

"Enough of that," Patricia says. "You've been under a lot of stress lately. Char coming home, and you waiting for her to cross over. It's been very hard on you. You've always been a worrier."

"You're right. It's probably just the stress."

Patricia sits on the couch, and pats the cushion next to her. "Why don't you sit and relax for a moment?"

I force a smile. "Yeah. That sounds nice."

I grab a pack of cigarettes from my pocket before sitting down. Patricia gives me one of her looks, the kind that's meant to shun me, but I ignore her. I pull out a smoke, and quickly light the end. My body sinks into the cushion, and I let the smoke fill the air above me. I'm exhausted. I nestle my head back, and close my eyes. I feel myself drifting away when Patricia nudges my side.

"Look," she says softly, pointing at the window.

I blink, clearing the blurriness from my eyes. "Holy shit."

Dust and wind pelt the glass, making it impossible to see. It's brown, and red, incredibly thick. The dust itself is made up of the smallest particles, but together they form a wall, pounding at my window. The sound is deafening. It's all I can hear. I turn to face Patricia. Her arms are waving. Her lips are moving, but whatever she is saying is lost in the sound of the storm.

I take another drag of my cigarette. "It'll be over soon."

Patricia shakes her head, and shrugs.

"It'll be over soon," I repeat.

Patricia shrugs again. She still can't hear me. With my cigarette resting between my lips, I push myself up from the couch and head toward the window. Something crunches beneath my feet as I walk. When I look down I see dust. A thin layer of red and brown dirt covers the floor. I bend down, and scoop some up into the palm of my hand. It's warm, and gritty. Behind me, I hear music. Soft, melodic music.

I whip myself around, but nothing is there. Still, I hear that music playing softly in my ear. I throw my hands over my head, and squeeze my eyes shut.

"Evelyn?" I hear the sound of fingers snapping in my ear. "Evelyn, are you okay?"

When I open my eyes I am standing at the window, staring out at the storm. Patricia is next to me, watching me with worry in her eyes. I take a deep breath. The window is in tact, and the storm is well below us. I must have dozed off while staring outside.

"I'm worried about you, Evelyn. You look pale," Patricia says.

"Don't be silly. I'm fine."

"I think you should come to my office tomorrow. We can run some tests. You were staring out of the window with a vacant look in your eyes. I was trying to get your attention for well over a minute and you didn't respond."

"It's nothing," I say. "I'm over tired, and I must have spaced out."

Patricia smiles, and puts a hand on my shoulder. "Go get some rest. I'll be fine here. I can let myself out once the storm is over."

"Okay." I walk to my bedroom door, my mind still a haze. "Hey, Patricia?"

"Yes, dear?"

"Do you happen to own a music box?"

Patricia stares at me, confused. "A music box?"

"Yeah, one of those... it's like a jewelry case that plays music when you open it. Do you have one? Or do you know anyone that has one?"

Patricia takes a deep breath, and smiles. "Get some rest, Evelyn."

CHAPTER TEN
Char Moore

Surreal. That's what it looks like when I step out of the tent. Archer and I were patrolling The Chasm when the sirens went off. Within seconds Archer set up our safety tent, and the both of us crawled inside. Besides the whistling of the wind, and the occasional buckling of the tarp, we were safe. Now though, stepping out for the first time, I realize how violent that storm was.

Just this morning the earth was covered in white snow. Now, that pure snow has become a withered skeleton, eroded by sand and wind. There are jagged indentations running along the frozen ground, with dirt gathered between. It is like that everywhere I look: dead winter, frozen and decayed.

"You see something new every day," Archer says, stepping beside me.

I nod, still surveying our surroundings. "I've never seen a storm during winter. Have you?"

"Like this? No," he says shaking his head. "They seem to be coming earlier and earlier."

I pick up a handful of dirty snow. "I've always hated the cold, but thought the snow was beautiful. Look at it now." I let the gritty slush fall in clumps between my fingers. "Even Felicity looks ugly from here."

Archer laughs. "I think those five minutes in the tent messed with your head. Felicity's always been hideous."

I look at Archer, and smile. "You and I have different definitions of hideous."

The radio transmitter on Archer's hip rattles out incoherent static. He removes it from his belt clip, and fidgets with the dials. A few seconds later, a female voice croaks, "Archer? Archer, are you there? Do you read me?"

Archer pulls the radio to his lips, and presses a button before speaking. "This is Archer. You're breaking up a bit, but I can hear you. Go ahead."

"We need you and Char to report to Calloway immediately. We have a situation. It's urgent."

"Address?"

"One Forty-Eight Liberty Road. This is a hostile environment. Be armed and ready."

"Got it. We're headed there now," Archer says. He clips the radio back on his belt, and looks at me. "Time to go. Still loaded up?"

I look at my belt, inspecting the gun and extra clips. "Yeah, everything's here."

Archer doesn't bother taking down the tent, which means whatever we were called to must be important. He waves his arm, telling me to follow him, and then we both begin our trek toward The Chasm.

"Liberty Road is at the back of town," I say, trying my best to match Archer's pace. "Even if we ran it would take us at least thirty minutes to get there."

"Then we should walk faster."

I grab him by the coat sleeve. "Archer, hold on."

He stops walking, and stares at me. "This better be important, newbie."

"We are all the way in Felicity. There are patrols stationed much closer to that part of Calloway than us."

Archer rolls his eyes and begins walking again, a little faster this time. "You just started, and you're already trying to get out of your duties."

"It's not that. I happen to think it's weird that they're requesting us specifically," I say, a little breathless. I have to jog in order to keep up with Archer's long stride.

"I think you're focusing on the wrong thing here. It doesn't matter why we're called. We go. End of story."

"I know, but—"

"My house was in that part of town. Perhaps they think I might know the person, or at least be familiar with the area. I have been here longer than most of the other patrols. I've got experience. They like to call in the patrols that know what the hell they're doing when the situation is dire. Or, maybe they're asking us to go simply because you are new. You still need to be shown the ropes, get you in on the action. Feel free to pick whichever one of those excuses will make you feel better."

"Okay, I get it. I'm sorry I said anything."

Archer sighs. "Look, I didn't mean to snap. We have to report first, and ask questions later. Anything else could get us killed. Do you understand?"

"I understand," I say, quietly.

We keep our pace as we head to the back of Calloway. There is a lot of destruction on our path, uprooted trees, branches strewn about, windows shattered. I can hear the hushed voices of the older children trying to calm the youngest ones who are wailing with fear. The storms are frightening for everyone involved, but it's worse for the ones whose homes are already in shambles.

"You alright?" Archer asks, frowning.

"Yeah, I'm fine. Keep moving."

"You're upset. I can read it in your face."

"After we're done, do you think I'll have time to stop by my brother's place? I'd like to make sure he and Harry are okay."

"After our shift is done, as long as we're still in the area, I don't see why not. Provided we're not walking into some crazy shit, that is."

Liberty Street is at the far end of Calloway, near the border of trees surrounding the city. The crisp, winter air is tainted with the scent of burning wood. It stings my nostrils. I look at Archer, whose face is hardened into a grimace. The closer we get to our destination, the stronger that stench grows. I can feel my pulse rising, pounding out through my temples. I've never smelled anything so horrid.

The house is hard to miss. It's tilted, like the earth is trying to swallow it back down, ashamed of how it looks. Every window is missing, and no one has bothered boarding them up. The front door is gone, and the frame where it once stood is cracked. Smoke rises from the roof. It's stale, like the aftermath of burning embers.

Four patrols stand out front. There are two women with their guns drawn, holding them toward the two male patrols holding a young teenager by his arms. The kid is flailing, and kicking. He is shaking his head back and forth, screaming.

Archer leans in close to my ear. "Do you know him?"

"No," I say, shaking my head.

"Me neither," he says.

Archer motions for me to follow him, and we jog up to the patrols. The two that hold the boy look tired and worn. The other two lower their guns as we approach.

"Thank goodness you're here," the girl with red hair says. She has freckles covering her bright pink cheeks. "We don't know what to do."

The boy cranks his head, and tries to look around. Archer and I are too far to the side for him to see us. He flails his legs to try to get a better view. "Is that her? Where is she?"

"What's going on?" Archer asks.

"A neighbor reported smoke coming from the house," the other girl replies. She has brown hair, cropped short. "When we arrived, half the kitchen was charred. Took all four of us to get the fire out. When we were done we found him standing in the hallway, shouting."

The boy doesn't look much older than my brother. It saddens me to see him, disheveled and desperate. He is still screaming at the top of his lungs, and kicking with such force that the two patrols holding him struggle to keep him upright.

I walk over to the boy, and stand as close as I can without being hit. "Who are you looking for?"

Immediately the boy begins to calm. His body goes limp. I see him breathing slow, steady breaths. He slumps forward, his chin resting on his chest. "Char. I am looking for a girl named Char. That's you, isn't it?"

I take a step back. Out of the corner of my eye I see Archer talking with the red haired patrol, their voices nothing more than a whisper. Now I know why they called us down here.

"Yes, I'm Char," I tell the boy. "What do you want?"

The boy looks up at me with steel blue eyes. I feel sick when I look into them. They are empty, void of any emotion. But still he smiles at the mention of my name.

"You threw my sister into The Chasm," he tells me, his voice calm.

Archer walks over to me, and places a hand on my shoulder. "Your sister was trying to cross the bridge. It's against policy. Char did what she had to do."

The boy spits at Archer, barely missing him. His lips curl into a smile. "Go fuck yourself. I wasn't talking to you. I don't give a shit about you."

Archer pulls his gun, and points it at the boy's head. "Go ahead. Do something like that again."

The boy laughs, and shakes his head. "Or what?"

I step in front of Archer, putting myself between him and the boy. "Archer is right. Your sister was doing something wrong. I was there to cross over the bridge. Nothing more. It wasn't my plan to throw your sister into The Chasm, but her and her friends murdered a guard that day. I couldn't let her go."

The boy nods his head. His eyes are red and swelling with tears. "She had to get over the bridge. She had to. She had to."

I chew my bottom lip, and tuck a strand of hair behind my ear. "What's your name?"

"Sam. My name is Sam."

"Sam, you and I both know that no one is allowed over that bridge."

Sam's face melts into a scowl. He sucks air deep into his lungs. "She was trying to help you!" He screams so loud his voice begins to crack. Then he tilts his head back and looks up at the sky. He slowly rocks himself back and forth, swaying in the arms of the patrols struggling to keep him still.

"I'm sorry, Sam," I say. "I've never met your sister before that day. You must be mistaken."

"Her name was Emily." His sings her name. "Emily, Emily, Emily."

"This is fucking stupid," Archer says, nudging me to the side. "Your sister was a nobody. She did something wrong and she got punished for it. End of story. You don't try to burn your house down, and then cause a scene, all because of a foolish decision your sister made. Where is the sense in that? What the hell are you trying to accomplish? You're fucking crazy. You're insane."

Sam's top lip curls into a snarl, but he doesn't say a word to Archer. He keeps his eyes locked on mine. When he speaks, his voice is low and his words difficult to understand. "Listen to me, Char. Listen carefully. She wasn't trying to live in Felicity. There was something there she needed. She was going to get it, and bring it back to me. Things were going to change. Things need to change, don't you see?"

I take a deep breath, and run my fingers through my hair. Maybe Archer is right. Sam is crazy. "I'm sorry about Emily. I really am. But you were both mistaken. There was never anything in Felicity worth dying over."

"Let's go. This is a waste of time." Archer turns to the other patrols, and twirls a finger in the air. "Take him to The Chasm."

Sam begins struggling with the patrols again, kicking and trying to wriggle out from their grip. They begin to drag him away when he shouts, "I know about your father!"

My heart stops. "Stop! Bring him back!"

"Let it go, Char. He's obviously lost his mind," Archer says.

"Tell me what you know! Tell me about my father!"

Sam struggles harder against the patrols, jerking his arms up and down, trying to escape. He tries to pull back, but one of the patrols stomps on his ankle, causing Sam to cry out in pain. I try to run to him, but Archer holds me back.

"He was murdered!" Sam shouts. The patrol holding his left arm tightens his grip, wrenching Sam's arm. "Fuck! You can't let them do this, Char! Your father knew!" The red haired patrol raises her gun to Sam's temple. "They killed him before he could stop it! He could have saved us all!"

"Let him go," I try to shout, but my words are drowned out by the sound of the gun. I watch as Sam's body goes limp, slumping forward, blood dripping on the ground by his feet. They killed him. I turn my back on his dead body, and put my head in my hands.

"Fucking hell," Archer mutters. He runs over to the patrols, and tells them something, but I can't hear him over the sound of my own heartbeat pounding in my ears. A few moments later, Archer is back in front of me. He puts a hand on my shoulder, and looks me in the eyes. His face looks out of focus, and blurry. "Pay no attention to him, Char. We get crazies like that all the time. I see them every day."

"I need to see my mother," I whisper.

"Char, you're not taking this seriously are you?"

"No." I shake my head. "I just want to see her."

"Well, we're going to need to write a report about what the hell happened before we can go anywhere," Archer says. He sighs. "Pull yourself together. Let's go check out the inside of the house real quick."

"Yeah, okay," I say, still in a daze. I take a deep breath and slowly exhale.

The smell is the first thing to hit me when we walk through the front door. I can't place it exactly, but it's enough to make my stomach turn. It smells like urine, or a dead animal, mixed with burned wood and plastic. I pull the sleeve of my coat down over my hand, and use it to shield my face from the stench.

Archer and I move through the living room. The walls are charred. I can see bits of wooden bones peeking out from behind scorched flowery wallpaper. The storm made it's way inside of the house. Snow and dirt litter the ground, crunching under our boots as we walk. Everything is sprinkled with the remnants of the storm: the smoking, half-burned couch, the broken tables, even the visible wooden beams in the walls have dirt caked upon them. Standing inside of the house sends a shiver down my spine.

"He really torched the place," Archer mutters.

We walk through the narrow hall to the back of the house. The bathroom is the first room we encounter. The door is wide open, and the tile floor is cracked and broken. There is no toilet here, only a sink. It's filled to the brim with brown, murky water. The longer we stand in the doorway, the more my eyes begin to burn.

"Let's move," Archer says, making a face.

There is only one more room down the hall. The door lays askew, broken from the hinges. We step over the bits of splintered wood as we enter. The first thing I notice are the blankets, nothing better than tattered rags lining the floors. Some of them are soaked with who knows what, others are molded. The smell is horrid, seeping through the cloth of my coat. I try to hold my breath to keep myself from getting sick.

Then I look at the walls.

"Oh my god," I whisper.

"I told you. Crazy," Archer says.

Every wall, from top to bottom, is plastered in paper. Mostly handwritten notes scribbled in ink. They've been wet. The black

91

has begun to run, dripping down half the wall before drying. The papers are shriveled, and yellow. Nothing is legible. Torn pages of books are stapled up here and there, between the handwritten notes. I try reading the pages, but nothing makes sense. One is about horse farming; another appears to be about astronomy.

I take a step back, and scratch the back of my head. I feel sick. There is nothing here but the ramblings of a mad man. Archer was right. I take a deep breath, and try to pull myself together. When I turn around to look at Archer, he is staring at the back wall, the one by the door. It's the one spot I hadn't looked yet. Archer's muscles are tight, and his body rigid. He raises a stiff arm, and points.

There on the wall, written in blood, are the words: We are the forgotten. Directly below, in small black letters: Rest in peace, Charles Moore.

CHAPTER ELEVEN
Alexander Moore

I brush the dust off the couch, and plop myself down on the cushion. The front window is broken from the storm, and now there are traces of its destruction everywhere: the floors, the counters, the furniture. Even the walls have a thin coating of dirt. I pat the cushion next to me, and a cloud of dust flies into the air.

"Why don't you guys sit? You're making me nervous," I say.

"My lungs still hurt," Harry says. "How much time did you waste trying to pull that damn thing out? Was it worth it?"

I glance at the brown leather case propped up against the wall. The side with the bullet hole is turned away because I couldn't stand to look at it any longer. One lonely bullet hole, with blood still caked around the edges. The other side is worn, but smooth. There is no exit wound, so to speak, which means the bullet is still lodged inside the case. Whoever owned it must have been shot in the back with the case clutched to their chest. That's the only explanation that makes sense. Whatever it holds must have been important, at least to one person.

"I won't know that until we open it," I say.

"Maybe it has a name printed on it," Mara says. "Have you checked?"

I shake my head. "To be honest, I don't want to look at it right now. It's creeping me out."

Harry throws his hands up in the air. "Oh great! So glad you nearly killed us for it then."

"Shut up, Harry. You'd have done the same thing."

"Not a chance."

"That's enough you two," Mara says. "Arguing won't change what happened. We are all alive and well. Did you see some of those houses while we were coming back? Did you smell the smoke? All you've got is a broken window, and some mess to clean up. I'd say we ended up pretty lucky, all things considered."

Harry crosses his arms over his chest, and looks out the broken front window. "We need to stop worrying about the case, and start worrying about the radio. That's the reason we were at the dump in the first place."

I've forgotten all about the damn radio. Only four more days left. I sigh, and head into the kitchen where the radio is still open on the counter. I blow inside the casings, clearing them of any dust that might have gotten in, and then I quietly work on getting all the pieces put back together, inspecting as I go. I'm certain all it needs is a new set of batteries to get it to start working again.

"What's wrong with it?" Mara asks, peeking over my shoulder.

"Nothing, as far as I can tell. Just needs power."

Harry plops the batteries down on the counter next to me. "Here."

I finish putting the last screw in, and focus on taking the cover off the battery pack. It clips off easily; a light pinch of the tab sets it free. I pick up two of the batteries, look them over, and slide them into position. Mara gasps as I click the power button on.

Static.

I play with the tuner, turning the knob and watching the little red tab slide left and right. Nothing I do seems to help. I whack the radio out of frustration, and then pound my fists on the counter.

"Dammit," I mutter.

"Looks like you were right. Works fine to me," Harry says.

"No, Harry. It's not working at all!"

"Open it up and check inside of it again," Mara suggests.

I clench my jaw and hang my head. "No. There's nothing wrong with it internally. I can tell by looking at it. Nothing's burned, or shorted out. No wires are tattered, or torn. The transformer looked fine, and so did the transistor chip. The capacitor wasn't damaged. On the surface, everything looks fine."

"It's the same with those televisions you fixed," Harry says. "There's nothing wrong with it, but it still doesn't work. Only broadcasted noise, right?"

"That's not the point. Adam said he wants the radio fixed. This isn't fixed."

"It's never going to work, Alex. Not the way he wants it to."

"Then we're screwed."

"What about the antenna?" Mara asks. "You asked for us to look for something metal to use as an antenna. I had one, but I dropped it while we were running. I could go back out and look for it. Would that help?"

I squeeze the bridge of my nose, and close my eyes. The radio is turning on, but it's not picking up a signal. Maybe there are no signals out there for it to pick up. That's the worst-case scenario, and the one I refuse to believe. I have to get the radio fixed. I have to.

I turn the radio over in my hands, looking it over one more time. There is no bump of broken metal where an antenna would have gone. That means there was never any external antenna to begin with, and a stick of metal never would have helped. But the radio must have been useful at one point. I need to figure out how it was picking up a signal before.

I root through the kitchen drawers, their insides rattling. I frantically go from one drawer to the next, digging through the junk inside, looking for something sharp. A knife, some scissors, anything that can cut through wire.

"What the hell are you doing?" Harry asks.

"Do we have a knife anywhere? A sharp one, not one of those crappy butter knives, or any of those dull pieces of shit we keep around. I need a good, sharp knife."

Harry holds up a finger, and dashes out of the kitchen. I look at Mara, who shrugs. He's not gone long before he returns, holding up a knife.

"I was freaked out after Adam left. Grabbed the sharpest thing I could find, and shoved it under my pillow."

I pluck the knife from his hand by the worn, wooden handle, and place it down on the counter. "You idiot. You'd end up stabbing yourself in the face before you ever got the chance to use the damn thing."

"Shut up," Harry snaps.

"How about you shut up, and then go grab the lamp out of Char's room," I tell him.

"The lamp? How's that going to help?"

"Just do it. You'll see."

Harry hurries off to retrieve the lamp while I work on opening the radio back up. I'm almost finished removing the last screw when Harry returns.

"One lamp as requested," Harry says, placing it on the ground beside me.

"Take that knife," I motion towards the counter where I placed it down, "and cut the cord off the lamp. As close to the base as you can get it."

"What can I do?" Mara asks.

"You can hold the base for him, and stretch out the cord as tight as it will go. It'll make it easier for him to cut."

Mara nods, smiling. She places her foot on the lamp base, and pulls the cord with her hands as hard as she can. "There you go, Harry. Don't chop my toes off. Or my fingers. I need all of them."

Harry chuckles. "No promises."

I take the last screw out of the back of the radio, and pry it back open again. I scan the inside for some thin, metal coils. If there is no external antenna, there must have been an internal one.

"We murdered the lamp," Harry says, holding up the long power cord.

"Harry!" Mara shouts, trying to contain her laughter. She whacks Harry on the arm. "We cut its tail off, that's all."

I can't help but smile. "I don't care what you call it. Give me the cord, and the knife."

Harry and Mara watch closely as I lay the cord out on the ground. I crouch down beside it, and try my best to find the exact middle between the top and bottom ends. The cord is made of two sets of wires, separated by a thin layer of plastic down the center crease. I use the tip of the blade to pierce that thin plastic. Then I run the knife from the middle of the cord all the way to the bottom end in order to separate the left side from the right.

"I'll need something metal that will stick inside the wall, like a tack or a nail. Try the junk drawer. I keep a lot of odds and ends in there. Even a leftover screw would work."

As they run off, I get to work on stripping the plastic from all three ends of the wire: the two sides I just separated, and the top part I left intact. A little delicate trimming with my knife, and all the wires are exposed. I only needed an inch or so off the two smaller pieces, but a good six inches off the other. By the time I'm finished, Mara and Harry are back.

"Two screws," Mara says, holding them out in her hand. "They're a little rusted though."

"That's perfect. The rust won't matter." I grab the two small ends of the cord, and stand up with them. "Harry, can you grab my screwdriver over there and start screwing them into the wall? Put a good two or three feet between them."

Mara grabs the screwdriver from the counter, and hands it off to Harry. "What are you trying to do?"

"I'm building an antenna."

"Using a lamp?"

"Using the metal wires in the lamp cord," I correct her.

"How do you know it'll work?"

"I don't."

"Then why are you doing it?"

I look at Mara, who watches Harry screw the last screw into the wall. "I have to try something, right?" I try to smile, but she doesn't notice. "Back when I was fixing a television set for one of Char's friends, she told me about how she found this book once, some how-to guide about electronics. She explained that she saw this tutorial on how to build an antenna out of scraps around the house. I tried it for the set I was fixing at the time, but of course it didn't work. It was a brilliant idea though."

"You know what's not brilliant?" Harry tosses the screwdriver onto the ground. "Making me put two damn screws in the wall for something you're not even sure will work."

"Or," I say, wrapping the exposed metal from one small end of the cord around the right most screw, "it actually might work. Here, take that end there and do what I just did, but on the other screw."

Mara holds the cord for Harry as he starts twisting the metal around the screw. As he's working on that, I grab the still-opened radio and sit on the ground at the thick end of the cord. I twist the bits of exposed wire around each other, until everything is thin and uniform. By the time I'm finished so are Harry and Mara, who sit down on either side of me. They steal a glance at each other while I connect the wire from the lamp cord to the antenna coil inside the radio.

I hold my breath as I click the power button.

Still static.

"Shit," I mutter.

I grab the radio, and scramble to my feet. The cord is spread out like a Y: the top two points attached to the screws, the bottom point attached to the radio. I move to the side a bit, and fidget with the tuner a little. The more I turn the dial, the louder the static gets. I turn it the other way, and the static fades out a little, but comes right back.

"I told you it wasn't going to work," Harry says.

"Hush for a second," Mara tells him.

I keep moving the tuner knob as slow as I can. After each small movement of the dial, I shift myself to the right another inch. The rhythm of the static keeps changing. It's loud one second, soft and wavering the next. I hit a spot, about a foot from where I was originally standing, where the static is accompanied by a high-pitched screech. Standing still, I move the tuner a little more, from one side to the next. The sound goes in and out, the screeching replaced with a deep rumbling noise. I shift my weight to the right a fraction of an inch. Within seconds I hear the faint noise of a woman's voice rattling through the static.

"Hel.... we... en... The... s... s..."

"Who is that? I can't understand her," Mara says.

"I don't know. Hold on."

I turn the dial as minimally as I can, then wiggle the cord. I step to the right a fraction of an inch. The hissing white noise becomes duller, and the voice of the woman grows clearer. Now it's obvious that it is not the voice of a woman that we are hearing. It's the voice of a little girl. Mara places a hand on my arm, and squeezes.

"Help. I repeat: We need help," the radio cries.

The girl's voice fades into static, her message disappearing. I turn the dial, and move a little to the side. My hands are trembling, the parts of the radio rattling in my hands.

"My name is E—"

A loud screech breaks through the girl's voice. I frantically try to move the tuner enough to make the static disappear, but not enough to lose the voice. The sound fades, and again the girl's words become clearer.

"Please. If you can hear me, if there's anyone out there, we need your help. I repeat: We need your help. We—" The radio falls silent, void of even static. After a fraction of a second the white noise returns. I turn the dial a little more, and the girl's voice rises. Her message repeats. "Help. I repeat: We need help..."

CHAPTER TWELVE
Evelyn Moore

My name is Evelyn Moore.

I take a glass from the cabinet, and slam it on the counter in front of me. It clanks against the marble, threatening to shatter. I wrap my fingers around the rim, turn the glass clockwise, and then back again. It makes a swishing sound against the countertop as it moves.

My name is Evelyn Moore. Felicity will not be destroyed.

I throw open the liquor cabinet. Not vodka. Not wine. Those won't do. I push them aside and grab the small bottle of whiskey hidden at the back. I wave the bottle in front of my face, watching the brown liquid slosh back and forth, ramming against the sides of the bottle like a hurricane.

My name is Evelyn Moore. There is no storm.

The smell of whiskey is as soothing as the taste. I close my eyes, and breathe in deep. I have never needed anything more than I need this. I reach for the glass, and quickly pour myself a drink. The taste of whiskey burns my throat as it goes down, but that doesn't stop me from pouring another. This time I sip it slow, reveling in the sweet sting of alcohol.

My name is Evelyn Moore. There is no music.

I slam the empty glass back down on the counter. One small drop of whiskey was left resting at the bottom. I dip my finger in it, picking up the remains. Then I shove that same finger in my mouth, making sure every last bit is where it needs to be.

I stare at the bottle, trying to decide whether or not I should have another. Two glasses in, and I can already feel the warmth spreading faster and faster through my insides. Without even thinking I pour myself another drink, and quickly gulp it down. I lick my lips and close my eyes. This should do for now.

Every time I close my eyes I can feel the earth spinning, faster and faster. I throw my eyes open and the world straightens itself back out. Now, I'm the one that seems to be spinning. I steady myself on the counter for a moment. Have to make sure I don't fall down. It's hard to stand still when everything spins.

I straighten myself up and grab the bottle of whiskey one more time. It's hard to remember how many shots I've drank so far. Was it two? Maybe it was three. Three is okay, but four is too much. Four would not be good. I need enough to forget. Too much, and I won't be able to remember.

Remember what?

One more drink. I pour it fast, most of it spilling over the edge.

"My name is Evelyn…" I take a deep, labored breath. "Evelyn Moore."

I stumble back, and stare at the overflowing glass of whiskey. My insides ache for more drink. My throat burns in anticipation. I rub the back of my neck, and chew my bottom lip. I can't remember when I decided to start drinking. I can't remember why. I suppose now, all these years later, the reason doesn't matter. All I know is what is in this moment, and right now I need this more than anything.

I walk forward, concentrating hard on placing one foot in front of the other, trying not to fall. I scoop the glass up in my hand, and hold it out in front of my face. It looks the color of amber: Beautiful, and full of fire.

"My name is Evelyn Moore." The words come out strange, all mumbled and fuzzy. Or maybe that's how it sounds in my head. My mouth feels like putty as it moves. I take a labored breath, and mumble, "I need this fucking music to stop."

I pull the glass to my lips right as my phone begins to ring.

"Shit," I say, putting the drink back down.

I lean against the counter and pull the phone from my back pocket. The blue glow of the screen looks abnormally bright. I have to squint in order to look at it. There is no name or number flashing on the screen, only the word UNKNOWN blinking white. I reject the call, and put the phone down on the counter next to the glass of whiskey. I decide that the drink is a much better option to pick up instead. I put the glass to my lips as the phone goes off again.

"Dammit." I slam the glass back down. This time it topples over, spilling its contents everywhere. I grab the phone and slam my finger on the accept button hard enough to make me wince. "What the fuck do you want?"

All I hear is nervous breathing on the other end. My head is spinning, and I can't be sure if it's from the alcohol. I don't think I've had more than two.

"Hello?" I rub my temple with my free hand. "I know you're there. I can... I hear you breathing, you moron."

"I don't have a lot of time," the male voice on the other end mutters. His words sound distorted, like he is speaking with his hand clasped over his mouth.

"Great. Me neither," I say. I slide my back down the counter, scraping over the knobs on the cabinet doors. The flesh on my back stings, but the throbbing in my head is even worse. "Who are you?"

"I can't tell you that."

"Then why the fuck—" I take a long, labored breath. "—Why'd you call me?"

"It's time for you to remember."

I pull the phone away from my ear, and stare at the screen. Remember what?

"Evelyn? Are you there?"

I put the phone back against my ear. I squeeze my eyes shut, trying to keep myself from spinning, but instead the rest of the world spins for me. The darkness behind my lids begins to fade, eclipsed by shades of red sand, and brown dust. I think the man on the phone calls out to me again. It's getting harder to breathe. The phone drops from my hand, and rattles against the marble floors. I tuck my knees close to my chest, and cradle my face between the crease in my legs.

"Hello? Evelyn?"

I reach for the phone with a trembling hand. Tears are streaming down my face. I don't remember crying. Why am I crying? My fingers are rigid, and numb. I try to pick up the phone but it fumbles from my fingertips. I try again, and still can't grasp it. My thumb bashes the speaker button instead.

"I'm here," I say, my voice weak. "What is happening to me?"

"You are slowly beginning to remember. Evelyn, listen to me very carefully. I don't have much time." There is rattling on the other end of the line, and another muffled voice in the background. A few seconds of static, and the man's voice is back. "Things are going to be changing very soon. You can't hide from it."

"I... I need help. I feel like I'm going insane." My throat tightens. "I need—"

"Follow the music, Evelyn. Everything will be answered soon. I've got to go."

The line is dead. The voice is gone. But the music, the constant chiming of bells, that will always remain. I let my body slump to the side. The marble tiles are cold beneath my cheek. I close my eyes, and listen to the music echoing all around me.

My name is Evelyn Moore. And I think I've gone mad.

CHAPTER THIRTEEN
Char Moore

My legs are moving. I can see them going forward and back. The problem is that I don't feel them. Everything is numb. There is no sensation in my arms as they swing, or my lungs as they breathe. Calloway is going by in a flash as Archer and I head back to The Chasm, but all I can see are words of red and black.

We are the forgotten.

Rest in peace, Charles Moore.

"Snap out of it, newbie," Archer says. "You have a report to file. You need to be on point. You can't look so jaded. Understand?"

I clear my throat. "Yeah, I understand."

Archer reaches down and unclips the radio from his hip. "This is Archer Evans, with Char Moore. We have an ETA of about fifteen minutes. Can you make sure to get all appropriate shit together before we get there? I don't want this to take all damn day."

I look down at my hands. I flex them open and close, trying to regain feeling in the tips of my fingers. The inside of my cheek feels raw. I must have been gnawing on it more than I realize.

"Now listen," Archer says, coming to a halt. "I know what you saw is going to bother you for a long time, but you have to let it go. You cannot let the other patrols know how much that shit is bothering you. If word gets out that you can't perform your duties, things will not turn out well for you."

"I got it. I'm fine," I tell him.

"No, you're not. That was some crazy shit back there. But whatever you think is going on, whether you choose to believe that Sam is pulling your leg or not, you must keep it to yourself. I cannot stress that enough."

"What would happen to me if they found out I was lying?"

Archer takes a quick look over his shoulder, and then his eyes lock on mine. "You wouldn't survive long enough to know they found out."

I lower my voice to a whisper. "Tell me what you believe, Archer. You were there. You heard what Sam said. You saw what was written on the wall."

Archer tilts his head up to the gray sky. "Any other day, and I would have an answer for you. I don't know what to believe."

"You know as well as I do that something isn't right."

"Maybe. Maybe not." Archer takes a deep breath. "Do you remember what I told you about my sister?"

"Yes," I say. "I remember."

"After I became a patrol, some people in Calloway liked to use her death to taunt me. The things they said to me..." Archer clenches his jaw, and stares off into the distance. "One day I got called to a house in the back of town. When I got there, there was this beady-eyed girl being restrained by two patrols, screaming about how what she did was right. She insisted on only talking to me, and no one knew why until I showed up. This sound familiar?"

"Yes," I say, quietly.

"That bitch took one look at me, and I'll never forget the way her lips curled into a smile. She told me she was the one that murdered my sister. There was a look of pride on her face, like she had solved some strange world mystery that everyone else had been too dumb to figure out. I took my gun out right then and there and shot her in the head."

"But—"

"The point I'm trying to make is this: There are some people in Calloway that look at us like the villain. They think that by becoming a patrol we are betraying them, leaving them behind. That's why that bitch was so happy to tell me about my sister. Do you see what I'm getting at? Sam wanted nothing more than to make you feel pain. He wants those lies to brew inside of you until you hate yourself as much as he did."

I let those words linger in the silence between us, giving them time to settle in.

"Archer." I place a hand on his forearm. "I am so sorry about your sister. Nobody deserves to know that kind of evil."

Archer's eyes drop to the ground. "I know what you're going to say."

"I think our situations are different. This felt like something else, like a warning. Sam knew about my father, Archer. Even I didn't know how he died until last night. It doesn't make sense."

"It might not make much sense, but that doesn't mean it isn't true. Besides, you're missing one key piece of the puzzle."

"What's that?"

"You killed his sister." Archer turns his back on me and begins heading towards The Chasm. He waves a hand at me, signaling for me to follow. "We are going to be late if we don't hurry. Remember our conversation. Don't say anything stupid."

"Yeah, okay," I say. My throat feels tight. I was so focused on what Sam said about my father, that I forgot all about Emily.

"Oh, and Char?"

"Yeah?"

"There wasn't anything written on that wall."

I feel my stomach swaying at the thought of those words, big and bold, standing out against the decaying paper. When I first saw them I felt sick. I had to excuse myself from the house and get some fresh air. Everything was spinning.

"There's no point in lying. Another patrol will come along and see it."

"No, they won't."

I look at Archer, who doesn't bother slowing down, or stealing a glance my way. He keeps his sights on the bridge with his head held high. We both stay silent until we reach The Chasm. Once our feet hit the crumbling dirt, a younger patrol jogs to our side.

"Archer, Char, you're here for the review?"

"Yep," Archer says.

"Great. You guys are set up in House Three with Tyler. I'll take you there now."

We follow him to House Three, one of the few abandoned homes inside of The Chasm that has yet to fully collapse. It is a faded red house with boarded up windows, and a makeshift front door. The wood frame has rotted, and looks soft to the touch. The entire house has broken free of the foundation, and is tilting dangerously too far to the left. Opening the door makes the entire place creak.

The inside of House Three reeks. It smells as bad as the outside looks, like it's moments from death. It is a one-roomed shack, with a small table and four chairs sitting directly at the center. When we walk inside, Tyler stands and motions for us to sit down. I pull out a chair across from him as Archer leans against the wall behind me. I cringe when I see him shift his weight from one foot to the next, worried that the house might finally collapse.

"I am here to take your official report of the incident that happened earlier this afternoon, at one forty-eight Liberty Road," Tyler states. "Everything you say will be noted in your official file, as well as the official record for the patrols. You were both at that address, correct?"

"Regretfully so," Archer says.

I look over my shoulder at him with wide eyes. He looks down at me, and smiles. I turn my attention back to Tyler, clear my throat, and try my best to maintain composure. "Yes, sir. We were called there by the other patrols."

"Thank you, Char," Tyler says. He gives Archer a stern look, and I can hear him snickering to himself behind me. Tyler scratches his jaw before turning his attention back to me. "Can you please tell me what transpired when you arrived?"

"When Archer and I arrived we noticed an unruly male resident being held back by a couple of patrols, also male. I did not catch their names. Two female patrols were standing guard."

"Holy shit, I'm falling asleep already," Archer says. "We showed up, the kid yelled like a crazy person, the patrols shot him, now we're here. Can we go?"

"I'm glad to see your attitude is still intact," Tyler says. "But as you are well aware, those kinds of jokes will get us nowhere. Has this ever been that simple of a process?"

"It could be if you'd let it," Archer says.

"While I appreciate your coming down here, please control those little outbursts of yours. It'll make things go quicker. Char, please continue."

"Yes, sir."

I try to concentrate on what Archer told me before we arrived, even though I want nothing more than to break down and scream. I want to tell Tyler about my father, the words written on the wall. I want him to help me find out what Sam knew, but I know what Archer said was true: breaking down now would mean I believed that crazy kid who lit his house on fire, and who scribbled words in blood. I take a deep breath, and try to keep my voice steady.

"The resident, who claims his name was Sam, was screaming rather incoherently. It was hard to understand exactly what he was saying. I know that he wanted to see me, specifically. His sister was one of the four that tried to escape the day I crossed over. She was the one I threw into The Chasm. As you can imagine, Sam was quite angry with me."

"The other patrols informed me that you shouted at them when they tried to remove Sam from the situation. You wanted them to let him go. Explain yourself."

I try my best to maintain eye contact with Tyler. "He was in the middle of talking when they began to remove him from the situation. I wanted to let him finish speaking. What if he gave away important information? I wanted to make sure our reports could be as accurate as possible. Certainly we would want to be fully aware of all relative events regarding the situation, in order to prevent it from happening again in the future."

Tyler shuffles in his seat, and exhales loudly. He taps his fingers on the table, drumming them in rhythm. Then he stares deep into my eyes as if trying to search my memories. I feel my heart racing in my chest, and I silently beg for it to not give me away. After a moment of torture, Tyler slumps back into his chair and scratches the side of his chin.

"I suppose that makes sense. Did you two check the house after the other patrols brought Sam's body to The Chasm?"

"Yes, we did," I tell him. "The walls were a bit scorched, and the house itself was rather disgusting. Other than that, I noted nothing of interest."

Tyler looks at Archer. "Anything you want to add?"

"Nope. Sounds like she covered it all," Archer says.

Tyler hesitates a moment before scooting his chair back. The wooden legs screech against the warped floorboards. "Then we're done here. I'll mark your files as soon as possible. If either one of your see or hear anything else, I am to be informed immediately. Understood?"

"Understood," I repeat.

"Good. Get back to work," Tyler says.

I wait for Tyler to disappear out the front door before I slap Archer on the arm.

"What the hell was that about?" I ask him.

"What?"

"I'm falling asleep already," I say, mocking Archer's low voice. "That's what."

Archer laughs. "Do you know how many of these report meetings I've been to? If Tyler saw me acting any differently, he'd know something was up. I was doing you a favor."

"It made me uncomfortable."

"Of course it did," Archer says with a grin. "You did good though. Very believable."

I cross my arms over my chest. "Great."

"You ready to get back to work?"

"No."

"Tough shit. Time to move on."

"When do I get to see my mother? Or Alex?"

Archer rolls his eyes and pushes the door open. "Dammit, you're relentless. Soon. I promise. You'll get to see them soon enough."

CHAPTER FOURTEEN
Evelyn Moore

The screech of the speakers, loud and shrill, awakes me from my dreamless sleep. I peel my face off the tile, and sit up. My head is throbbing. My mouth is dry, and my breath stale. I look around and see my phone on the floor next to me. The screen flashes LOW BATTERY in bright white.

"Good morning residents of Felicity: The weather forecast for the day is mild wind, with clear, sunny skies. The overall threat level for the day is elevated. Please exercise caution, and keep your eyes and ears open for any suspicious activity. We thank your for your cooperation."

I rub my temples, trying to soothe the headache at the front of my skull. It's radiating down through my jaw, exiting out the back of my neck. Must be the way I slept.

I grab the counter top and use it to pull myself to my feet. The kitchen is a mess. It's hard to remember what happened before I drifted off. I was drinking, that much I can tell. The room reeks of alcohol. I grab the empty glass, and toss it into the sink. Then I pick up the near-empty bottle of whiskey and put it back in the cabinet, hiding it behind bottles of wine.

I bend down to grab my phone. A groan escapes my lips. The pressure in my head is unbearable. I squint one eye, and tap the phone screen. There are three new text messages. The first one is from Patricia. It reads: Everything okay? I've been worried about you. - Patty. I open the second message, which is more of the same. Patricia is worried about me, wants to know if everything is okay, and this time demands an immediate reply.

I open the third message expecting to read another annoyed note from Patricia, but this one is from an unknown number. Don't forget. That's it. That's all it says. Suddenly, my throat feels tighter. My fingers tremble as I try to punch in a reply. I only get the chance to type: Who is, before the phone dies.

"Shit," I mumble to myself.

I hurry into my bedroom and plug the phone in next to my bed. Don't forget. I try to remember last night, to think back to the conversation I had with that mysterious man. I remember the drinks, I remember the phone ringing, and I remember his muffled voice. But what did he tell me? What am I forgetting?

I can't help but laugh at myself. I am getting worked up over nothing. What I need is some fresh air, a nice walk to clear my mind. Today I can finally think straight, which means it's time for me to get out of this house. I grab my pack of cigarettes off the bedside table, throw on a jacket, and hurry out the door.

It's beautiful outside. The sky is clear. Not a cloud to be seen. The sun is still rising, and I take a moment to enjoy its golden hue beneath my lids. I take a deep breath, and let the air slowly escape my lips. The wind blows gently, and smells of spring: fresh cut grass, and blooming flowers. I turn to look at my building. The lights that cascade down the corners are no longer blue for winter, but purple for the first hint of the new season. The cold was gone faster than I expected.

There's something else different about the building. I squint, and take a few steps closer, my face almost touching the exterior. I run my fingers over the stone, feeling the tiny divots and holes. The smooth white concrete has been eroded in spots, showcasing the rough texture beneath. The damage is barely noticeable, but I still feel a chill crawl down my spine.

I shake my head. Fucking dreams have gotten me all worked up. I shove a cigarette between my lips, and light it fast. I keep my head down as I trek toward the library, not bothering to look up. There aren't many people out this early in the morning, but I don't want to have to stop and make small talk. I can't risk making accidental eye contact with anyone.

I still keep my eyes on the sidewalk as I approach the library. When I finally look up, the streets are filled with patrols. They are packed on every corner, looking in windows, talking in hushed voices. The ones that aren't on street corners are huddled in front of the library door. I remember this morning's announcement. The threat level for today was elevated. That must be the reason for all the patrols. I throw my cigarette down on the ground, and snuff it out with my foot. Then I brush my hair with the tips of my fingers, and continue marching forward.

"Hey! You there. Stop," a male patrol shouts.

I look over my shoulder and see a tall, dark-haired patrol waving me down. I give him a nod and a smile, and then I keep walking with my head down.

"Hey!"

I stop where I am and wait for the patrol to catch up. All of the other patrols have begun to make their way to the library. They seem to be flocking to it like an insect to the light.

"I told you to stop," he says.

"Did you? I'm sorry. I must have misheard," I say with a smile.

"What are you doing out this early?"

"I'm always out this early," I tell him.

A second patrol jogs up, and stands at her colleague's side. She has curly black hair, and a small frame. Freckles cover her face, which is stern and unforgiving. Her hand is readied on her gun.

"What is your name?" she asks me.

"Evelyn. What's yours?"

She looks up at the other patrol and raises her eyebrow.

"She asked you for your name," he says. His top lip curls up enough for me to notice his missing front tooth. "Your full name."

I slide the packet of cigarettes out of my pocket, and take my time lighting one up. I take a deep drag, and tilt my head to the sky to exhale a giant puff of smoke.

"Can you put that thing out?" the girl asks, waving a hand in front of her face. "I asked you a question."

"There aren't laws against smoking," I say.

"I'm going to ask you one more time before I haul you to The Chasm," she says. "Now, what is your name? Where are you headed?"

I sigh, and cross my arms over my chest, the tip of the cigarette warming my skin. "My name is Evelyn Moore." I watch as the two patrols exchange glances. "I'm trying to get to the library, so if you'll please excuse me—"

The tall patrols steps in front of me, blocking my path. "I'm sorry, but the library is closed."

"Closed? The library is never closed."

"Maintenance," the girl states.

"Then I'll go sit on one of those benches and wait for whatever is wrong to get fixed. Shouldn't take long, right?"

I try to step around the tall patrol, but he holds an arm out to stop me. I peek around his shoulder and see all of the patrols filing into the library, one after another.

"You heard the announcement," he says. "Threat levels are elevated. Even if the library weren't closed, we would still be sending you home. Why don't you just turn around, and stop causing trouble?"

"You're the ones causing the trouble here. I just want to—"

"Look," the girl states. "The only reason we haven't dragged your ass in yet is because your daughter is a patrol. If your last name were anything other than Moore, you'd have been arrested by now. Stop wasting our time, and our patience, and go home."

The girl stares at me stone-faced, waiting for me to leave. I look back at the library, trying to catch sight of that familiar short blonde hair. "Is Char here? Is she in the library?"

"You know we can't disclose specific locations," the tall patrol states.

I take a final drag of my cigarette and then throw it to the ground. "Fine. Fine. I'll go. But I'm coming back later. You can't keep the streets empty forever."

I don't wait for them to reply. I turn on my heels and begin to walk back the way I came, another cigarette lit. I walk as slow as possible, taking my time, enjoying the quiet in the streets. My feet carry me mindlessly back to Meadow Court. I can see my building jutting into the clear blue sky, the very tip disappearing into a blur.

"Evelyn! Wait up!"

"Hey, Patricia," I say as she jogs to my side. "What's up?"

"I should be asking you that question. I've been trying to get ahold of you. Where have you been? You look like shit."

"My phone died. I forgot to charge it last night. Didn't sleep well."

"Again? You said the same thing last time I saw you. I've been worried."

I open the doors to my building, and Patricia follows me inside. "There's nothing to worry about."

"That's easy for you to say. You didn't see that look in your eyes last time we talked. It was like you were possessed," Patricia says. She purses her lips, and shakes her head. "And then you don't answer your phone. You can see how I'd be worried."

We step onto the elevator together. I lean against the back wall, arms crossed, while Patricia presses the floor number. Seconds later the doors open, and we step out.

"I said there's nothing to be worried about." I walk inside my front door, Patricia closely behind me. "Let's drop it."

Right away Patricia heads into the kitchen and clasps a hand over her nose. "Evelyn, have you been drinking again? It smells awful in here."

"What I do in my own home is my own business."

Patricia walks over to me, and places both hands on my shoulders. "This isn't normal behavior. You should stop by my office so I can give you a proper diagnosis. You've been smoking more the past week than I've ever seen you smoke before. When was the last time you brushed your hair? Or had a decent night's sleep?"

"I said I'm fine. I've got to take a piss."

I shrug out from beneath Patricia's hands, and head into my bedroom. I grab my phone from the nightstand, and light up a cigarette. The phone's powered back on now that the battery is charged. The front screen flashes THREE NEW MESSAGES. I sit down on the edge of my bed, turning the phone over in my hands. I look over my shoulder, and hear Patricia cleaning the kitchen. The faucet is running. I can hear the clamoring of metal pots, and clinking of glasses. I turn back to the phone and open the first message.

UNKNOWN: You don't have much time.

I place the phone on the bed, and stare at the wall. I don't have much time for what? I pick the phone back up, and open the next two messages. It's from the same blocked number. They were received only moments ago.

UNKNOWN: Hello?

UNKNOWN: Are you there?

I think for a moment to myself, wondering if it's worth my time to respond. Before I know it, my fingers are typing the reply.

ME: I'm here. Who is this?

It only takes a second to receive another message.

UNKNOWN: Have you already forgotten?

ME: Forgotten what? I'm losing patience.

UNKNOWN: Follow the music, and you'll remember everything.

ME: This isn't funny. My daughter is a patrol. Leave me, alone or I'll report you.

UNKNOWN: This isn't a joke.

ME: Then tell me who this is. What do you want?

UNKNOWN: Trust no one.

ME: What the fuck does that even mean?

I stare at my phone waiting for the reply. Seconds go by, and then minutes. Nothing.

"I cleaned your kitchen for you."

I jump at the sound of Patricia's voice, and scramble to my feet. She is standing in the doorway, drying her hands on a dishtowel. I smile, and slide my phone into my back pocket.

"That's great," I say. "Thanks for that."

"What were you doing in here?"

"I told you. I had to use the bathroom. Decided to use the one in here so I could check my phone at the same time. I wanted to make sure no one else was trying to get ahold of me."

"And?"

THE FORGOTTEN

I fake a smile, and push a strand of hair behind my ear. "Not a thing."

CHAPTER FIFTEEN
Alexander Moore

I sit on the couch with my head in my hands. Mara and Harry gave me the night to decide what to do about the radio signal we picked up: One whole night of no sleep, of fretting until I felt sick, and I'm still conflicted.

Harry paces back and forth across the living room floor with his arms crossed over his chest. "I think we should find Char. The patrols need to know what we found. It could be important."

"I don't know," Mara says. "What if there's something else going on, something we shouldn't be getting involved in?"

"But this is Char we're talking about," Harry says. "We take it to her first. She would know if we've gotten our hands on something important. She'd tell us if we've done something wrong. If that happens we can destroy the damn radio, and tell Adam to go to hell."

"Char is a patrol now. Patrols first, family second. You know that."

Harry stops pacing, and stares at Mara. "Char wouldn't do anything to put us in danger."

"She might not have a choice."

"Alex, are you listening to this shit? Tell her she's wrong."

I peel my face out of my hands, and see them both standing in front of me, anticipating some sort of answer. "I don't know what to say."

Mara plops down on the couch next to me. "I think we should hand the radio over to Adam, without the antenna you built. The radio works by definition. That's all that matters."

"There was a girl calling for help," Harry says. "Are we just going to pretend we didn't hear it?"

"I don't think we should be worrying about it," Mara says. "That's what I'm saying. Where would a signal like that even come from? Not from Calloway. That would be impossible. It wouldn't come from Felicity either. The voice was too young. Where was it coming from?"

Harry stares at the floor for a moment, lost in thought. Mara's ideas are based on logic, and you can't argue with logic. No one in Calloway would have the technology to both build a radio, and transmit a signal. Even if they could, the signal was too weak to have originated from here. It didn't come from Felicity either. There are no children there. Those are simple facts we cannot ignore.

"I agree with Mara," I say. "If it didn't come from Calloway or Felicity, then it's none of our business."

Harry's face hardens. He still stares at the ground, his arms still crossed. "What if it came from The Chasm?"

"You can't be serious," Mara says. "The Chasm? That's where people go to die. No one survives that fall."

"Of course," Harry says, his voice quiet. "How stupid of me."

"It's not stupid," Mara says. "It's an interesting idea. But I don't see how it could be possible."

"It is interesting," I say. "I think all of us have wondered if there's something down in The Chasm. But even if it were true, it wouldn't explain what we heard. If someone happened to survive the fall to the bottom, how would they be able to broadcast the signal?"

"You're right. I didn't think about that," Harry says. "Besides, they would most likely be dead by now without food or water. And the patrols wouldn't risk their lives to save someone they threw down there in the first place."

"I think we can all agree then. We give the radio back to Adam, and forget this whole thing happened," Mara says.

"I think that's for the best. We wait until our five days are up, and we give it back to him. Tell him it works, but there's no signal," I say.

"It doesn't feel right," Harry says.

"We're out of options," I tell him.

"I still think we should tell Char. Not because she's a patrol, but because she's your sister. She would want to know what we found, even if it's meaningless."

"I'll think about it," I say. "But I don't want to get her involved in something that might put her or her job in jeopardy. Let's see what happens in the next couple of days first."

"I think that's fair," Mara says. She walks to the front door, and puts her hand on the knob. "If it's okay with you two, I'm going to head out. I saved up a few dollars and want to head to the store to get some new soap now that the weather's warm. I've been out for days."

"That's a great idea. It looks like a nice day today," I say. "But make sure you're careful out there, okay?"

"Keep us posted if you hear anything," Harry adds.

Mara smiles, and opens the front door. "I will. Let me know what you guys decide to do with the radio. I'll be back later, and I expect an update."

"Noted," I say with a smile.

Mara waves and shuts the door behind her. Once she is gone, Harry sits himself down on the couch next to me. He sighs loud enough to get me to notice, and then leans back into the cushion.

"What is it?"

"I've been thinking," Harry says.

"Did it hurt?"

"Shut up. I'm serious. Don't you find this all strange?"

"The radio thing? It's weird, yeah, but what does it matter? It's not our problem."

"That's not what I meant. Yes, this whole radio thing is weird. That cry for help? It freaked me the hell out. I couldn't sleep at all last night because I couldn't get that voice out of my head. But... I don't know. I feel like there's more to it."

"I think you're overthinking it."

"I think you're not thinking enough! Which is not like you if we're being totally honest with each other. Since when do you brush shit under the rug like this? The Alex that I grew up with would never do that."

"What are you trying to say?"

"I think you're scared."

I roll my eyes at him. "Oh, please."

"You can roll your eyes and deny it all you want. I know you better than that. I know that if I've been up all night thinking about it, you've been up all night too. I know that if I've connected the dots, you've connected them too. Long before I have. Probably the moment you heard that girl's voice."

My cheeks grow flush, and my heart races. I try to swallow, but the lump gets caught in my throat. I look down at my hands and interlace my fingers to keep them from trembling. I didn't want to think about it again. I don't want to say it out loud.

"I don't know what you mean." My voice sounds shaky, distant.

"Adam shows up on our doorstep the night Char leaves for the patrols. He has a radio that he tells you is broken, and that he knows you will want to fix. Not only because he threatened you, but also because you like doing shit like that for some stupid reason. He knows you'll go to the dump to find what you need, because that's where everyone goes. Am I right?"

I clear my throat. "Yes."

"So, you're at the dump, and you're rooting through all the crap there, and what do you find? A briefcase. Looked out of place, even you admitted that. It's why you grabbed it. I know you didn't think anything of it at first. If you did you probably would have left it behind. But I think once we got back home, you started to realize what was happening. That's why you haven't touched it."

I look at the case, still leaning against the wall.

"Once the radio worked, once you heard that girl's voice asking for help, you had it all figured out," Harry continues. "Adam knew you'd fix the radio, and he knew you'd find that case. He put it there where he knew you'd see it."

"I know," I say, staring at my hands, avoiding eye contact. "This must have been how it was planned all along."

Harry shifts to the side, and leans in close. "I didn't want to say anything while Mara was here, but that's exactly why we need to find Char. We have to tell her everything. She's the only one that can help us. If we don't figure out what all of this is about, bad things are going to happen. Adam will be back in a couple of days. We don't have much time."

"I don't think Adam's coming back," I say. "I think he's dead."

"What the hell, Alex? Why would you say that?"

I run a hand over my buzzed hair, and sigh. "I thought about that last night, too. When he first came to our doorstep, when he pulled the gun on me and demanded I fix his radio, I mistook his desperation for fear. I figured that maybe he promised to fix the radio for someone else and got in over his head, and came to us for help. But it doesn't make sense anymore. He knew something bad was going to happen to him. That's why he was desperate. He knew his fate. And that, Harry, is why I'm scared."

"Fuck," Harry mumbles. He stares at the ceiling for a moment, and then suddenly leaps to his feet. "Is that why he said we had five days? Five days until we... until we end up like him?"

I shrug. I can feel the lump in my throat growing, my insides turning. "I don't know."

"Shit. Shit. Shit. We need to get rid of the radio." Harry is pacing again, back and forth across the living room floor. He's speaking an octave higher, and his words fall out fast. "We can bring the case back to the dump. No one was there. No one saw us take it."

"Calm down. It might not mean anything," I tell him, but even I have a hard time believing it.

"We need to get to The Chasm. We need to tell Char. You can put the radio back together so no one knows we opened it. You can tell her... I don't know. Tell her everything that happened. We can leave out the part about the girl and the signal. No one would know we actually got it to work. Char can convince the patrols that we had no idea. Some crazy kid showed up one night with a radio and a gun, that's it."

Harry continues to ramble, but I've stopped paying attention. I'm staring at the briefcase, wondering what secrets lie inside. It meant something to the person whose blood stains the outside, and it must have meant something to Adam.

"We have to open the case," I say.

"Are you completely insane? What the hell happened? You wanted nothing to do with any of this a few seconds ago. I know what I said about you ignoring all this, but that was before—"

"It's not you. I changed my mind on my own."

"I don't get you, Alex. There's nothing wrong with being afraid. It's okay to walk away from this one."

"I'll open it tomorrow so you have time to think about it. Adam wasn't looking for both of us. He was looking for me. I'm not going to drag you into this. Find somewhere else to go if you don't want to get involved. I won't get mad."

I think Harry is yelling at me, but I'm not listening. I walk to the case, my mind a blur. Adam, the case, the radio, they've made their way to me for a reason. Whatever feelings I might have, whether I am frightened or not, shouldn't matter. Something is going on, and it's up to me to find out what that something is.

Tomorrow. Tomorrow I will open the case.

CHAPTER SIXTEEN

Char Moore

I'm sitting in the library with a hard metal chair digging into my spine. I don't remember how I ended up here, or when it happened. I can remember the call that brought us to the library. I remember standing out front, wondering what was going on. What I don't remember is filing inside. I don't remember sitting down. My heart begins to race, my skin growing flush. What else have I forgotten?

I look to my left and see Archer sitting with his hands folded in his lap. To my right is a blonde-haired patrol with pale skin and high cheekbones. Her eyes are glazed over, and she stares straight ahead. I follow her sight to the front of the library, but there is nothing there. All I see are rows and rows of patrols, sitting and waiting the same as I am.

I lean in close to Archer, and whisper as quiet as I can. "What are we doing here?"

He puts a finger to his lips, and makes a hushing sound. I turn and look behind me. There are dozens of more patrols all lined in a row, sitting, waiting. A few patrols stand around the door with their hands resting on their guns.

"Excuse me," I say to the girl on my right. "Why are we here?"

"Tyler called us here," she says, her eyes still focused straight ahead.

I try to tally the number of patrols around me, but there are too many to count. The library is packed. The air has begun to grow hot and dense with the heat of all the bodies. When the library is empty, the inside looks boundless in size. With all these people filed inside it feels like a matchbox.

I tap the girl on her shoulder. "Sorry to bother you again, but are there any patrols actually patrolling right now?"

She turns and stares at me, her pale blue eyes cutting through me. "Of course there are."

"Right." I clear my throat. "Of course."

"Can you be quiet, please? Tyler's here," the girl says, turning her attention back to the front of the room.

Tyler stands before the crowd, his lips curled into a half smile. He nods at a person in the front row, and waves at another in the back. Hushes ring out through the crowd, everyone quieting everyone else, not realizing they're the ones making the most noise. Soon the entire library falls quiet. All eyes are on Tyler.

"First and foremost, I would like to thank you all for coming here. As most of you are aware, today marks the end of my term. It has been an honor to serve by your side. I want to thank you, each and every one of you, for serving your land well. Because of you, I am proud to call myself a patrol."

The crowd erupts in cheers. A patrol at the front stands up, points at Tyler, and shouts something incoherent. The ones around him begin cheering even louder, some of them stomping their feet. Someone behind me whistles, loud and sharp. It pierces my eardrum, and rings through my head. The sound makes me gnash my teeth together. I notice that Archer is the only person staring at the ground, the only one that remains silent.

Tyler waves his hands in the air with a smile on his face. I can see his mouth move, but can't hear the words over the constant cheers. Someone in front screams for everyone to shut up, and slowly the crowd begins to quiet.

"That's enough. Everyone calm down," Tyler says. "As it turns out, three years will sneak up on you quick." His eyes scan the room until he settles them on me. "Sticking with tradition, the newest member of the patrols will be the one to end my term. Char, that person would be you. Are you willing to accept this task?"

I shift in my seat as all eyes turn toward me. My throat tightens, and my cheeks grow flush. I feel like a fool standing here, staring at Tyler, not knowing what to say. No one told me Tyler's term was ending. No one told me I'd have to be the one to do it. Archer clears his throat beside me, loud enough for me to notice.

"Yes. Yes, I accept," I say.

"That is wonderful news," Tyler says, his voice soft. He rubs the side of his jaw for a moment before continuing. "With that out of the way, I wanted to inform everyone that our maintenance issue from this morning has been fixed. Thank you to those who helped out, and thank you to everyone else who sat patiently by for the past couple of hours while it was being attended to."

Couple of hours. I feel an ache developing over my left eye. I've been here for a couple of hours. That's impossible. I lean close enough to Archer that my lips lightly brush his ear. "Why don't I remember coming here?"

Archer shrugs. He brushes a hand over his pants, smoothing out invisible creases. Tyler is still up front talking to the crowd, but I've stopped paying attention to what he says. Instead, I stare at Archer and wait for him to reply. When I catch him looking back at me from the corner of his eye, he slumps his shoulders and leans in to my side.

"We need to talk," he whispers in my ear. "After."

Archer raises an eyebrow at me, and I nod to let him know I understand.

"Char," Tyler says. I look up and see him staring at me again. "You and I will reconvene at The Chasm in exactly one hour. Don't forget your gun, and don't forget your breather. I will need Archer there as witness, along with two other patrols of my choosing. You will know who you are when I come and speak to you directly. The rest of you must get back to work immediately. There are cities to patrol."

The front row is the first to stand. The patrol that riled up the crowd earlier is now instructing everyone to file out and leave. A few people walk up to Tyler before they go, and shake his hand. I'm still sitting, staring at Tyler, when Archer grabs me by the elbow.

"Come on. It's time to leave," he says, pulling me to my feet.

We are one of the last people to leave the library. Archer and I stand out front, still on the stone path. My hands are in my pockets as I stare at the ground.

"You'll be fine," Archer says. "It's not a big deal."

"Not a big deal," I repeat. "Why the hell didn't anyone tell me? I had no idea. You should have said something. Unless you did, and I can't remember. Seems to be a problem with me."

"It slipped my mind."

I laugh. "Slipped your mind?"

"Yeah. Look, I'm sorry. But we need to talk."

"Not right now. Look! I'm shaking." I hold out my hand to Archer, showing him the way it trembles. "I didn't have time to prepare. What am I supposed to do?"

Archer grabs me by my wrist, and pulls me off to the side. He looks over his shoulder, and then looks over mine. I see him smile and nod at a young patrol as she walks past. As soon as she's gone, his face grows hard.

"Char, look—"

"Archer, we don't have time for this. I'm sorry. Whatever it is can wait. It takes us almost an hour just to walk to The Chasm from here. I can't be late."

Archer drops my wrist, but I can still feel the way his fingers squeezed the bone. I rub the skin with my other hand as he mumbles an apology. I smile to let him know it's fine, and then we begin our walk to The Chasm. Even though Archer's content with silence, I can tell that something is bothering him. It's the way he chews on his lip, and can't seem to stop fidgeting. He checks his belt, pulls out his gun then puts it back, runs his fingers through his hair, cracks his neck, straightens out his shirt. Every once in awhile he clears his throat. When he isn't staring at the ground, his eyes dart back and forth over the horizon.

After what feels like an eternity of dead silence, the tension finally gets to me.

"I know you're upset. I know you have something to say. I want to get this all over with first. I've got too much on my mind right now to deal with anything else."

Archer nods. His cheeks are puffed out, filled with air. He blows the air out through his lips, which makes a deep whistling sound. The action makes him look ridiculous. I look up at the sky. The hour is almost up. We are already at the outskirts of Felicity, amongst the dead trees and decaying houses.

The air around the bridge feels more dense than usual. The weather in Felicity was beautiful, but here it's hard to breathe. My skin feels coated in sweat, the fog settling into my pores. There are only a few patrols on this side of the bridge, most of them hovering around the gate. I look around for Tyler, but he's nowhere to be found. Archer jogs up to the nearest patrol, a stocky man with black hair and a crease in his chin, and pats him on the shoulder.

"Any idea where Tyler is?"

"He's over the bridge," the man says. "He crossed over a few minutes ago."

Archer looks at me, and nods. "You ready?"

I pull the gun from my belt, and give it a quick inspection. "Ready."

Archer waves at the guard, and the gate swings open. I only take three steps before I'm forced to use my breather. I pull it from my pocket, and put the square tip in my mouth. Three pumps of air, and one deep breath, and my lungs don't feel as tight. Archer is fairing better than I am, because he hasn't bothered touching his breather yet.

The air is even worse as we approach the center of the bridge. The fog is dense enough to prevent me from seeing the other end of the bridge, and I can hardly make out Archer's silhouette as he walks beside me. I scoot a little closer to his side, enough that our shoulders touch. I've never been near The Chasm during weather like this. The fog drifts up from the giant crevice beneath us, smothering everything it touches. I can feel it, taste it. I hear Archer beside me pumping his breather, and taking a long, deep breath.

The air begins its return to normalcy once our feet touch soil in Calloway. Archer takes a quick look around The Chasm for Tyler. He spots him standing to the left of the bridge, his toes close to the jagged edge of the hole. Tyler doesn't immediately turn around to face us when we approach him. He keeps his sights set on the black abyss below.

"It seems to never end," he says. "The darkness goes on for eternity."

"Everything has an end," Archer says.

"That it does." Tyler turns to face us, a weary smile on his face. "Are you ready, Char?"

"Yes, I'm ready. I—"

"She's nervous," Archer says. "You should have seen the way her hands were shaking."

I look at Archer, eyes wide. "They weren't that bad."

Tyler laughs. "There's nothing to be nervous about."

"She's afraid she's going to do it wrong. If she doesn't stop trembling she might shoot the tip of your nose off," Archer says, smiling.

I shake my head. "That's not true! I never said that!"

"You have to keep steady, or you might shoot his neck. That'd be an awful mess."

"Archer!"

Tyler laughs as he slips an arm around my shoulder. It's strange to see him like this, smiling and at ease. I've grown used to his hard edge, and tough demeanor. "Ignore Archer. He thinks he's funny, but he's actually rather irritating."

"You laughed. I saw you laugh," Archer says.

"All jokes aside, there's nothing to worry about. It's an easy job. I've done it. That guy over there has done it." He points to a patrol wandering in the distance. "Archer's done it three times. There weren't a lot of new recruits after he joined, so he had to pick up the slack a little more."

"It's because they were intimidated," Archer says with a smile. "I'm a tough act to follow."

"Call it whatever you'd like," Tyler says. "The point is, Char, we've all been in your position before. If I'm not worried about it, you shouldn't be either."

"Tell me what I need to do," I say. "What's going to happen?"

Tyler retracts his arm from around my neck, and takes a step back towards The Chasm. "I'll stand about right here." He gestures to a spot in the dirt, right by the edge. Then he lifts his hand, and points at the center of his forehead. "You shoot me here. It should drive me backward into The Chasm, but if it doesn't, you will need to direct me. A quick kick in the chest should do."

I feel sick. Imaging myself shooting Tyler in the head, and my boot pressing into his chest, makes my stomach turn. It all seems so pointless. I knew what I was getting into when I joined the patrols. I know I shouldn't question it. But like my first steps inside of Felicity, this too doesn't feel right anymore. Tyler's only crime was keeping the cities from destruction. Why does he have to be punished?

"Got that, newbie?" Archer asks, nudging me in the arm.

I clear my throat. "Yeah. I got it. Not a problem."

"Great. The two other witnesses are arriving now. Shawn, and Lauren."

I recognize the two patrols walking up to us. They were both there the day I encountered Sam outside of his smoldering, broken down shack. Shawn was one of the patrols who held him back. Lauren was the one that put a bullet in his head. My heart races at the sight of them. I can still picture the way the blood splattered on their uniforms as Sam met his end. Lauren nods at me as she walks past. They stand by Tyler, who gives each of them their instructions. While they talk, I take the time to grab Archer by the arm and drag him off to the side.

"What is he playing at?" I ask.

Archer frowns. "What the hell are you on about now?"

My throat is tight. I look over my shoulder, and notice Tyler staring at me as he speaks to Shawn and Lauren. "Out of all the patrols here, he picks those two. Is he trying to tell me something? Is he mocking me?"

"You're thinking too much into this." Archer pats me on the shoulder. "They're both experienced. They've both been in the patrols for a long time now. Regardless of what happened, they know how to file a witness report, they know how to do the job. That's why they're here."

I look down at the ground. "Yeah. That makes sense."

"Relax, newbie. You're all wound up. Grab your gun. Tyler's ready for you."

I pull the gun from my belt, and look it over one last time. It's loaded, and the safety is off. I follow Archer back to the edge of The Chasm. Tyler's welcoming smile makes my stomach turn. He backs himself as close to The Chasm as he can get, and motions for me to come close.

"Everyone else stand back a good ten feet. I only need you to watch, not participate," Tyler says with a quick laugh. I hear footsteps shuffling behind me as the three witnesses take their positions. Once their movements stop, Tyler looks me in the eye. When he speaks again, his voice is low. "They need to watch you do this, Char. They need to know who you are."

I search Tyler's face for answers. "What are you saying?"

Tyler takes a deep breath. "You'll find out soon enough. We don't have much time now. Raise your gun."

I nod, and raise my gun until it is level with Tyler's forehead — right in the center, just as he said. I pull back the hammer, and concentrate on keeping my hands from shaking. The gun rattles in my fingers.

"When this is done, you need to find your brother."

My arm relaxes, the gun slowly falling. "Alex?"

"Put your gun back up."

I straighten myself up, and raise the gun back to Tyler's forehead.

"Don't become another one of the forgotten, Char. Tell Evelyn to follow the music."

"My mother? Tyler, what—"

"I've wasted too much time already. They'll know something is wrong. Shoot."

"Tyler, I—"

"Do it, Char. Pull the trigger. NOW!"

The gun fires. The bullet lands in the center of his forehead, exactly as it should. Tyler's eyes glaze over. He stumbles forward once, and his body begins to crumble. He's falling, but he's not falling back. I raise my foot, and shove a boot hard into his chest. Then he falls, eyes still wide open, into the blackness below. As the darkness devours his lifeless body, all I can think about is Alex. I need to find my brother.

THE FORGOTTEN

CHAPTER SEVENTEEN
Alexander Moore

I look over my shoulder, down the hall where Harry stormed off a few hours ago. I can hear him shuffling about in Char's old bedroom now, the floor creaking in rhythm with his steps. He is walking back and forth, pacing. I'm surprised he hasn't worn himself out by now.

I shift my weight from my left side to my right. The floor is uncomfortable, and my hip has started to go numb. I click the radio back on, the sixth time I've done so in the past hour. I don't know what I was expecting to happen. Nothing changes. Nothing has ever changed.

"Help. I repeat: We need help."

There is static, like there always is.

"My name is E—"

The radio screeches a high-pitched, awful noise. I don't bother moving, or turning the dial. It won't make a difference.

"Please. If you can hear me, if there's anyone out there, we need your help. I repeat: We need your help. We—"

Then, silence. I put the radio back on the ground in front of me, and lean back, stretching. I crank my neck to the left, then to the right, and then I push my chin into my chest. I can feel my muscles pulling at the top of my spine. I lay down on my back, and stretch my legs out in front of me like a V. I look up at the ceiling and listen to the girl's voice, her message repeating.

"Help. I repeat: We need help."

There is a bang at the front door. It's hard enough to rattle the walls, loud enough to drown out the static of the radio. Before I have the chance to move, Char bursts in. She is panting, her chest heaving up and down. There is red splattered on her face. It looks like blood. Behind her is another patrol, with steel blue eyes and curly brown hair. He's the one that brought Harry and I home the night Char crossed over. He is stone-faced, with a hand readied on his gun. I think his name is Archer.

"Ch...Char." I scramble to my feet, tripping once before finding my footing. "What happened to you? Is that blood?"

Char is silent, staring. She is still out of breath, gasping for air. I hear Harry running through the hall and within seconds he is standing at my side, our elbows touching.

He looks at Char, and gasps. "What the hell is going on here?"

Archer steps forward. "You may or may not remember me. I helped you get back home when your sister crossed. Char has been working closely with me these last couple of days. She requested we check on you."

Char eyes narrow, and she points at the radio. "Is that what this is all about? Is that why I'm here?"

"I don't know why you're here," I tell her.

Harry elbows me out of the way and moves in front of Char. "I told him we should have came to you first, but he didn't want to listen. I told him—"

"Everyone shut the hell up," Archer says. He tilts his head to the side, his eyebrows furrowed. "Listen."

"Please. If you can hear me, if anyone is out there..."

"Oh my god," Char whispers. She pushes a hand into her forehead, and shuts her eyes. When she opens them again she looks different, angry. Her face is red and her chest is heaving, even though she's long caught her breath. "What have you done?"

"I... I was going to tell you. I—"

"You." Char stomps over to me, and pushes a finger into my chest. "You complete idiot. Do you realize what you've done?"

"Char, I'm sorry. I didn't know."

Char grips my shoulders so hard I wince. Her fingernails dig into my skin, and I have to

bite my cheek to keep myself from crying out. She pulls me against her, and stares into my eyes. Her hot breath is inches from my face.

"I have been gone three days," she snarls. "Three fucking days, and the world is falling apart."

Archer grabs her arm, and gently pulls her away. I rub my shoulder, feeling the sting in my eyes, and the sting in my flesh. My skin throbs where her nails dug in. I think she drew blood.

"I know you're angry," Archer says, his hand still gripping Char's arm. "But you need to shut the hell up for a second. There is something going on here. Listen."

147

Char opens her mouth to argue, but stops when Archer puts up his hand. I hold my breath as everyone stands still, listening.

"My name is E—"

I watch Char's face as the screech belts through the radio. It startles her slightly and she jumps the littlest bit, but her eyes never leave the ground. They seem to twitch, scanning themselves over the fibers in the carpet as she waits for the voice to come back.

"Please. If you can hear me, if there's anyone out there, we need your help. I repeat: We need your help. We—"

Silence falls over the room as the girl's voice disappears. Char stands as still as stone, staring at the floor. Archer stares too, somewhere off in the distance, maybe at the back wall. His hand still grips Char's arm, so tight that his fingertips have turned white. She doesn't seem to notice.

"Help. I repeat: We need help."

There is static, like there always is. Char shifts her weight from one foot to the next, and Archer loosens his grip enough to let her move. Harry hasn't left my side. He's staring at Char, waiting for her to respond.

"My name is E—"

"That's it," I say over the loud screech. "The message keeps going. That's all there is to it."

"We don't know who that girl is," Harry says. "We don't know what she wants."

Char tucks a strand of hair behind her ear. "She sounds—"

I cut her off. "Alone?"

"No. Familiar," Char states. "I've heard that voice somewhere else."

Harry and I exchange glances. "Where?"

Char shrugs. "I don't know. Maybe I'm imagining it."

"She gives her name," Archer says. "What is it?"

I shake my head. "I don't know. Her voice cuts out when she says it. I've listened to it over and over again, hoping to hear something more. It cuts her off at the same spot every single time, no matter what I do."

Archer takes a deep breath, and puffs out his cheeks, exhaling slow. "There's nothing you can do to fix it? To make her voice more clear?"

"It's not the radio," I say.

"What is it then?" Archer asks.

"I'm not certain." I bite my bottom lip, not sure how to explain myself without sounding crazy. "All I know is that no matter what I do to the antenna, or the tuner, nothing changes. I don't think it's because the signal is bad. I think the message is corrupted."

Behind me, I hear Harry slide his body down onto the couch. I hadn't had the chance to give him that bit of information yet. He was too busy pacing a hole in the floor.

"You didn't have the radio when I left," Char says. "Tell me how you got it."

"From some asshole named Adam," Harry says.

"That's the gist of it," I say. "The night you left, some kid named Adam showed up on our doorstep. He asked me to fix the radio for him. At first I told him no, but—"

"But he pulled a gun on us!" Harry says. "A fucking gun!"

"He demanded we fix it, and told us we had five days. He didn't tell us why."

"Shit," Char says, rubbing the back of her neck. She exhales loudly. "Archer, can you leave us three alone for a minute?"

"Char, you know I can't do that."

"Archer?" His radio calls out. "Archer, do you read me?"

He removes the radio from his hip, and gives Char a strange look before bringing it to his lips. "This is Archer. Give me a minute." He clips the radio back on his belt. "I'm going to step outside to take this. Whatever you do while I'm gone is none of my business."

Char smiles, and mouths thank you to Archer as he leaves. Once he's gone and the door is shut, she waves her arms at Harry and I, telling us to come in close. We both huddle as close as we can to my sister.

"Look, there's some really weird shit going on," she says. "Right after the storm, Archer and I were called to this really crappy house at the back of Calloway. Four other patrols were there, restraining a teenager. He was your age, Alex, maybe older. He was screaming all this nonsense about our father."

"Our father?" I take a step back, but Char grabs my hand and pulls me back to her.

"Yes, our father, Charles Moore. This kid was screaming at me, telling me how our father was murdered, and how he could have helped everyone. Then one of the patrols shot him before he could say anything else."

"Our father's dead?" I didn't know. Why didn't I know?"

"Yes. He died when you were little."

"Why didn't you tell me?"

"That's not important right now."

"Okay," I say, rubbing a hand over my hair. "Okay. So, that kid, Sam. Did you know him?"

"Him? No. But his sister was the girl I threw over The Chasm the day I crossed over. He mentioned that too, before he was killed. He said that his sister had only wanted to come find some sort of proof, I don't know. Nothing really made sense."

"You're going to get in trouble for telling us," Harry says.

Char looks over her shoulder, back towards the front door. "I don't think anyone will know. Listen, there's more to the story. After the patrols dragged him away, Archer and I went inside of his house. It was a mess. His bedroom was covered with paper, really nonsensical. But on one wall he wrote the words: We are the forgotten. Then under that, it said: Rest in peace, Charles Moore."

"Holy shit, Char," Harry says. "Is that why you have blood on your face? Did someone confront you?"

"What?" Char laughs. "No, nothing like that. The blood is from something else, from another patrol that ended his term today. He... before he was shot, he said the same thing that was written on that wall. He told me not to become one of the forgotten."

I can feel my pulse racing. "One of the forgotten. I don't like how that sounds."

"Who else knows about all of this?" Harry asks.

"Archer knows a lot because we've been assigned together. He's with me constantly. I had to tell him that our old lead, Tyler, told me to come see you. Otherwise, I don't think he'd let us deviate from our orders. I haven't told him anything else yet. I'm worried he wouldn't take me seriously. It's all a bit crazy sounding, isn't it?"

"What do you think it all means?" I ask. "What does it have to do with the radio we fixed?"

"I'd say that girl sounds pretty forgotten to me," Harry states.

"You might be right, Harry. I don't know. The radio was a surprise to me. Tyler told me to come find you, but he didn't have the time to tell me why. That's the reason I'm here. If one patrol knew what you've found, others might find out as well. The patrols are going to be watching you very closely. I'm going to do what I can, but in the meantime, you two need to watch your ass."

Archer walks back in. His eyes are red, and his jaw is clenched tight. He avoids eye contact with everyone in the room, staring only at the back wall. I'm the only one that seems to notice him. Both Char and Harry are still huddled together.

"There's something else," Harry says. He looks at me, and raises his eyebrows. "The briefcase."

Char eyes move between Harry and I. "Briefcase?"

I sigh. "When I went to the dump to grab some batteries for the radio, I found a briefcase."

Char raises an eyebrow. "What's so special about a briefcase?"

"Well," Harry says. He walks across the room where the briefcase still leans against the wall, and holds it up for Char to see. He makes sure to turn the case so the bullet hole is what she notices first. "Look for yourself."

"I think it was planted in the dump for me to find," I tell her.

Char snatches the case away from Harry, and rushes to the kitchen counter to set it down. "Have you opened it yet?"

"No," I say, shaking my head. "I was waiting until tomorrow."

"Archer, do we have the time?" Char asks, turning to Archer. He leans against the front door, his head is hung low, his eyes on his feet. He nods, slowly, without saying a word.

"You're going to open it now?" Harry asks. "Right now?"

"There's something weird going on, and I want to find out what it is," Char says. "Now's as good of a time as any."

Char examines the rusted metal lock. She tries to strong-arm it open, but it doesn't budge. She tries wiggling the lock loose, but that doesn't work either. She picks the case up, and tucks it beneath her armpit. After it's secured, tucked tight, she rams her nail inside the keyhole, and tries to turn the lock that way. It pains me to watch as her nail tears off close to the skin. Apparently, it bothers me more than it bothers her, because she bites the rest of the broken nail off with her teeth.

After everything else fails, Char raises the case high above her head. Right when I think she's going to throw it angrily against the back wall, she brings the case down and whacks the lock against the kitchen counter. Once. Twice. Three times. The damn thing doesn't budge.

"You need something stronger, and you need a better angle." I open the drawer to my right, and pull out a hammer. "Here, try this instead."

Char grabs it with a smile, and positions the case so the lock hangs over the edge of the counter. I grab Harry by the shirtsleeve, and pull him back a few inches. We watch as Char holds the hammer over her head, and then swings it down hard on the lock. It bends, but doesn't open. She raises the hammer again, and slams it one more time into the lock. It rattles as it hits the tile floor.

"There," Char says, smiling.

She hands the hammer off to me, and I put it back inside the drawer. I hold my breath as she runs a finger over the clip that holds the case closed. She flips the tab with her finger, and the case springs open.

"What's in it?" Harry asks, looking over my shoulder.

"Papers," Char says. "And a bullet"

Char plucks the small metal casing from inside, and holds it up, examining it. I hold out my hand, and she places it down in my palm. At least I got something right. The bullet was still lodged inside. I roll it around between my fingers. It's heavier than I thought it would be.

"Is there a name inside?" Harry asks. "Does it say who the case belongs to?"

Char pulls out a stack of papers and neatly places them down on the counter. She squints, and pulls the case a little closer to her face. There's a small metal plaque attached to the bloodstained felt, maybe two inches wide and half an inch tall. It's caked in dried blood. Char licks her thumb, and rubs it over the plaque.

She throws a hand over her mouth. "Shit," she whispers through her fingers.

"What? What's it say?" I nudge her out of the way. I squint and tilt my head to the side, trying to read the plaque. When I see the name my breath catches in my throat, and my knees feel weak. "Charles Moore. I… I can't believe it."

"Holy shit," Harry says, throwing his hands in the air. "Are you messing with me? Does it really say that?"

I step away from the case, and motion for Harry to come look. When he reads the name his face falls. He grabs his stomach, and takes two slow steps backward. "I don't believe it. That's your dad's case. We were right about Adam, about him putting the case there where you'd find it. He must have known who owned it."

I run my fingers over the inside of the bullet hole. This was my father's case, and he died with it clutched to his chest. Shot in the back. The inside of me is seething, hatred brewing. For who, I don't know. Perhaps I never will. All I know is that whoever it was is nothing more than a coward. You have to be to shoot a man in the back.

"Look at this, Alex," Char says, holding out a sheet of paper. "Do you know what any of this means?"

I take the paper from her. It's covered in equations that I don't understand, and diagrams with strange labels. His handwriting is chaotic, like mine. Hard to read. I flip the paper over, but the backside is blank. I hand it back to Char.

"Looks like he was trying to work out some problems, but I don't really know what they mean without more context."

Harry picks up a large piece of thick paper that's been creased neatly in half. He unfolds it, and holds it out in the air. "Anyone know what this is?"

"That's a blue print," I tell him. I grab the paper from him, and spread it out over the floor. "Looks maybe like it's for a building."

Char stands over me, casting a shadow down on the blueprint. She tilts her head to the side, and then crouches down next to me. "That's the library. I can tell by the dome on top."

I silently run my fingers over the sketch, curving them over the arch, and back down the side. It's strange to touch something my father made, to feel the way his pencil dug into the paper, every line and indentation. "Look at this line work. This over here," I point to the detail in the dome, "I can see what it looks like perfectly in my mind. Does it work like a prism?"

"Yes," Char says, quietly. "How can you tell?"

"This over here," I move my finger over to the triangle etched on the side of the paper, "it's got the angle of incidence and the refraction angle written inside of it. The law of refraction. I read about it once."

Char smiles, and grabs the blueprint off the ground. "Of course you did."

Harry laughs. "That's why we keep him around."

Char puts the blueprint for the library back inside the briefcase, along with the first paper she handed me. Harry steps up beside her and grabs another sheet. The paper looks similar to the one from the last blueprint, only smaller in size.

"Here's something else," he says. "Any ideas?"

I shrug. "It looks like a box with two flaps."

"Seriously? You figured out prism from a triangle on the last one, and this one looks like a box with flaps," Harry says. "I don't get you."

"It looks like a container I guess, with some sort of mechanism inside. Is that better?"

"Not really."

"Well there aren't books on mechanical boxes around town, so this one's more tricky."

Harry looks up at my sister. "What do you think, Char?"

I look over at Char who stares at the small blueprint with a scowl on her face. Her eyes flicker over the lines and tiny details of the paper, searching for familiarity. All of a sudden her eyes grow wide. It looks like someone clicked on a light switch in her mind.

"I know what that is."

I make a face, and shake my head. "What?"

"That's a music box."

CHAPTER EIGHTEEN
Char Moore

I grab the sketch of the music box away from Harry, and pull the blueprint of the library back out of the briefcase. I roll them both up and tuck them into the back of my pants, under my shirt so no one else can see them. I don't tell anyone why I take them, only that I want to look them over a little more to be sure. Evelyn must follow the music. That is what Tyler told me. I may not understand what he meant right now, but I have a feeling I will soon. Finding a blueprint of a music box seems like more than a coincidence. Maybe Evelyn will have a better understanding than I do.

"We've been here too long. The other patrols will begin questioning us," I say.

Alex crosses his arms over his chest, and looks at the radio. It's still playing its cry for help. Over and over, the girl's voice calls out to us. I put a hand on Alex's shoulder and give it a soft squeeze. Then I walk to the radio, raise a boot in the air, and stomp down hard.

Alex grabs my arm and tries to pull me away. "Stop!"

I brush him off and scoop the broken pieces of plastic into my arms. Balancing the radio in one hand, I yank the antenna cord hard enough to dislodge it. I throw it to the ground beside me. Alex balls his hands into a tight fist, knuckles white, and tries to take a swing at me. I hunch my shoulder and turn to the right. His punch lands at the top of my back.

"I can still fix it. If you stop right now, I can put it back together. Please," Alex says. His voice trembles. His body shakes. When Harry tries to pull him away, Alex throws an elbow behind him and tries to knock him back. It hits Harry in the center of his chest. Without flinching, Harry adjusts his grip and wraps his arms around Alex's upper body, keeping him still.

"It'll be alright," Harry tells him.

I clench my jaw. "I'm sorry, Alex."

I bring the radio high above my head, and throw it hard into the ground. Everything that was once intact has now been destroyed, lying in tiny pieces on the kitchen floor. Alex slumps in Harry's arms, shaking his head from side to side.

"No, no, no," he repeats, his voice hoarse.

I turn my back on him, and keep my eyes set on Archer. He is still leaning against the front door, his eyes on the ground. They look empty, unmoved. I watch his chest, counting the rhythm of his breath. It's fast. His heart is racing. And yet, those vacant eyes and relaxed jaw make him look uninterested. Something is wrong.

"The radio had to be destroyed," I say, still watching Archer. "You said yourself that the message never changes. You tried everything, that's what you said. The only thing that radio is good for is bringing you trouble. Get rid of the pieces. Throw it in an old flour sack and drop it off at the dump. Douse it in oil and burn it. I don't care what you do. Just get rid of it."

I can see Harry in the reflection of the window. He drops to his knees, and pulls the broken pieces of plastic together into one pile. He pulls out the antenna cord, and wraps it into a tight little ball. Then he finds the two batteries, and puts them off to the side.

"She's right, Alex," Harry says. "The radio isn't important anymore. It was the message that was important, and getting rid of the radio doesn't get rid of what we heard."

"I worked so hard to get that thing to work," Alex says, his voice soft.

"No one else would have been able to do what you did," Harry says. "That was absolutely brilliant. But it's over now."

"It's time to go," I tell Archer. I reach my hand out, offering to help him up. When he grabs hold, his palms are covered in sweat. I keep a tight firm on his hand, and once he is on his feet I pull him in close. "Everything okay?"

He leans in to my ear, and whispers. "There's been a murder in the alley behind the general store. A young girl. No one's been able to identify the body."

Now I understand. The way he sat quietly in the corner, waiting for me to say goodbye to my brother. Why he didn't intervene when I selfishly wanted to stay longer, all so I could open a briefcase. He was doing his best to stay calm, to remain levelheaded so as not to give himself away. My heart drops, and I feel my throat growing tight. I feel like a fool.

I give Archer a quick nod to let him know I understand, and together we leave Harry and Alex to clean up the mess I left behind.

"You should have told me," I say once we are outside. "We could have left sooner."

"Don't worry about it," Archer says. His voice cracks the smallest bit. "As far as the other patrols know, we were still by The Chasm. If we got to the scene too quick they'd realize we were wandering off."

"I don't regret coming here."

"You shouldn't regret it. You made the right decision destroying the radio."

"I know I did. He's going to be pissed off at me for quite some time though."

Archer shrugs. "He'll get over it."

"What do you think it all meant?"

"Don't know. Could mean anything."

I keep my eyes on my feet, watching them move forward and back. "I suppose."

Archer shakes his head, and rubs the back of his neck. "You said Tyler told you to check on your brother. Did he tell you anything else? You need to be honest with me."

My heart flutters a little faster. I clear my throat. "No. He told me to find Alex. That was all he said."

"Tyler probably knew about the radio, and wanted to make sure you got rid of it before anyone else found out," Archer says. "You and I still need to talk. Don't forget that."

"You still look pale. You going to be okay?"

"I'm fine. It's always tough when there's been a murder."

I give him a wary smile as we round the corner in front of the general store. The front door of the business is being guarded by two patrols. To the right of the store is a small alley, no wider than a few feet. There, two more patrols stand guard around a small body. The patrol on the right is Shawn, but I don't recognize the other. The two of them stand side-by-side, blocking wandering eyes from seeing what lies behind them. All I can see is a pair of bare feet peeking out from between them, relaxed, sprawled out in the shape of a V. A small patch of dried blood is caked on the sole of her left foot.

"Fuck," I hear Archer mumble. He comes to a staggering halt before turning his back on the scene. He leans forward, hands pressed against his knees.

"Take a few deep breaths," I say while patting him on the back.

It only takes a moment for Archer to straighten himself back out again. He stands tall with his lips pressed tight together. He cracks his neck, and gives me a hardened smile. "Let's go see what happened."

I nod, and smile back. That was the first time Archer has shown me weakness. Here is a young female victim lying dead on the ground. Her shoes are missing. Exactly like his sister. I bet he was the one that found her limp body, lying in the same way, with the toes pointing up in the shape of a V.

Archer walks up to Shawn, who watches us intently as we move. His gun is out of the holster, and is hanging in his hand down by his side. Even up this close I cannot see the body behind him. All I can see is a messy bit of blonde hair flowing over the ground like a river.

"Alright, Shawn. Give me the details," Archer says.

"Curtis, the owner of the general store, said she came in a couple of hours ago," Shawn says. "After she left he saw her talking outside the door to someone he didn't recognize. Said he was unfamiliar. When he took the trash out a little while later, he found her dead in the alley. Claims he didn't hear or see any signs of a struggle."

Archer frowns and rubs his chin. "Lauren told me they've been unable to identify her. You have no idea who she is?"

"Though Curtis claims she's been in several times before, he never knew her name," the other patrol says. "She was quiet. Got what she needed and left."

"I assume she purchased something while she was here this time," I say. "Does he remember what it was?"

"A bar of soap, and a small piece of candy," Shawn says. "Neither of which was found on the body."

I look down at the girl's bare toes poking out from between the two patrols. "And they took her shoes?"

"No," Shawn says. "Well, not both of them at least. One boot was found a little ways up the alley. The other is still missing."

"Let me get this straight," Archer says, rubbing the back of his neck. "She was murdered over a bar of fucking soap and a piece of goddamn candy?"

"There's more to it than that," the other patrol says. "You'll have to take a look for yourself."

Archer flares his nostrils as he takes a deep breath. "Alright. Let's see."

The two patrols share a look before they each step to the side. I let my eyes slowly wander down to the body of the girl sprawled out before me. The first thing that I notice is her pants, cut short above the ankle. They must be two sizes too small. My heart thumps loud inside my chest. My throat begins to tighten. I have to swallow the lump back down, to keep myself from suffocating.

I see her light pink shirt that dulls her already pale skin. It's ripped at the neck and crumpled at the front. Deep scratches run down her arms. I can hear my heartbeat in my ears. It is loud, chaotic. I try to take a deep breath, but my chest is tight. I make a wheezing noise when I inhale. I close my eyes for a moment and try to count to ten. I need to calm down. It's not her. It can't be her. I won't let it be her.

When I open my eyes again my stomach clenches. I can feel the bile rising up my throat. Blonde hair is matted against her face, caked with blood. Her brown eyes are wide, her mouth agape. Everything begins to spin. The alley, the patrols, the girl, they are nothing but a blur as they whirl around me. I stumble back, hand clutching my chest.

It's her.

"Mara," I whisper.

Archer catches me as I fall to my knees. He wraps his arms around my shoulders, keeping me upright. He is saying something. It doesn't make sense. His words are jumbled, muffled. I can't make them out. I press my face into his chest and scream. The sound tears through me, rattling my chest. Suddenly I feel a sharp pain radiating from my jaw. The side of my face is throbbing. I see Archer in front of me, holding a hand in the air. He brings his palm down and slaps my cheek one more time.

"Get it together. Breathe."

I take three loud breaths. Deep, deep breaths that make my chest swell with air. Archer clutches my coat and pulls me to my feet. He puts a hand against my chest and presses down, harder and harder, until my breathing is even and light.

"There you go," Archer whispers. "You'll be okay."

I look in his eyes, my head still throbbing. I try to talk to him, but my mouth won't move. The sounds won't come out.

"I know," Archer says. "But you have to pull yourself together. We will find out who did this, and they will suffer for what they have done. I'll make sure of that. In the meantime, we need you to identify her. Who is she?"

My mouth is dry. I taste blood at the back of my throat. "Her name is Mara Matthews." My voice cracks as I speak. "She was my brother's friend."

Archer's body stiffens. He looks over at Mara, then back at me. "Fucking hell."

"Yeah," I say.

"No. You don't understand. I need you to do me a favor. Look at her shirt. Can you do that for me?"

"Her shirt?"

"Yes. Her shirt. Only her shirt, okay? I won't make you look at anything else."

I nod. Holding my breath, I turn to look at Mara one last time. Only her shirt, like Archer said, because I don't think I could bare to see her broken, empty face one more time.

When I first saw Mara I noticed that her shirt was crumpled down the front. Her clothes were a mess, like someone had them clenched in their fist. Now, one of the patrols has taken the time to smooth out the front of her shirt while I was having a meltdown. My eyes catch sight of something large, and black. I take one step closer and tilt my head to the side.

Between the splotches of blood and torn cotton there is a message.

Written in black jagged letters, the words: Let them forget.

CHAPTER NINETEEN
Evelyn Moore

The inside of the Riot Cafe is filled with music loud enough to make my teeth rattle. The noise makes the place appear busier than it is. In actuality, there are only a few patrons sitting around the coffee bar, sipping the last remains from the bottom of their cups. Late afternoon is a strange time for the cafe. It is too early for dinner, and too late for lunch. Perfect for someone who wants to be alone.

I situate myself at the back of the room, at a small table made of rusted metal. I slide myself down into the red leather seat with a notebook clutched to my chest. I pull my phone from my pocket, and place it face-up on the tabletop. Once I'm settled in, I grab the pen I tucked inside the notebook's spiral spine, and turn to the first page.

What do I remember?

That is all I've had the chance to write down so far. The phone calls, the strange messages, they have to mean something. When I try to piece it together in my head I am left confused. Not because I don't know what's going on, but because the act of remembering begins to wear me down. My head aches. I get tired. The music starts up again. Things begin to grow hazy, like I'm staring at memories through patches of fog. The more I try to grasp them, the farther they float away. Writing them down seems like the best solution.

I tap my pen on the table, and gnaw at my bottom lip.

"What can I get you?"

The waitress is standing over the table, arms crossed over her chest. She's an older woman, in her late sixties. Her hair is pulled into a tight bun at the top of her head. Her worn, blue eyes are lined with deep wrinkles, and her mouth is pursed in a permanent scowl. She smells of old cigarettes covered up by too much perfume.

"A cup of coffee would be nice," I say.

"That it?"

"You guys still have those lemon muffins? The ones with the bits of sugar on top?"

"Yep."

"Then I'll take one of those, too."

"Nothing else?"

"Nothing else."

"Fine. I'll be back in a sec."

I turn back to the notebook as the waitress shuffles off.

I read the words again: What do I remember?

Beneath that I write, Charles. My children. My home. Patricia. Music.

I underline the word music three times. When I look up I see the waitress weaving her way back to my table. She holds a cup of coffee in one hand, and a bright yellow muffin in the other. I lean to the side, covering the notebook with my forearm as she approaches.

"Here," she says, placing the items down on the table. The plates clank against the metal, threatening to shatter. "Anything else?"

"Can I smoke in here?"

"If you want to smoke you can go outside. Anything else you need?"

"No. I suppose that's it."

The waitress shakes her head, and mumbles something incoherent under her breath before she leaves. Good thing I didn't choose this place for its hospitality. It happens to be the farthest cafe from my home, situated at the front of Felicity, close to The Chasm. When I look out the window I can see the faint silhouette of dead, brittle trees on the horizon. In the middle, the bridge rises up in the air, fading as it crosses the gap.

I write down the word Calloway, and then immediately cross it out. I don't remember my time there. I don't remember crossing the bridge. Sipping my coffee, I look back out the window and watch an elderly woman cross the street. She gets to the curb, and has a hard time stepping over. A young patrol rushes to her side, offers an elbow, and helps her over the ledge.

I write down My Parents, and cross that out as well. I'm sure there was a time I could remember their faces, or their names, or what they did while they lived here. That memory died alongside so many other memories, forgotten through time. I break off a piece of muffin and pop it in my mouth. It's dry, like it's been sitting in the open, humid air for far too long. The lemon tastes sour. I make a face, and take a sip of my coffee to wash it down.

Drinking. I write the word twice. The second time I write it, I scratch it out. I remember drinking, but I have been doing it for so long that I don't remember when it began. I don't remember why. Could be the reason my memory is failing me already. Perhaps I began drinking the moment I came to Felicity. I must have missed my life over the bridge.

My phone chimes, and the screen glows blue. It's a message from Patricia asking where I've gone. I double-check the time. I've only left the house forty-five minutes ago. I type a quick message with the simple words I'm out, and turn my attention back to the notebook.

Nothing makes sense yet. I close my eyes and rub my temples, trying to think. This isn't working. It's time for a new approach. I flip to a blank page, grab the pen, and write down my daughter's name.

Char.

Below that, I begin to write all the things I know about her. She has blonde hair and hazel eyes. She is a patrol. She appears timid, but is strong. She doesn't like Felicity. I could read that on her face. She does not like Patricia. I could read that on her as well.

I tap the pen on the edge of the table, and then I frown. That's all that I know about my daughter. I pull the pack of cigarettes from my pocket, and place them down on the table. My fingers itch to pull one out; my lips crave the feel of paper between them. Even my lungs ache at the anticipation of the smoke. I drain my cup of the last bit of coffee, and look around the cafe for the waitress. She is sitting at the front counter watching me. When she notices me looking, she leaps to her feet faster than I thought someone her age could do. She hurries behind the counter, grabs the pot of coffee, and heads back to my table.

I cover the notebook with my arm again, the same as I did last time. She doesn't seem to notice as she pours me another cup. When she's done, she puts the pot of coffee down on the table next to mine, and reaches into her apron pocket.

"I never do this, but it's pretty empty in here, and you look like you need a little pick me up." She places a small, metal ashtray down in front of me, and then winks. "Don't tell no one."

I don't have the time to thank her before she turns on her heels and walks back to the front of the cafe. I take a quick look around me. Everyone else has cleared out. I grab my pack of smokes, pull out a cigarette, and light it as quick as I can. I close my eyes and tilt my head back as the smoke coats my throat. It tastes better than ever. This should help me think.

I scribble down the word Alex and immediately add a question mark after his name. All I know is what Char told me, which leads me to believe he is a lot like his father. I write down Charles' name. My memories of him have grown more distant over time. I do not remember when we first met. I don't remember our wedding. The pictures I once had of us were stolen by the patrols that dragged him from our home, so there is very little left that reminds me of him.

He is dead, I write that down first. I try to remember the day they stole him from me. It was the middle of the night, and we were both asleep in bed. My hands begin to shake. I try to concentrate on keeping the pen upright between my fingers. What happened? One patrol dragged me into the kitchen, and held me up against the wall. I feel a pain growing at the base of my skull, radiating down my spine. My head is throbbing. The rest of the memory whirls by in a blur, like it's playing in fast forward. The screaming, the way I tried to fight the patrol that held me back, the others dragging Charles away.

The room begins to spin around me. The pen slides from my fingers, and rattles against the table. I close my eyes and rub my temples. I try to concentrate on the loud music blaring through the cafe, so loud that I should be unable to hear anything else. But I do. I hear it, right at the back of my mind. That same damn music I heard the night Char crossed over. The same soft chiming sounds that I had in my dream, that I had the night that mysterious man called me.

This time I listen. A smile creeps upon my face. The music is soft, and it is beautiful, and it reminds me of him. It is familiar. I take a deep drag of my cigarette, letting the taste linger on my tongue. I pick my pen back up, and hold it so tight between my fingers that my nails turn white from the grip.

I let the cigarette hang from my lips as I listen to the rhythm of the music that no one else hears. Slowly I begin to remember. The night before Charles was taken from me, before we laid our heads down for the night, he knew of his fate. I can see him now, standing in front of me, his hands on my shoulders. Those beautiful blue eyes look deep into mine, and he tells me something. If only I could remember what that something was.

I place my pen against the paper, and think. My trembling fingers create small sporadic lines on the page. I take a deep breath. The memory is there. I know it is. But the harder I try to remember, the more difficult it is to hold.

I take another drag of my cigarette. The paper warms my lips. Smoke lingers in the air in front of me like morning fog. Thin and light. Exactly like the fog that hung in the air outside my window that night. I remember pulling up the shade, and staring down at the empty street below our building. Charles put a hand on the small of my back. When I turned around to stare into his eyes they looked heavy with burden. He placed his hands on my shoulders, and he spoke low and quick.

I push my pen into the paper, and write down his last words to me - I have left a present for you. I can feel his arms around my waist, pulling me close to him. I can still feel his lips pressed against my forehead. One day you'll remember where I've hidden it. Find it for me when you do.

"But be careful," I whisper, snuffing out my cigarette in the ashtray. "Once you find it, you can never go back."

CHAPTER TWENTY
Evelyn Moore

I place some money down on the table, and leave the noise of the Riot Cafe behind me. My phone is gripped tight inside my fist as I walk. I can feel it buzzing against my palm. Bombarded by messages from Patricia. It's always Patricia. She wants to know where I am, when I will be home, where I've run off to this time. I place another cigarette between my lips, and stop walking long enough to light the tip.

I watch the smoke drift off into the empty sky, red with the glow of the low-hanging sun. It casts a strange shadow down upon the buildings that surround me. The windows glow as if they are on fire; the walls look like rust-stained stone. There will be a storm tomorrow, as violent as the last one. I've learned to recognize the signs over the years. In less than twenty-four hours there will be dust. I would bet my life on it.

My phone buzzes again. Three small, quick vibrations tickle the palm of my hand. Not a message this time. It's a phone call. I take a quick glance at the screen, long enough to confirm the call is from Patricia, and then I let it go to voicemail. I toss my notebook in a garbage can as I walk past, too afraid to hold on to it, and then I begin to walk faster. My thighs ache from the strain of my deep stride. It's not long before I drop the cigarette to the ground and begin to sprint. My heart is throbbing and my chest aching. The urge to find what Charles left behind drives me forward. I have to find it.

By the time I round the corner of my street, my lungs feel seconds from collapsing. I halt on the corner, put my hands on my knees, and take a few deep gasps of air. My head is pounding. My blood vessels feel on the verge of bursting. I stand up straight, and arch my back. I take a few, slow breaths and my heart rate begins to calm. I walk down Meadow Lane, closing in on my building, when I see three patrols standing by the front door: A tall, towering woman and two shorter men.

"Excuse me," I pant, still out of breath, as I shuffle between them.

I enter in my code, and step inside the building. My footsteps echo against the tiled floors as I walk to the elevator. Behind me, I hear the pounding of the patrol's heavy boots inching closer. When the elevator doors open I step inside. I turn to see all three patrols right behind me. They walk inside the elevator before I have the chance to close the doors.

"What floor?" I ask.

I'm answered by silence. I bite my bottom lip and press the button marked 42. My phone is buzzing in my hand. I shove it into my pocket, and stare at the numbers flashing by on the elevator's display.

"In a hurry?" the woman asks.

175

"It's a beautiful day. Finished up a nice jog," I say.

"In jeans?"

"Yep."

The woman raises her eyebrow. "You're Evelyn Moore."

"That's right," I say. "What's it to you?"

"We need to ask you some questions," she says.

I glance over at the patrol to my left. He is a short, stocky man with white hair. His jaw is tight, and his eyes narrow. The other patrol is on my right, slightly taller than the one on my left, but not as tall as the woman. His cheeks are flushed, and he looks at me with a threatening stare.

"You're more than welcome to come back tomorrow. I've got some things to attend to."

The elevator beeps, and the doors slide open. I step out into the hall, and hear the patrols step out right behind me. I pull a key out of my back pocket, but stop short of unlocking the front door. Instead, I spin on my heels and face the three patrols still following my every move.

"Like I said," I tell them. "Today isn't a good day. Come back tomorrow. I'm free all day."

"We aren't going anywhere," the white-haired patrol says.

"It will only take a few minutes," the woman adds.

"My daughter is a patrol. If you talk to her, I'm sure—"

"Char Moore is busy attending to other matters," the woman says. "We will be more than happy to inform her of our inquiry once it is over. All we need is your cooperation."

"Well, I'm not cooperating. So, if you'll excuse me."

It takes a lot of concentration to unlock my front door without trembling fingers. When I hear the lock click, I try to push the door open only enough to slide myself through without the patrols following me. When I try to shut the door behind me, the woman shoves her boot in the crack. I pull the door open and try to slam it shut harder, but the other white-haired patrol shoves his shoulder into the entry, letting the door bounce off his body.

"You can't come storming in here like this. Get out of my house!"

"Hold her," the woman says.

The third patrol wraps his arms around my waist. I struggle against him, throwing my elbows back, and leaning my body forward. It only makes him hold tighter.

"Sit still," he growls.

"I want your names! I'll fucking report you!"

The woman raises her eyebrows at me, and smiles. "You want our names? Mine is Alma, that one's Greg," she points to the white-haired patrol, "and that one behind you is Cameron. Report us all you want. We're here on orders."

"Whose orders?"

Alma snickers and turns her back to me. "It has come to our attention that there may be items of interest in your possession; things that should have been removed from your home years ago. Things that belonged to your late husband."

"Whoever told you that is a goddamn liar. Charles has been dead for ten years."

"Sometimes shit gets overlooked," Cameron says. His breath is warm on my neck. It makes me cringe. "We are going to take another peek."

Alma and Greg both nod at each other. They walk into the living room and begin pulling the cushions off the couch. They're throwing everything to the ground: the pillows, the cushions, the ashtray that sits on the side table. They kick over the coffee table, and pull the pictures off the walls.

"What the hell are you doing? Don't touch my things! There's nothing here. I've already told you. You're ten years too late. Everything's gone," my voice cracks. "Someone made sure of that a long time ago."

They don't care. It doesn't matter what I say, or how I say it. Alma and Greg are in the kitchen now, throwing the contents of the cabinets out onto the white tiled floor. Red wine and brown liquor begin to seep into the grout, running across the floor like tiny streams of blood and dirt. Piles of broken plates and shattered cups lie in heaps. I watch through tears as they take the last dish out of the cabinet and throw it into a pile with the others. It breaks in half when it lands.

"This isn't right," I whisper.

Cameron tightens his grip around me as Alma and Greg make their way to the back of my home. They walk into my bedroom and disappear behind the walls. I pull against Cameron, trying to fight my way down the hall. He's strong, too strong to let go. I jerk my head back, and slam it into his nose. It makes a sickening thud when it connects. Cameron screams out in pain, and his grip loosens. I stomp down on his foot and free my arm enough to throw an elbow into the side of his head.

He brings his hands up to his face, and I use that time to run. I reach my bedroom door in time to see Alma ripping the sheets off my bed. We lock eyes for a brief moment and she smiles. I press my lips together, and begin to march forward when pain shoots through the back of my head. I'm being yanked away by my hair, led back to the front of my home.

"You're not going anywhere, bitch," Cameron snarls.

I shout out in pain as he pulls me back hard enough to make me lose my footing. He drags me up by my hair and pins me up against the wall, his forearm pressing against my throat. His face is inches from mine. I notice his nose has already swollen to twice its size. There are dark bruises forming beneath his eyes, and a red welt on the side of his head.

"There's nothing here," I try to say, but I can't breathe. I grab Cameron's arm, and try to pull him away enough to help me breathe again.

"Then what the hell are you so worked up for? If there's nothing here, then you have nothing to worry about. So shut your damn mouth, or I'll put a bullet in your head."

"Keep your cool, Cam," I hear Greg say from down the hall. "No fucking bullets."

Cameron pulls his top lip into a sneer, and he makes a sound resembling a low, rumbling growl. In my pocket I can feel my phone vibrating. I try to shift to the side enough to remove it, but

Cameron grabs it first. He presses a button to silence it, and chucks the phone against the wall.

"Are you guys almost fucking done?" Cameron shouts.

"Fuck off. We're working on it," I hear Alma shout back.

Cameron pushes his forearm down harder into my throat, and I struggle to take a breath. Every second that passes feels like hours as I fight to pull him away. The more I strain against him, the harder he pushes down. My head is throbbing, pounding against my skull. My eyes begin to water. Right as I begin to feel myself slipping away, the front door swings open.

I take a loud gasping breath. "Patricia."

Cameron pulls his arm away and I fall to the ground, holding my throat, struggling to catch my breath. Patricia is standing in the doorway, her phone still clutched in her fist. She is panting, her eyes searching the room. I can still hear Greg and Alma tearing apart the back rooms, unaware. Cameron takes a step toward Patricia. I grab the bottom of his pant leg and try to pull him back. He kicks his free leg into my forearm, and I am forced let go.

Patricia's jaw tightens, and she holds the phone out in front of her. "You have exactly five seconds to get the hell out of here before I call someone to have you removed."

Cameron's lips curl into a grin. "Yeah? Who exactly are you going to call?"

Patricia shrugs. "The patrols, of course. Unless you can prove you're here on official business."

"This was a waste of time," I hear Alma say. Her voice grows louder as she approaches the front room. "We didn't find—"

Right as they reach the end of the hall, Greg throws his arm out in front of Alma. They both stop short with eyes wide. Alma looks between Cameron and Patricia. When she notices the phone, her shoulders slump forward.

"Who the hell are you?" Greg asks. "How did you get in here?"

"That doesn't matter," Patricia says, straightening her back, and lifting her chin. "All you need to know is I'm three seconds from reporting the three of you to the patrols for corruption. If it's not official, it's against policy, everyone knows that." She presses three numbers on her phone, and raises her eyebrow. "Get the hell out of here before I finish."

I use the wall to pull myself to my feet. My head is throbbing. The back of my scalp is sore. It's hard to stand upright. I take a deep breath and straighten my back, trying hard not to shout out in pain. Every move I make sends another bolt of pain shooting through my head. I rub the front of my throat. It's sore to the touch, and it burns whenever I swallow.

Alma takes a step forward. Her lips are pressed tight together. I can see the way her muscles move as she clenches and unclenches her jaw. Cameron stares at me from the corner of his eye, his nostrils flaring. Greg sighs, and tugs on Alma's coat sleeve. She jerks her arm away and licks her lips. After a few seconds, she looks at Greg and nods.

"Time to go. There's nothing here anyway," she says.

Patricia steps to the side, and nods at the door. She holds her phone out in the air, and taps her foot. Greg is the first to leave, followed by Alma. Cameron hangs back, staring me down, before he turns to leave. When he gets to the door, he puts his hand on the frame, and looks back at Patricia.

"This isn't how it ends. Your days are numbered. Both of you."

He slams the door behind him as he leaves. The walls rattle. The only picture left hanging slides down the wall and shatters when it hits the ground. Patricia hurries to the door and locks it. She glares through the keyhole, and only when she is sure they have left does she run to my side. She slides her arm around my shoulders and guides me to the dining room table. She picks up an overturned chair, and pats the seat.

"Thanks, Patricia," I say as I slide myself down into the chair.

"Are you okay?"

"Yeah," I say, rubbing the back of my head. "I'm alright."

"Next time answer your phone."

"Right." My eyes wander to the disaster in the kitchen. "I need a smoke."

Patricia rolls her eyes, and heads into the kitchen to root through the mess. When she finds my pack of cigarettes she holds them up and smiles. "Here we are."

I grab the pack away from her, pull one out, and place it between my lips. I close my eyes and revel in the taste of tobacco. There is a click, followed by a flicker of light behind my lids. Patricia has lit the end of the cigarette for me.

"Thank you," I say.

"You going to explain what happened here?"

I shrug, and take a deep drag of my cigarette.

Patricia grabs another chair, turns it upright, and sits down beside me. "Look at this place, Evelyn. What did you do to piss them off enough to warrant something like this?"

"Not me," I say, slouching in my seat. I rest my head on the top of the chair and look up at the ceiling. "It's Charles."

Patricia leans forward and places her hand on my knee. "Oh, honey. Did they say why?"

I swallow hard, wincing at the pain. "Looking for something."

"Didn't they take everything ten years ago? Even the pictures. There isn't anything left."

"That's what I told them."

"Then they have no reason to think you're lying. Not unless you're keeping something from them. Is there anything you want to tell me?"

"No."

Patricia leans back in her seat and crosses her arms over her chest. "I saved your life. Don't you lie to me."

"I'm not lying."

"As both your doctor and your friend, I can tell when you're lying."

"We all have our faults."

Patricia scoots her chair back hard. It screeches loud against the tiled floor. She towers over me with her hands on her hips. Her lips are pursed, and she stares down at me with a scowl.

"Stop bullshitting me, Evelyn. Three patrols came into your home. One of them nearly choked you to death. Your throat is purple, and I can still see that piece of shit's marks on your neck.

Either something is going on that you don't want to tell me, or you've lost your damn mind. Neither of which is ideal. Tell me what is happening so that I can help you. I'm the only friend you have."

I take another drag of my cigarette and then put my head in my hands. "Nothing I say will make any sense to you. But, Charles left me something the night before he died. I don't know what it is. I don't know where it is. All I know is that he left something for me."

Patricia puts her hand on my shoulder and gives it a gentle squeeze. "We need to get you out of here, Evelyn. Come home with me and we can talk about it there. I've got a bad feeling about all this, like those three patrols will be back and something bad might happen. Let's go. We can file a report at my house."

"I can't leave until I find it."

"Evelyn..."

I snuff my cigarette out on the dining room table, not caring about the black mark the ash makes. Stepping over piles of broken memories, I begin searching through the kitchen cabinets. They've all been stripped bare. I run into the living room and look under the couch, and inside the table drawers.

Patricia puts a hand on my arm. "Evelyn, stop."

I move away from her and pick up the couch cushions off the floor, one by one, and squeeze them against my chest. They're all soft, and I can't feel anything hidden inside of them. I reach my arm beneath the couch again, and run my hand over the bare floor. Nothing. I stand up, brush a piece of hair from my eyes, and put my hands on my hips.

"It's not going to be in here," Patricia says.

"How the hell would you know?"

"Because look around you. They've already torn it apart. Besides, Charles wouldn't hide anything in here where anyone else could find it. He'd want it to be more intimate than that."

Patricia bites her bottom lip and looks around, thinking. Suddenly she grabs me by the wrist and pulls me down the hall toward my bedroom. My throat tightens when I see what's become of my room. The blankets and pillows have been slashed. Feathers lie in piles around the floor. The bed is overturned and the mattress thrown on it's side. Everything in my closet has been pulled out: clothes, shoes, art supplies. They're strewn about the room, covering every inch of the floor. When I walk inside, I have to be careful not to step on anything.

Patricia bends down and grabs a small wooden picture frame. A picture of her and I sits crumpled behind shards of broken glass. "They're monsters."

I kick a pile of ripped clothes out of my way and tip the mattress over until it lies flat. I drop to my knees and run my hands over the outside, looking for anything unusual. Patricia shuffles herself beside me, and holds out her hand.

"I can guarantee you they've done that already," she says.

I grab ahold of her hand and pull myself to my feet. "Then what the hell do you suggest?"

"Look," she says, pointing to the box spring still sitting in the bed frame. "It's the only part of the room they haven't touched."

"You're right," I say, walking along the edge of the bed.

I run my fingers over the fabric, feeling the edges of the wooden frame bumping against my fingers. I find a spot in the center, where the cotton is thinner. A small tear has already started to form.

"Here," Patricia says, holding out a jagged piece of glass from the broken picture frame. "Use this."

I carefully take the shard of glass from her and ram it into the fabric of the box spring. The cloth rips in two as I tear a hole right down the center. I toss the glass aside and shove my hand inside the fabric. I feel around between the wooden frame, searching. Something brushes against the back of my hand. I position myself a little closer, stick my other hand inside the hole, and wrap my fingers around a small box.

"Did you find it?" Patricia asks, peeking over my shoulder.

"I think so," I say, pulling out the box.

"I told you," Patricia says, waving a hand in the air. "That was the only spot they didn't touch."

I inspect the box in my hands, getting a good look at each side. It's a simple box, made of light pinewood. The texture of the outside is rough and jagged. There is a single clasp at the front holding it together, and two rusted hinges in back. I give the box a little shake and the contents inside rattle.

Patricia leans forward, her face inches from my ear. "Well. Go ahead then."

I look at her and smile. I press the box into my chest and walk out into the hallway. It's the only spot left that isn't piled high with junk. I place the box on the floor and kneel down beside it. When I unclasp the lock, the top springs open.

The inside of the box is made of four mirrored walls that angle down to one central point at the center. The glass mirrors shine as though the sun is directly above them. Tilting the box from one side to the other projects a small prism on the ceiling above me. In the middle, where all four mirrors come together, sits a cylindrical bronze wheel with holes and divots running along the outside. I tilt the box to the right and notice a small metal crank attached to the side of the wheel.

It's hard to grip the handle with my fingers, but I manage to use the very tips of my nails to turn the crank. When I let it go, the wheel starts to spin. As it does, a melody is played: Soft, sweet music like the gentle chiming of bells.

"Oh my god," I whisper.

Patricia places a hand on my shoulder and kneels down beside me. "I can't believe it's been here all those years."

"It's beautiful," I say. I pull the box into my arms and stand, the music still playing. I close my eyes and listen. "Somehow I knew I would find something like this. I knew it was here. I could hear the music, Patricia. It's been playing in my head for days. I know that sounds crazy, but it was like I knew it was here all along, waiting for me to find it. Why did it take me so long to remember?"

Patricia smiles and rubs my back over the top of my shirt. "I don't know, hon. Memories fade over time. They get lost somewhere in our minds and we're content with never having them, until something reminds us what it is we're missing. No matter how much we think we've forgotten something, the memory is never truly gone."

187

"But why would I want to forget something like this?"

"Look," Patricia says. She bites her bottom lip, and runs a hand over the music box. It's still playing its beautiful melody. "You started drinking a lot after Charles died. You wanted, needed, to forget about him. I don't blame you one bit. That was a horrible time in your life."

"But I drink as much now as I did back then. There's no reason for me to remember it now."

Patricia takes a strand of my hair in her fingers, and tucks it behind my ear. "Maybe it's because Char is back. She does look like him, doesn't she? Her and her brother are the one thing that still connects you to Charles."

"You're probably right." I clutch the box a little tighter.

"Come on," Patricia says. "Let's get you out of here. I'm worried about the patrols coming back. That music box must be what they were after, which means it has to be important. They'll be back for it, and for you. Take the box. We'll figure out what it means later."

Patricia helps me to my feet, and guides me to the front door. I step out into the hallway and look back inside my home before we leave. Everything is destroyed; everything is as good as gone. I feel an ache deep in the pit of my stomach. The rough edges of the music box dig into my chest. The top is closed, but I can still hear the music playing.

Patricia shuts the front door, but the memory of my disheveled home lingers in my mind. There's no sense in sending someone out to clean up the mess. I don't think I'm coming back.

CHAPTER TWENTY-ONE
Alexander Moore

I grab the old burlap sack off the floor, and sling it over my shoulder. I trudge over to the window, and look between the shards of splintering glass. The sun has begun to take its spot in the sky, slowly rising above the horizon. The rooftops of the surrounding homes emit auras of red, and burnt orange. It clashes with the gray clouds that hover high in the air against the deep blue sky. Soon it will be morning.

"Most of Calloway should be asleep," I say. I turn back to Harry, and slump the sack on the ground by my feet. The broken radio rattles as it lands. "Whatever we need to do with this radio, we should do it now."

"I want to go back to bed," Harry says. His eyes are red and swollen, and he struggles to keep them open. "Did you have to wake me so early? We can take it to the dump later."

"You heard what Char said. We need to be more careful than that. If we wait until the rest of the city is awake then we're likely to be seen."

"Fine. Fine," Harry says, scratching the back of his head. "I'll get my shoes. But I'm not happy."

"You're never happy," I say with a smile.

Harry makes his way down the hall to the small closet. He leans against the wall as he opens the door, and grunts when he has to bend down to grab his shoes. I roll my eyes and look back out the window. The sun has risen a little higher, and the sky is steadily growing brighter. I crane my neck to the side to get a better look down the street.

Most homes are still dark, but a few have a light on inside the front window. They're probably used as a theft-deterrent and are nothing to worry about. The streets are empty, except for a single patrol. From what I can tell, he has dark, slicked back hair. His uniform is tight, and it looks like the buttons down the front of his green shirt might burst if he breathes a little too deep.

I turn around, and lean my back against the door.

"We're going to have to go out a back window. There's a patrol outside."

"On our street?"

"Yeah. A few houses down."

"But they never patrol our street."

My eyes wander down to the sack with the broken radio inside. I nudge it with my foot. "Maybe he's looking for something."

Harry groans. "Oh come on, man. It's too early for this shit."

"Grab the bag. Meet me in Char's room."

Harry nods, grabs the sack, and lugs it over his shoulder. Once it's secured, he takes off down the hall towards Char's old

191

bedroom. I look back out the window one last time. The patrol is only two houses away. It looks like he's whistling to himself, smiling. He looks inside the window of the small green house across the street, cupping his hands around his eyes to get a better view.

"Are you coming?" I hear Harry shout.

"Yeah, one second!"

My eyes dart around the living room for one last quick inspection. I hid the near-empty briefcase under my bed after Char left, and cleaned up the mess from the radio the best I could. It doesn't look like any bits of black plastic have been left behind. No evidence. I head off into the back bedroom, and see Harry standing in front of the opened window.

"You sure he won't see us going out this way? I don't want to get caught," Harry says.

"It's better than taking our chances going out the front door," I say.

"Can't argue with that." Harry picks up the sack, and shoves it through the open window. It thumps when it hits the ground. "You go first."

I place one foot through the window, and try to steady my weight against the frame of the house. I shift my torso to the left, and bend forward enough to squeeze my top half through next. Then I pull my other leg through, balance on the window ledge for a moment, and drop down to the ground. It's not a long fall, only a couple of feet. Once I steady myself, I sling the sack over my shoulder and move out of the way. Within seconds Harry is standing next to me on the ground with a smile on his face.

"That was kind of fun," he says.

"Here," I say, handing over the bag. "You take this. Fun part's over."

"Why do I have to take the damn bag?"

"I built it. You carry it. That's how it works."

Harry sighs loud enough for me to hear, then mumbles nonsense under his breath. Once he has the bag in hand, he throws it over his shoulder. I take a quick look around, and groan.

"Oh man. Someone took my bike," I say.

Harry laughs. "Are you serious?"

"Yeah. I had it chained up to the back railing. They even took the chain." I frown, and purse my lips. "Forget about it. We've got more important things to worry about."

Harry pats me on the shoulder, and we begin walking towards the back of town to where the dump resides. After a few minutes, Harry perks up. "I wonder if Mara's up."

"I doubt Mara even sleeps," I say with a laugh.

"We should stop by her place and see if she wants to come with then. Unless you think she's mad at us."

"Why would she be mad at us?"

"I'm not sure, but she hasn't been around in two days. That's not like her."

I shrug. "Maybe she doesn't want to get involved in whatever we have going on right now. I wouldn't blame her if that were the case."

"I don't know, Alex. I've got a bad feeling about it. Maybe she found something out, something we don't know yet, and she's angry with us."

"You worry too much, Harry. Her place is only a couple of blocks away. Let's go talk to her and find out."

Harry stares straight ahead with his eyes narrowed. He slings the bag from one shoulder to the other, and his chest expands and drops with a silent, but heavy, sigh. We round the corner of Hollow Lane, the street that Mara calls home, and see her tiny red house in the distance. No lights are on that I can see.

I look at Harry right as the speakers let out their rattling screech. We both stop walking long enough to listen to the morning announcement.

"Attention residents of Calloway: The weather forecast for the day consists of mild temperature, strong winds, and a high chance of storms rolling through this afternoon. The threat level for the day is extremely elevated. It is advised that all residents remain indoors until further notice."

Harry's face twists into a puzzled frown. "What the hell does that mean?"

"Something must have happened," I say while rubbing the back of my neck. "They wouldn't force us inside unless something bad happened. Maybe someone went missing."

"Should we go back home?"

I shake my head. "It's still early. Hopefully everyone else will be inside so we won't be seen. We have to get this radio to the dump."

"Shit, Alex," Harry says, his eyes on Mara's house. "I can't tell if you're stubborn or stupid."

"Probably both."

Harry laughs, and drops the burlap sack to the ground by his feet. He rubs his shoulder, and then shakes out his wrist. "I think this bag is heavier than the radio."

"Give it to me," I say, holding out my hand. "I'll carry it for a bit."

Harry picks the sack back up and hands it over. I immediately sling it over my shoulder, and we begin walking toward Mara's house again. The problem isn't that the bag or the radio is heavy. The problem is the way we have to carry it, slung over one shoulder, muscles flexed, and wrist bent at a strange angle. The bag is simply too large to carry any other way. It would have been easier to transport if I had a small box, or even a smaller bag, but this old flour sack was all I had.

"You don't think that patrol I saw on our street will try to come into our house, do you?" I turn to Harry and frown. "I hope he doesn't."

Harry's eyes are still focused ahead. He grabs me by the arm and tugs it hard enough for me to stop. The sack flops noisily against my back. "Do you see that?"

I follow Harry's sight to the front of Mara's house. The lights are still off, but I notice the front door is ajar. I squint, and use my hand to block out the glow of the rising sun. That's when I see green. At least three bodies dressed in patrol gear move about the shadows. I can see them standing in front of windows, and walking back and forth in front of the door.

195

My eyes wander to the other homes lining the street. Small, single room houses that are so close together they practically touch. Most are dark, but some have a light or two on in the front window. All of them have closed, or boarded-up doors. Not a single other house has the same patrol presence.

"Something is wrong," I say.

"I told you, Alex. We haven't heard from her in days, and now there are a shit ton of patrols around her house." Harry turns to me, his face pale. "Maybe they took her in. What if they brought her to The Chasm?"

"We should turn around. We should get this sack to the dump as quick as possible."

"No," Harry says. His face is turning red, and his fists are clenched at his sides. "We have to find out what's going on."

I lower my voice, and lean as close to Harry as I can. "You know that's not a good idea right now, Harry. We have to get rid of this radio."

Harry presses his lips together in a tight line. He looks back down at Mara's house and shakes his head. "Fuck the radio," he mumbles.

"What are you expecting to do? Walk up there with the radio in hand? We shouldn't even be outside right now. You heard the announcement. So not only will we waltz up to the patrols with criminal evidence in a nice package for them, but we'll also be advertising the fact that we're breaking the law and wandering around the city when the threat level is—"

"Holy shit," Harry whispers. "The threat level."

"It's not for her, Harry. It can't be."

Harry stares at me with eyes wide, and lips pressed firm. He reaches forward so fast that I flinch, and before I know it he is yanking the bag away from me. My wrist and arm bend to the side, and I'm forced to let go. I watch in horror as he walks to the nearest house, and begins kicking in the front door. I pull my arm into my chest, and rub my swollen, tender wrist. I hobble after Harry, trying to shout at him without making too much noise.

"Harry, stop it. What the hell are you doing? Bring me back the bag."

"Fuck you, Alex. You're not in charge anymore." Harry kicks the door harder this time, and it swings open. He tosses the bag inside, and brushes his hands off on his pants. "There. Now it's not our damn problem."

Harry marches past me with chin up, heading straight towards Mara's house. I hurry after him, and grab ahold of his arm. I pull back hard. He stumbles, almost tripping over his own feet as he does. When he regains his footing he whips himself around and shoves his hands into my chest. I trip over the edge of the road, and tumble to the ground. My palms scrape against the gravel.

"Mara is our friend," Harry says, his voice high and quivering. He points a trembling finger in my face. "We don't abandon our friends, Alex. Mara wouldn't hesitate to come to our aid if we needed her help. She's been there for us every single fucking time we've needed her. Put your bullshit logic away for just this once, Alex. Forget about the radio."

I push myself to my feet and brush the pebbles off my hands using the front of my shirt. I inspect my palms, and pull out the smaller rocks that embedded themselves in my skin. As I pluck the last piece of gravel from the inside of my hand, Harry stands in front of me with his arms crossed. I look down the road and see one of the patrols walking out of Mara's house. It's hard to tell, but I think she says something into her handheld radio.

"You're right," I say. I take a deep breath and drop my hands to my sides. "I'm sorry."

"Let's go see if we can find out what happened. If Mara is in trouble it's up to us to help her. We can grab the sack on the way back. If the owner of the house finds it first, they'll probably freak out and take it to the dump anyway. Then it won't be our problem anymore."

"Fine," I tell him, trying my best to give him a smile. It's too late to turn back. All I can do now is hold my breath, and hope for the best. I don't know what will happen next, but I do know the patrols will not be happy to see us.

"Good," Harry says. "Let's go then."

I can feel my fingers growing numb as we inch closer to the house. My heart is racing, my blood pressure rising. Harry clears his throat beside me. I can hear the air quivering through his lungs as he breathes. I squeeze my eyes shut for a moment, and let my feet guide me. The threat level is not elevated because of Mara. It can't be. Harry rams an elbow into my side, and my eyes snap open.

There is a patrol standing on the broken concrete stair that leads to Mara's front door. When he sees us his eyes grow wide, and his freckled cheeks glow bright red. He is frozen with the radio held inches from his lips.

"Wh…what are you two doing here? You heard the announcement. All residents must remain indoors," the patrol says. The closer we get to him, the younger he looks. He must be new. He runs a hand through his disheveled red hair, and looks back inside the house. "You have some explaining to do."

"We were on our way here when the announcement was made," I say. I try to keep my voice as steady as possible. "I thought we'd be safer waiting things out here, rather than try to make it all the way back home again."

"Is everything okay?" Harry is standing on his tiptoes, trying to peek around the patrol. "Is Mara inside? Did something happen?"

The patrol bites his bottom lip, and raises an eyebrow. "You guys know the owner of this residence?"

"Yes. Mara Matthews. We've been friends with her for almost five years," I say.

The patrol looks over his shoulder, and I see his eyes scanning the inside of the house. When he turns back to us his face is pale, and his voice quiet. "When was the last time you had contact with Miss Matthews?"

I try to swallow down the lump in my throat. "Two days ago, I think."

"Is Mara missing?" Harry's voice is loud and hoarse. He takes a step forward, inching his way toward the front door. "Is that why you guys are here?"

The patrol looks back over his shoulder. When he turns forward again his eyes are squinted. He bites his bottom lip, and shakes his head slowly. "I don't think I'm allowed to give that information out."

I see a shadow creeping up behind the patrol. It lingers in the doorway for a moment before stepping out onto the stair. It's a woman with dark hair pulled up into a high ponytail. She takes one look at us, then grabs the other patrol by his collar, and pulls him inside of the house.

"You've had enough outside time," she tells him. He crawls back inside the shadows of the house and disappears. When he's gone, she turns back to Harry and I. "Who the hell are you two? You'd better have a great excuse for being here."

"My name is Alex Moore. He's Harry." The more I stand here, trying to explain myself, the worse I feel. I have a picture of Mara's face, twisted in agony, clawing her way out of The Chasm. "This is our friend Mara's house. We were on our way over to check on her when the announcement was made. Thought we would be better off hunkering down here than trying to make our way back home again."

"I need to know where Mara is," Harry adds. "If you've taken her somewhere, if she's done something wrong, we have a right to know."

The patrol holds her hand up, palm facing out. She reaches her hand down to her belt. I take a step back, and my heart begins to pound against my chest. My throat is tight, and it's hard for me to breathe. But right as I think she's about to pull the gun from her belt and shove it in our faces, she unclips her radio instead. I audibly breathe a sigh of relief, and slump my shoulders forward.

"This is Megan," the girl says into the radio. "We have the two subjects here. Prepare a room for questioning. I'm bringing them in now."

"Bringing us in?" I look at Harry, and his face is hard as stone. His jaw is clenched, and his hands are in tight fists at his sides. "What do you mean you're bringing us in? We didn't do anything."

"You two are wanted for questioning in the murder of Mara Matthews." Megan clips the radio back on her belt, and pulls her gun from the holster. "Put your hands where I can see them, and slowly turn around."

"Murder..." Harry's voice sounds strained, like the words shoot through his throat like daggers. "M...Mara. She...she's..."

"Hands up," Megan repeats. She raises her gun, and points it directly between Harry and I. "Now."

I think I raise my hands to my ears, but I can't feel them. My body has gone numb. Even my lips have no feeling as I try my best to speak. "This is a mistake," I whisper. "Mara's fine."

"Turn around," Megan says. "Do it slow. No sudden movements."

"This is a mistake," I repeat.

I am supposed to turn around. I am wanted for questioning. None of those words make sense. They're not real. None of this is real. It can't be. It can't be real, because I can't feel anything anymore. The wind, the sun, the bits of gravel beneath my feet: they may as well be non-existent. I think the air is caught in my lungs, but my chest is numb. I think tears are falling, but I can't be sure, because my eyes don't sting.

All I know is the world in front of me becomes a blur. I can make out Harry's silhouette lunging forward. He shouts something, words I cannot hear because my own pulse is pounding too loud in my ears. I rub my eyes to try and clear my vision. My palms pull away wet with tears. My sight clears up long enough to see Megan raising her gun. I open my mouth to scream, but nothing comes out. Through the blur of my new-falling tears I can see her swing the gun down hard. It connects with the side of Harry's head. His legs buckle, and his body hits the ground with a thud.

My eyes close, and my hands drift up in the air.

"This is a mistake," I mumble.

Pain shoots through my head like a hammer to the nail, and I can feel myself falling.

The light fades around me as the sirens begin to wail.

The last thing I see is Mara, leaning against my front door with a smile on her face. Her mouth begins to open, and the scream of the sirens falls from her lips. Then she is gone as quick as she appeared. All I see is black

CHAPTER TWENTY-TWO
Char Moore

Wind pelts the side of the small, decaying house. The storm made its approach as I was in the middle of filing the report on Mara's death. I was allowed one single night to pull myself together, but I don't think I slept at all. Now the dust is ramming the small shack where Archer and I sit, filling out paperwork. The wind screams as it whips through the cracks in the foundation. The entire house creaks, and sways, threatening to finally crumble to dust. I sit on the floor with my back against the wall, feeling it move and shake with the rhythm of the wind. Every so often I can feel the blueprints in the back of my pants shift against my skin.

"Should be over soon," Archer says, shuffling the papers set in front of him at the table.

I tilt my head forward and back in a slow, methodical nod.

"I want you to know that I'm sorry you had to come down here," Archer says. "I know I've said it a dozen times already, but I'm sorry. It's protocol."

"I know," I say.

"You going to be alright?"

I shrug. "Probably not."

"I think getting back to work will help you heal. Help take your mind off of it."

I clear my throat. "Maybe."

"I've sent two of our best patrols to work on the case. We'll find out who did this."

I close my eyes and tilt my head into the wall. I can hear the storm pelting the outside like a hurricane. "Can we not talk about it?"

"Amanda Simmons is crossing over today," Archer says. "It's her time. She's being prepped in the house next door. I think Greg is helping her. I thought it was best if Amanda take some of Mara's things to her brother, Michael. He's been in Felicity for a couple of years now, and he deserves to know what happened. It would be a nice gesture."

I lean forward, and stare at Archer. "Are you fucking kidding me?"

Archer scratches the side of his head with a puzzled look on his face. "What?"

"I know who Michael is." I push myself to my feet, and begin to pace the floor. The warped wooden boards beneath my feet moan with every step. "Why do you think it's better to have someone that he doesn't know bring him his dead sister's shit? I should be the one handing it over, along with a giant fucking apology for being the person responsible."

"The person responsible? Char, you weren't the one that…that hurt her like that. This isn't your fault."

"It is my fault," I say. "Everything that has happened is my fault, Archer. You're too stupid to fucking see it. Sam's little message on his wall, his death, the radio that was given to my brother — they were all my fault. And after we're done here, I'm bringing the shit to Michael myself. I'm not about to let some stranger do it."

"You can't do that," Archer says.

"I sure as hell can."

Archer stares down at his fingers, and lightly drums them on the tabletop. "You're not allowed to enter Felicity."

I stop pacing, my eyes fixed on Archer. "What did you say?"

"There's a temporary ban in place, to keep you from entering Felicity." Archer doesn't look at me. He keeps his eyes on his hands. "At least for the time being. I'm sorry, Char. It wasn't my call."

I cross my arms over my chest, and press my eyebrows together. I stare down at my feet with my teeth clenched together. Tyler isn't around to make the call on something like this. Someone else made this decision. "Who was put in charge after Tyler died?"

"When the lead patrol's term ends, the one with the most experience takes their place. In this case, it was Shawn."

"Shawn? You're joking, right?"

"Like it or not, it's protocol," Archer says.

My heart is pounding fast against my ribs. The anger spreads through me like venom with every beat. Shawn: the patrol that dragged Sam away; the one that was there to witness the end of

Tyler's term. He was there guarding Mara's corpse, too. He looked like he was beaming with joy as he stood next to her limp body. Now, it is Shawn who is keeping me from crossing over into Felicity. This doesn't feel right.

"Shawn can't ban me from the other side without reason. I've done nothing wrong."

"I know." Archer grabs the pen from the table, and signs his name to the bottom of Mara's report. "He claims that allowing you into Felicity will bring potential harm upon the residents. It's pretty apparent you're the target of something we haven't figured out yet. Shawn wants to keep you in Calloway until everything blows over."

My stomach drops. I trudge over to Archer, and slam myself down in the seat beside him. "So the lives of those in Felicity are worth more than those in Calloway? Is that what he's saying? And you're letting him get away with that?"

Archer's back goes rigid, and his eyes narrow. "There is nothing I can do, Char. He's lead patrol now. He's in charge until his term is over. We have to follow orders."

I think about my mother, waiting for me in Felicity, wondering why the days have gone by without a word from her daughter. Outside, the wind begins to slow. The dust is settling in. On the other side of these walls sits The Chasm, less than twenty feet away. I remember the exact spot where Tyler's term ended. I remember him standing before me, warning me about the others.

They need to watch you do this. They need to know who you are.

I listened to Tyler when he told me to find my brother. He was right about Alexander. But in that whirlwind moment, Tyler also mentioned my mother. Evelyn waits on the other side of that Chasm. I need to get to her. I have to give her his message.

"Fine," I say as I shoot up out of my seat. The chair falls to the ground behind me, thumping against the floor. "Are we done here?"

I stand and wait as Archer looks over the paperwork. He shuffles one page after the other, his eyes reading line after line. After a few moments he folds the paper in half, then stands. He grasps my shoulder in his hand and squeezes.

"I'm going to figure this out," Archer says. He runs his hand down my arm, straightening out the creases in my shirt. "You might think this is entirely your fault, but I'm to blame as well. I was there with Sam, too. I saw what was written on that wall. I was stupid to disregard it. It's only a matter of time before witnesses start coming forward. Someone has to have seen something."

I give him a weary smile. "I said I didn't want to talk about it. But, what you're doing means a lot to me, Archer. You should know that."

"Yeah, well, keep it to yourself, okay? I've only got six months left. I want to stretch that out as much as possible."

"You'll have to bring the paperwork to the library for me," I say.

"I'll file it on your behalf," Archer says. "But I'm going to make up my own reason why you can't do it yourself. I think writing gimp leg under the excuse log would be pretty funny."

"Gimp leg? Really?"

Archer laughs as he opens the door, and motions for me to leave. I step out onto the dust-covered ground, feeling the grit beneath my boots. Archer steps out beside me. He shields his eyes with one hand, and looks out over the horizon.

"That's the second storm this week. Thankfully, this one wasn't as bad as the last. If we're lucky we won't get another one for a couple of months." He pulls the radio from his belt, and puts it to his lips. "This is Archer Evans requesting the gate be opened. I have to cross over to file a report in the library."

"This is Mallory," the voice on the other end of the radio says. "You've received clearance to cross alone. I will radio the guards to have them open the gates when you approach."

"They're making sure I don't cross with you," I point out.

"Give it a couple of days and it'll all blow over," Archer says. "Walk with me to the bridge. It'll give them a good spook."

"Sounds like a plan," I say with a laugh.

It only takes a few minutes to reach the bridge at the center of The Chasm. Even the links that form the silver gate are covered with a thin layer of dust. The guard eyes meet mine as we get close, and he readies his hand on his gun. If I'm not mistaken, it looks as though he smiles at me for a moment. Archer nudges me in the side with a grin on his face.

"I told you they'd freak out," he says. Then he turns to the guard, and raises a hand. "Don't worry. I'm crossing alone. She's seeing me off."

The guard raises the radio in front of his mouth, and gives the all clear to open the bridge. As soon as the gate swings open, the Archer's radio belts out a bit of static, and then Mallory's voice is back.

"Archer, this is Mallory again. I've received word from Greg that Amanda is ready to cross over. We are requesting that you wait to enter Felicity until after she has crossed."

Archer gives me a puzzled look as he grabs the radio from his belt. "Any particular reason I need to wait?"

The other end of the line grows silent as Archer waits for his answer. I look out over the land stretching towards Calloway. Greg and Amanda are making their way down the path towards The Chasm. I squint my eyes to try and get a better look. Greg has his arm around Amanda's shoulders, and he is guiding her towards the bridge.

As they get closer, I can see that Amanda's eyes are glazed over. She seems lost, confused. In her arms she carries two bags: a worn, brown duffel bag, and a small pink backpack. I recognize the latter as one of Mara's old bags, the one she used to carry with her to our house when she intended to crash on the living room floor.

I take a few steps forward to get a better look. Archer must have noticed something was wrong, because he's following closely behind me. He grabs me by the shoulder and stops me in my tracks.

"What the hell are you doing?"

"What's wrong with Amanda?"

"There's nothing wrong with Amanda," Archer says. "You need to back up before you get yourself in even more trouble."

"Look at her eyes," I say. "She looks like she's sleepwalking."

"That's fear, Char. Nothing more."

I shake my head, and take another step forward. "That's not fear. I've seen fear before. What happens during prep? You said Greg was helping to prep Amanda. What does that mean?"

"That's classified information," Archer says. "But I assume the former resident is reminded of the rules, and gets a better explanation of life on the other side."

"You're saying you don't know?"

Archer shrugs. "There are three to four patrols whose specific job is to help prep those ready to cross over. They are the only ones that know what really happens."

Greg and Amanda cross in front of us as they head to the bridge. Amanda doesn't blink, or flinch when a gust of winds blows at her face. Her eyes are dead, like she is a walking corpse without direction. Greg keeps his eyes on mine as he passes, even craning his neck to stare at me from over his shoulder.

"Hey!" I shout after them. "Wait a second."

Neither of them stops. Greg continues to lead Amanda towards the bridge. Only a few more steps until Amanda has officially begun to cross. I jog to their side, with Archer right behind me swearing under his breath. Greg turns and looks at me, but Amanda keeps her eyes forward.

"I'm sorry," I say with a smile. "I had a small favor to ask. Since I can't cross to the other side, I was wondering if she could give a message to Michael for me."

Greg stops walking. He keeps his hands clenched tight to Amanda's shoulders, causing her to stop at the same time. I shuffle myself in front of them, forcing Amanda to look at me. Her eyes are still glazed over, and vacant. I smile at her, but she doesn't return the gesture. There is only an expressionless stare.

"If you could tell him I'm sorry about his sister, I would really appreciate it. I've known Mara for a long time." The air catches in my throat. "She was a great friend to my brother."

Greg rolls his eyes. "Yeah, sure. Now get out of the way."

"Sorry." I put my hands up in the air, and take a giant step to the side. "I didn't mean to cause delay."

I watch with contempt as Greg pushes Amanda towards the bridge. The lost girl takes a wary first step over The Chasm. She hesitates for only a moment before beginning her march into Felicity. As soon as Greg is confident enough to know that Amanda will cross on her own, he whips around and starts marching toward me, finger pointed.

"What the hell was that all about? You don't interrupt someone when it's their time to cross." Greg's eyes are narrowed, and his nostrils are flared. "You put all of our lives in danger when you hold one person up like that."

"She didn't mean it," Archer says, stepping up beside me. Greg begins to walk away, shaking his head. "Her friend died. Cut her some slack."

"Archer," Mallory's voice comes through his radio again. "We have to close the gates soon."

Archer rolls his eyes, and grabs his radio. "All the residents are indoors, Mal. There are two patrols at The Chasm, plus the guard, plus four patrols around the immediate perimeter. If someone were going to try to cross over they'd have a real bad time doing it. Tell the guards to chill out. I'll be there in a minute."

I look around The Chasm. The guard is standing nervously next to the gate, a radio in one hand and his gun in the other. Greg has disappeared somewhere out of view, either into a run-down house to file a report, or back into Calloway where he is to patrol. I turn back to look at The Chasm, watching Amanda's silhouette disappear into the thick fog.

The radio is silent for a second before Mallory speaks again. "Cameron is currently escorting a resident to The Chasm for questioning. It's best if you cross now, and let Char get back to her duties. She is to patrol outside perimeter today, by the tree line."

"That's not what her assignment indicated," Archer replies.

"Her assignment has changed."

There is a long pause as Archer bites the inside of his cheek, thinking to himself. After a few short moments he pulls the radio to his lips again. "Tell the guard I'll be crossing in a minute."

I throw my hands in the air. "That's it?"

"What the hell do you want, Char? You're on thin ice as it is. You really want to be arguing about your assignment right now? You've got bigger things to worry about."

I'm still staring at exposed bridge over The Chasm, wondering how easy it would be for me to cross to the other side. Never before have I thought I'd be in the position of one of the frantic residents - the ones that want to cross, and would be willing to risk their lives to do so. But I can taste the temptation of that bridge, it calls to me, tells me to run. I haven't been staring at The Chasm long when I hear Archer whisper the word fuck under his breath. There are footsteps approaching quickly behind us.

I don't know what I expected to see when I turned myself around, but my stomach drops at the sight of my brother. He is being led forward by a patrol, with his wrists bound together by rope. The left side of his head is covered in a deep, purple bruise, with a red welt right at the center. His eye is swollen shut, and he walks with a slight limp. I notice his clothes are covered with dust, and slightly more frayed at the edges than normal.

"Char," Alex croaks. The patrol shoves a hand into his back, and he stumbled forward. He looks up at me with bloodshot eyes. His voice quivers as he speaks. "Mara's dead. She's dead."

My hand instinctively falls to my gun, and I wrap my fingers around the cold, metal handle. "What are you doing with him?"

"Your brother is wanted for questioning," Cameron says, nudging Alex in the back.

"Where is Harry?" I ask.

"I don't know," Alex says, his bottom lip quivering. "I didn't see where they took him."

"Archer," Mallory's voice cuts through his radio. "I need an ETA on your crossing. We can't keep the gate open much longer."

Archer ignores Mallory's request, and steps out in front of me. "What are his charges?"

I don't realize I've unbuckled my gun's holster until I hear the click of the button unsnapping.

"That's classified information," the patrol says.

They've stopped walking now, and are standing before Archer and I. The patrol keeps a hand on Alex's back, and I keep my hand on my gun. Slowly, I begin to slide it out of its holster. Without thinking, I reach forward and grab tight to the ropes that bind my brother's wrists together. With a quick pull I jerk him forward. I raise my gun as Alex stumbles to the ground. I point my weapon at the patrol's chest. He doesn't even flinch.

"Whoa, whoa, whoa." Archer takes a step back, and holds his hands in the air.

"You and I both know what was going to happen." I crouch down, my eyes and gun still on the patrol, and help pull Alex to his feet. "And I'm not going to let you take him."

"What are you doing? You're going to get yourself killed," Alex pleads.

"Listen to your brother," Cameron says. He takes a step forward. "Interfering with another patrol's duties is considered treason. The punishment is death."

"Archer." It's Mallory, pleading to him through the radio again. "If you don't respond I will be forced to close the gate."

"I know you're on edge right now, Char, but you need to put the gun down," Archer says softly. "Let's talk about this before you make any rash decisions. We can fix this. Just put the gun away, okay?"

I can feel my arm trembling. The gun grows in weight, and it suddenly feels too heavy for me to hold. I try to take a deep breath to steady myself. My heart is pounding, and sweat is dripping into my eyes. I know I've lost. There is nowhere for me to go. I let the gun fall to my side. As I do, I see Cameron drop his arm. He moves so fast that it takes a moment for me to register what he is doing.

Cameron's arm is a blur of green uniform and black metal as he is quick to raise his gun. I turn my back to him, and pull my brother into my arms, protecting him with my embrace. I prepare for the heat of the bullets as Alex's body trembles against mine. My eyes close, and my body stiffens as a shot rings out.

A body thuds to the ground behind me. When I turn to look, I see Cameron collapsed on his back, with a bullet hole in his chest. Archer falls to his knees. He presses a hand into Cameron's chest and tries to stop the bleeding with his hands. Red is pouring out from beneath his palms. I know that what Archer does is of no use. Cameron's eyes are void of life.

"Run," I hear a man say behind me.

I turn to see the guard standing with his gun raised, still pointed at the lifeless patrol. "I..." My head is spinning. It's hard to breathe. "What?"

"Both of you," the guard says. "Both of you need to run. Get to the other side of the bridge. You won't find any resistance from the guard over there. Find Evelyn. She is at fifteen hundred Rose Lane, floor twenty, room two forty-two. Repeat that back to me."

I take a deep, quivering breath and look back at Archer. His chest is heaving, his hands are covered in blood, and he is looking at me with concern in his eyes. He doesn't need to speak for me to know what is running through his mind. This is a bad idea. The guard can't be trusted. You don't know what you're getting yourself in to. You're going to do it anyway, aren't you?

215

I have no other choice.

"Fifteen-hundred Rose Lane. Floor twenty," I say.

"Room two forty-two," the guard states.

"Room two forty-two," I repeat.

"Go. Before the other patrols come."

"What is happening?"

"I said go!"

"We need to run," I say to Alex. I grab him by the shoulders, and pull him in for a quick hug. "Are you okay to run?"

Alex nods. His body is still shaking, but we don't have time to wait for the nerves to leave. We have to go. I grab him by the arm, and together we run.

CHAPTER TWENTY-THREE
Evelyn Moore

A slight breeze is all that is left of the storm. Every so often it softly knocks against the window in Patricia's spare bedroom. I sit on the floor with my back propped up against the frame of the bed, and the music box is clutched to my chest. Outside of the room I can hear Patricia banging dishes together, preparing a late breakfast. It seems no matter how many times I've informed her that I'm not hungry, she has decided to prepare some food anyway. That is what Patricia does. Anything to keep her mind off the present.

The kitchen becomes quiet, and I count the seconds until Patricia knocks on the door.

One. Two.

Three small, quick knocks rap against the bedroom door. I smile to myself.

"Evelyn? I've made some eggs. There's also toast, and raspberry muffins. I've brewed some coffee, or there's orange juice, if that's what you want. You should come eat something."

I decide it's best not to argue. "I'll be right there."

The floor was starting to hurt my back anyway. If I don't come out of my room and at least try eat something, I will never hear the end of it. I dig my heels into the ground and push myself to my feet. I place the music box at the foot of the bed, and flip the top open with my thumb. There is more to this box than the music, but I have yet to figure out what. I turn the small crank one last time, and hear the soft chiming music once again. I take a deep breath and slam the lid back down. Then I shove the box under my pillow, out of sight.

The smell of food hits me the moment I walk out of the room. My mouth is watering, but my stomach is uneasy, like my insides are sloshing around in my belly with every step. I give a wary smile to Patricia, who is standing in the kitchen doorway with a plate full of food in one hand, and a cup of coffee in the other.

"Starving yourself isn't going to solve anything. Sit down, eat something," she says.

I walk into the dining room and sit myself down in one of the padded leather chairs, my mind still on the music box. Patricia wastes no time sliding the plate and coffee down in front of me. She turns on her heels and hurries back into the kitchen. "You need some orange juice."

Patricia has already set the table with silverware, and empty glasses etched in gold trim. She returns a few seconds later with a pitcher of orange juice. I shake my head, and put my hand up. The thought of the orange juice, with all it's acidity, sloshing around in my already queasy stomach, makes me feel sick. More than I already am. Patricia frowns, and puts the pitcher at the center of the table.

"You shouldn't worry so much," Patricia says as she sits down in the chair next to mine. "They were curious patrols, and that's all."

I can feel myself growing livid, like her words are laced with venom. "Curious patrols that force their way into my home? Is that it? They were so curious they had to destroy every inch of living space? That wasn't curiosity, Patricia. That was deliberate. They were looking for the music box."

Patricia's eyes soften, and she puts her hand over mine. "I've thought about it, and I think it's nothing more than a coincidence. There is nothing special about the music box, Evelyn. The patrols were there because they were curious about Charles."

I pull my hand away from hers. "What's wrong with you? One minute you're sympathetic, and the next you're siding with the patrols. Even if it was curiosity, being curious does not give them the right to destroy my home. It does not give them the right to put their hands on me. The patrols are supposed to be there to protect us, Patricia."

"You're still emotional. I get it. You'll feel better soon, once you've had the time to calm down."

Patricia doesn't wait for me to respond before she hurries off into the kitchen. Her words are seething inside of me, and I know she can read the anger on my face. Like always, she believes that I am overreacting. I am emotional. I am not thinking straight. The fault lies with me. I don't care what Patricia might think, that music box is not simply a music box.

I scoot my chair away from the table. The wooden legs screech against the black marble floors. Frankly, I hope it leaves a mark. I stand up and begin heading back to the spare bedroom when there is a loud knock at the door. I pause in my tracks, and turn to stare at the door as if I could somehow see behind the wood. Three more loud, frantic knocks fill the air. They hit hard enough to make the wall shake.

Through the kitchen door I see Patricia wiping her hands off on a towel. She plucks a few stray curls back into place, and straightens out her shirt before she heads to the door.

"Don't open it," I say.

She waves her hand and brushes me aside as she unlocks the front door. Her smile turns into a frown, as the door swings open.

"Char," I gasp.

My daughter is standing in the doorway. Her patrol-green clothes are drenched with sweat, and her hair is matted against her forehead. Next to her stands a lanky teenage boy, much too young to be in Felicity. He has bruises on his face, and one eye is swollen shut. His hands are bound together in front of him by thick rope. They must have run here as fast as they could, because his chest is heaving up and down.

"I need a knife," Char says as she pushes her way past Patricia. She keeps the boy close by leading him by his elbow.

I can't seem to make sense of the thoughts racing through my head. Who is this boy? And why does he look so familiar? What happened to him? Why is he here? I want to ask a million questions, but instead I watch, silently, as Char grabs a knife from the counter, and in one quick motion she slices the bindings from the boy's wrists. His skin is red and bruised where the rope was pressing into his skin. He rubs the tender flesh there, wincing.

There is something familiar about the way he moves, as if I've witnessed those exact movements before. I can see that he is trying to avoid eye contact with everyone around him. He glances cautiously around the room, his chin low. It's when he tilts his head up that I finally get the chance to look into those soft, blue eyes. Then it hits me like a punch in the chest.

"Alexander," I say quietly. I take a step forward, my knees weak. "Is that really you?"

The boy looks at Char, who smiles down at him with softness in her eyes. She loves him. Of course she does. He is her brother. That is my son. A numbing sensation flows through me, starting at the top of my head, spreading down to my chest, my arms, my legs. For a moment I believe I must look crazy to the boy, to my son, who is watching me with intense curiosity, as I look him up and down. It only takes a moment for him to put the pieces together. When he does, his eyes grow wide. He grabs ahold of Char's arm as if she is the crutch that keeps him from falling.

"Is that?"

"That's your mother, Alex," Char says.

"Isn't this a lovely surprise," Patricia says, clasping her hands together. "He broke the law so he could come visit you."

221

"The guard let us through on his own," Alex says. His voice is both timid, and forceful. "Both guards, on both sides of the bridge. We were told to cross, and we were told to come here."

Patricia makes a face. "That doesn't seem likely."

Char steps forward. "He's not lying. That's exactly what happened." She turns to me and I notice for the first time how tired she looks. "I understand that this is strange, and I can imagine there is a lot going through your mind right now, but we need to talk."

"Is everything okay? What happened to Alexander?"

Char takes a quick glance at Patricia. "Is there some place we can be alone?"

"Patricia..." I begin to say.

Patricia waves her hand in the air, and begins to walk into the kitchen. "Fine. Fine. If either of you are hungry you know where to find me. There's plenty left over."

"Thank you, Patricia. I mean it," I say. Then I turn back to Char. "We can go into the spare bedroom."

Both Char and Alexander follow me into the back room where I slept last night. I pause outside the door, and let them walk in before me. I try to smile at Alex as he walks past, but he stares at the floor as he walks. I take a second to compose myself before I step into the room behind them. When I do, I catch Alex whispering something to Char. He is quick to cut himself off when he sees me watching, and he stares back down at his feet.

"We don't mean to barge in like this. Alex and I, we have no other choice." Char looks at Alex, and places a hand on his back. He looks up at her and smiles, then goes back to staring at his feet. "I know this isn't the way you wanted to meet each other. Because of that, I recognize that things are going to be a bit weird. Evelyn... mom, I mean, before we continue I need you to understand that however you feel right now, Alex is feeling much, much worse. It's going to take him awhile to come around."

I nod in understanding. "Tell me what happened."

Alexander shifts his weight from one foot to the other. He adjusts his shirt, which looks a few sizes too small. He runs a hand over the top of his pants, smoothing out the wrinkles that look to have been there for years. I watch as he then tucks his hands inside of his pockets, pockets that are so small that only the tips of his fingers fit inside. I notice one of his fingers poking out of a small hole on the right side. My heart aches to hold him, to comfort him, to let him know that everything will be okay. But I don't know that boy standing in front of me. I gave him his name, and nothing more.

There was a time when I crossed over, timid and scared the same as he is. Even though I don't remember that time, I know I was much older than Alexander. Eighteen. That is when we are all supposed to cross over, when our minds are mature enough to handle the city around us. I can only imagine that this is the reason he looks afraid, and overwhelmed. I can feel his nervous energy pulsating through the room.

"First, can Patricia be trusted?" Char crosses her arms over her chest. "Or is she out there calling the other patrols for backup?"

"Patricia might not agree with you being here, but she would never do anything to compromise our friendship. We're safe. The better question is were you followed? Who else knows you're here?"

"We didn't take a direct route, and we didn't encounter any patrols. I know their general whereabouts, and where the more heavily patrolled areas are. It also seems the patrols around The Chasm knew we were coming over, because we had zero resistance from them."

"Now will you tell me what happened?"

Char hesitates at first, looking to Alexander for his approval. He quickly nods, and bites his bottom lip. I listen carefully as Char tells me about a boy named Sam, who burned his home, and shouting warnings before being killed by a patrol. She tells me of the messages on the wall, and I feel sick at the mention of my late husband's name. I decide to keep quiet and listen as she now tells me about the boy that forced Alex to fix a radio, and about the strange message that repeated through its speakers. She tells me about the briefcase as well, and that it once belonged to Charles. For some reason there were blueprints inside.

When she tells me about Tyler, and about his message to me, the room begins to spin. I clutch the side of the bed and have to concentrate hard to sit down on the edge without falling to my knees. My heart is racing, pounding, echoing in my ears. Was this the same man I spoke to on the phone? The same one who sent me messages? I'm still reeling when Char tells me about Alexander's friend, Mara. How she was found, murdered in an alleyway, with a note written on her shirt.

By the time she has finished telling me everything, my throat is dry. When I try to swallow it feels like sandpaper. I have to close my eyes, and squeeze the bridge of my nose in order to compose myself. I take a slow, deep breath.

"I have received the same message." It hurts to speak. Even my lips feel coarse and dry. "On my phone, through calls, and through texts. I thought it was someone trying to mess with me, someone trying to rile me up, but I couldn't figure out who would do that, or why. I've also been hearing the faint sound of music, like there was a symphony in my head that only I could hear. I thought I was going mad."

Char takes a step forward, her face pale. "You should have said something."

"They came to my house, Char. They destroyed it. Said they were looking for something Charles left behind. It wasn't until they left that I found what they were looking for."

"What is it? What did you find?"

I place my hands on the edge of the bed, steadying myself as I slide to my feet. Char steps to the side as I walk to the head of the bed with heavy feet and weak knees. I throw the pillow to the ground, and pull out the small wooden box. "This." I hold up the music box. "I knew that Charles had left me something, but I didn't know what. Unfortunately, it does nothing but play music."

Alexander clears his throat. When I look at him, his blue eyes are eager with anticipation. "That's the same music box from the blueprint."

"One of the blueprints you found in the briefcase?"

225

"Oh shit, you're right," Char says. She reaches behind her and pulls out two pieces of paper. One is large, the other is small, and they were both rolled up and flattened down. She places the smaller one down on the bed and spreads it open. "Look. This is the sketch of the music box. You can see the dimensions are exact."

Alexander smiles, and for the first time I can see just how much he looks like his father. "Can I see it?"

"Yes, of course," I say, handing him the music box.

Alexander's eyes flicker back and forth between the wooden box, and the sketch laid out next to him. With a flick of his thumb he flips the lid open, and then he places the box down on the bed. "You turn this crank here on the side to play music, but I'm sure you've figured that part out already."

I take a step closer to him, our shoulders almost touching. "Yes, I've listened to the music a few times already. Nothing happens."

Alexander runs a finger over the sketch, tracing the edges of the box, and tapping the handwritten math problems as he thinks. He turns his attention back to the inside of the music box, inspecting every detail. "This cylinder here in the middle rotates once you turn the crank. Pins fall from these holes, and pluck a metal comb as it passes by."

"Okay, so that's how it plays the music," Char says. "What does that have to do with anything?"

"I'm getting there." Alex glances at Char, and shakes his head. "If you look carefully at this sketch, you can see the holes on the cylinder are reversed. The pattern on the drawing has three dots, then two, then three, then one. If you look at the music box, it's one, three, two, three."

I've stopped looking over the blueprint and the music box, and instead I've begun watching Alexander. His eyebrows are raised, while still pressing together at the center. That's the same expression Charles made whenever he was working through a problem. I can't help but smile. I want to reach out and brush my hand against his cheek, and tell him how proud I am of him. Instead, I watch him figure out a problem that only Charles knew the solution to.

Alexander reaches inside of the box, and wiggles the cylinder loose. There is a small, square hold where it once was. Beneath it I can see the metal comb that Alexander had spoken of. I tilt my head to the side, and lean in close, trying to see behind the comb. A wall of mirrors reflects my image back to me, and nothing more.

"Let's see what this does," Alexander says. He turns the cylinder in the opposite direction, like it was in the sketch, and places it back where it belongs. Once it's snapped back into place he looks at me, and smiles. "Turn the crank."

I chew the inside of my bottom lip, and reach a trembling hand towards the small crank. I try to grasp it between my fingers, but it slips loose. In the end, I have to use the tips of my nails again to get a good hold of the crank. I turn it three times, and wait.

The music it plays is haunting. It sounds as if someone recorded the beautiful chiming bells, reversed them, slowed them down, and replayed them back. The tones are deep, and strange.

Still, nothing changes. The music box plays music, and nothing more.

"It takes awhile for the pins to pluck the comb," Alexander says. "With it reversed, it takes even longer. Give it two full rotations."

Char looks over her shoulder toward the closed bedroom door. "What's going to happen?"

Alexander laughs. "You're impatient. Wait, and see."

A few seconds later and the cylinder stops spinning. A loud click replaces the haunting sound of music. The center of the box, with the cylinder and crank, begins to rise. Three more clicks, and the cylinder starts to whirl at a rapid pace. As it spins, the insides of the box begin to move independently from one another. The mirrors pull away from the center, and start rising into the air. I can hear the tiny gears whirring and clanking as the mirrored edges open and stand on end.

Then suddenly it stops. The box is quiet. The cylinder no longer spins. The mirrors have opened up a gap in the middle of the box. I can see the metal comb clearly now, and the four mirrored walls that still surround it. Alexander reaches inside the box, unclips the cylinder, and lifts it out. This time, the comb comes with it, as if they were attached together to form the top of those four smaller walls.

Inside sits a lonely syringe, with a bright orange cap covering the needle.

Alexander scratches the side of his head. "What the hell is that?"

"It's an injection," Char answers as she takes the syringe. She squints one eye and examines the side. "There's something written here. It says, 'For Evelyn - only use if you want to remember.' Then it says, 'inject directly into vein.'"

"It can't be." It's hard to talk. My throat feels swollen and dry. "Let me see."

I hold out my hand, and Char places the syringe in my palm. The words are there, small but still legible.

"I thought Charles was an engineer," Char says. "Did he work in the medical field, too?"

I shake my head. "I... um... no. I don't... I don't think he did."

"You mean you don't remember?"

My legs are shaking. "I don't. I don't remember."

Char places a hand on my shoulder. It feels like a sack of bricks weighing me down. "Like how you don't remember your time in Calloway?"

I sit down on the edge of the bed. At least I think I sit. Maybe my legs have finally given in. "That was a long time ago."

"Calloway isn't something to forget. I don't care how much time has passed," Char says.

I place my head in my hands and press my palms into my eyes. The sound of my heartbeat echoes between my ears. I feel sick. I take a deep breath to fight off the nausea. If I have forgotten Calloway, and I have forgotten important details about my husband, what else am I forgetting? And why does the world insist on me remembering?

I swoop my long, matted hair to one side, and tilt my neck toward Char. "There's a large vein here. Hard to miss." I clear my throat. It sounds loud, much louder than it should. "Be quick about it."

Not wanting to look, I keep my eyes on Alexander.

I feel the cold needle against my skin.

"Are you ready?" Char asks.

"Hurry up and do it before I change my mind."

I can hear Char take a deep breath, and I imagine her holding the air in her lungs, too afraid to breathe, with the syringe trembling in her fingers. Or perhaps she's not trembling at all, and is instead ready for everything to end like I am. I feel a sharp prick, and a burning warmth spreads through me. The heat crawls through my veins, penetrating every inch. My lids feel heavy. My beating heart has gone from a chaotic rhythm, to a slow, steady patter. As the room dulls, the colors darkening, my children fading, I can hear the soft patter of dust pelting the window. In the distance I hear my father calling my name.

Then I am gone.

Everything is black.

CHAPTER TWENTY-FOUR
Evelyn Santos

"Evelyn. Evelyn, look at me."

My father has me by the shoulders, his nails digging into my bones. I am trembling. Beside me I hear my little brother whimpering. He is three, and he is more afraid than I am. I try to look at him, but my father holds me tight. I can't move. Outside I hear the storm pounding the walls. It's been three days. Three days and the storm hasn't ended.

"Evelyn, are you even listening? I said look at me, dammit."

My head snaps forward and back, and I realize my father is shaking me.

"Leave her 'lone," Noah cries. His tiny fist lands on my father's forearm.

"I'm sorry." My father sighs. His hands loosen their grip, and his fingers slide down my arms. "Can you please look at me?"

I lift my chin enough to look him in the eyes. I've never seen my father so afraid.

"We are running out of food," my father says. "Whatever crops we had left over from the drought have now been destroyed by this storm. People are dying, Evelyn. Shutting down isn't going to fix it."

"You said they would come." I can barely hear my own voice over the roar of the storm. "We were supposed to leave!"

My father drops his chin to his chest. "I know. I know. That's why I need you right now. The caravans were supposed to arrive this morning. I've got to go to the library, to the transmitter. I've got to get them a message. Something must have happened."

My chin begins to tremble, and my eyes well up with tears. "You can't go alone! I won't let you."

"You'll be okay." He grabs me tight, and pulls me into his chest. "I need you here to watch Noah. He needs you more than I do."

I shake my head. "Mom's here. Mom can watch him. I'll go with you."

"Your mother is sick, Evie."

The house creaks and moans with the force of the wind. I steady myself against the wooden doorframe as the walls begin to shake. We're running out of time. "What if you don't make it?"

"I'll make it."

"But what if you don't?"

My father stands up. He towers above me, and stretches his large hand down for me to take hold. I wrap my fingers around his thumb, and he pulls me to my feet. Noah grabs tight to my waist, and snuggles his snot-covered nose into my side. I pat the top of his head, and run my fingers through his curly brown hair.

"I promise you I will make it," my father says with a smile. "If for some reason I don't, I will need you to run to the neighbor's house. Find someone, anyone, and tell them to go to the library. The door code is zero, one, four, three. Repeat that back to me."

"Zero. One. Four. Three," I say.

"Good. Once they're inside they'll need to find the transmitter. It's in the third room on the left. Tell them to press the red button on the right of the control board. This will allow them to send out one recorded message. The layout can be confusing, but there's a manual taped to the bottom of the chair. Understood?"

"Third room on the left. Red button. Manual is under the chair," I repeat.

My father kisses me on the center of my forehead. "That's my girl." He holds me out at arm's length, and looks me in the eye. "You need to be brave for your brother, okay? Like I said, there's nothing for you to worry about. But, Evelyn, I need you to understand something. Your mother only has a few weeks left. Maybe less. She won't be around for much longer."

"I know, Dad."

"Yes, but do you know what it means if something were to happen to the both of us? If both your mother and I were to... not be around." He takes a deep breath. "It was set that after your mother passed, I would be the one to inherit her duties. The city would be mine to govern. If something were to happen to the both of us, that burden is passed on to you. Do you understand?"

I nod, slowly. The house shakes around us, and I fall into my father's chest. He holds me upright, with little Noah tucked between us.

"It's getting worse out there," he says. "Get your mother. The three of you need to get to the closet beneath the stairs. It's the safest place for you."

"Her medicine?"

"I put her injections in the room for you already. Make sure to give them once in the morning, and once again in the evening. You know what to do. Just get her beneath the stairs."

"Momma sleepin'," Noah says, wiping his nose on the back of his hand.

I pat him on the head, and smile. "Don't worry. I'll move a few blankets for her, and she'll go right back to sleep."

"Momma don't like be wakes up."

"I know," I say. "But she won't mind it this time."

Noah holds my hand, and we both follow my father into the front room. He stands by the door and slips on a pair of heavy brown boots. "Off you go now," he says as he pulls his coat from the pile of clothes on the floor. Once his coat is on, he buttons the front up to his neck, and pulls the collar up as high as it will go. "Hurry. I'll be back in an hour."

"Bye, Dada," Noah says, waving his hand in the air.

Our father smiles one last time, and heads out the door. The storm outside blows a pile of dust into the foyer, and the wind is so strong that the door almost bends as my father struggles to push it shut. Noah tugs on my hand.

"I dun' want Dada go," he says.

"Me neither," I say, trying my best to keep my voice steady. "Come on. Let's go get mom."

It has been six months since my mother fell ill. It seemed to happen over night, and every night thereafter became a constant downhill struggle to keep her alive. At first, she was content sleeping in her own bedroom, but after a few weeks of isolation she requested to be moved somewhere close by. My father built a bed from wood and cloth, and moved my mother into the sitting room. As I walk into the room now I can see she is asleep. Her skin is pale as it always is, and her body just as thin and withered.

There is a picture of my mother that sits on my nightstand. In this picture she is dressed in a gorgeous blue dress, with white buttons running down the front. Her dark hair is in curls that fall like clouds around her face, and she is smiling. The picture was taken during a meeting to discuss the storms. It was said to be the most important meeting of the decade, and it was in this meeting that my mother decided it was best for the entire town to evacuate. She devised a plan, and had spent the next year a half putting that plan into action. Our resources depleted, and the city went broke, but still the people supported her. My mother did all that she could to give the people hope.

Now she is reduced to nothing more than memories withering away in a broken bed.

"Momma, time go," Noah sings.

Outside, the wind is blowing hard. I walk to the window and peer out between the nailed up wooden boards. I think I see the faint silhouette of my father disappearing behind billowing clouds of red dust. I run a hand through my short, cropped hair. He'll be back. He promised he would be back. I turn my back on the window, not wanting a reminder of what is outside, and walk to my mother's bedside.

I nudge her on the shoulder. "Time to get up."

My mother's swollen, red eyes peer around the room. She looks at me, and smiles. "Evie. My darling."

"We need to get to the closet under the stairs."

"Is everything alright?"

I shake my head. I can feel the tears forming, my eyes stinging. "The caravans aren't coming. Dad's gone to the library to figure out what happened. He said the storm's real bad now."

She reaches up, and runs a chapped finger over my cheek. "Today is your birthday."

I grasp her hand in mine. "I know."

"How old now?"

"I'm ten," I say, forcing a smile.

"Such a smart girl for ten. Much smarter than nine."

She tries to laugh, but her voice is hoarse. It ends in a coughing fit.

"Come on, Mom," I say, grasping her hard by the elbow. "We have to go now."

"I help, too," Noah says, grabbing our mother's other arm.

Together we guide her through the front room, around a corner, and to the small room beneath the stairs. Inside, there are three small crates overturned to act as chairs. The floor is lined with old sheets and blankets. To the left of those blankets sits a small wooden box, the one that holds my mother's medication. It helps her to forget. Leaving the past behind is easier to do if you no longer remember it. That was her dying wish. At the time of her passing she will remember the love of her family, and nothing more.

I help my mother lie down, and then I cover her to keep her warm. Noah sprawls out next to her, his innocent brown eyes gazing into her worn, blue eyes. My mother wraps her arm around him, and he tucks himself close to her chest.

The house shakes again. I have to steady myself in the doorway to keep from falling down.

"I think I should go check to see if Dad's on his way back yet."

"You be careful," my mother replies.

"Evie no go," Noah says. "Evie has to stay."

"It's alright," my mother coos, softly stroking his hair with a trembling hand. "Evie's coming right back. Aren't you, honey?"

"Yes." My mouth feels dry. I try to swallow, but my breath catches in my throat. "I'll only be gone a minute."

Noah smiles and waves, and I give him a big smile in return. He closes his eyes and nestles his head into my mother's chest as I quietly shut them inside the closet. I press my back into the door. The vibrations of the storm can be felt through the wood. I straighten out my hair, and take three deep breaths to keep myself from screaming.

I walk to the window at the front of the house. The boards my father nailed up are closer together here, and it's hard to see between the spaces, but it's the best window facing the direction of the library. Outside, I see nothing but dust being carried by wind. I look at the clock hanging haphazardly on the wall, but the time has stopped hours ago. Back outside I see billowing clouds of sand hovering beneath the red sky, and I know my father won't make it.

I dig through the pile of clothes on the floor until I find my thick wool coat. It's one size too small, but it's the thickest piece of clothing I own. I put it on, and button the front up to my neck, just as I watched my father do. The hood goes up, covering my ears. I pile on a second pair of pants, and put on three pairs of socks to make sure my feet are well protected. Then I find my old winter boots, and tuck my feet inside of them.

I think about running back to the tiny room beneath the stairs, and telling my mother where I am going, and that I will be back soon. But, I decide against it. It'll only worry her, and little Noah would only get more upset. All I have to do is find someone to help. I'll be back before they even know I've gone.

I take a deep breath, and step outside.

The wind rips the door from my hands, and it slams against the house. It takes all of my strength to push it back shut. Dust whips through the wind, cutting through the air around me. It slashes at my skin, stinging every part of me it touches. I tuck my hood down as far as I can, covering as much of my face as possible, then I pull my hands inside my coat sleeves.

I look around. It's hard to see more than a few feet at a time. I turn my back against the wind, and run as fast as I can to Mister Sosa's house next door. The closer I get, the easier it is for me to see there is no house. Not any more. There is nothing left of it. It is now a pile of wood, and metal, and dust piled on top of dust.

I try to shout for Mister Sosa, but the sand goes in my mouth. I cough, and spit, but no matter how hard I try I can still feel the grit coating my tongue. All I can think about is Mister Sosa, buried somewhere beneath the rubble. I only hope he got out in time. But if he did, where would he go?

There is no time to think about that now. I need to help my father. My feet carry me to the next house, owned by a kind old lady named Mildred. The front door is open, and the entrance is piled with sand at least a foot high. I kick as much out of the way as I can.

"Miss Mildred! Miss Mildred are you in here? It's Evelyn!"

Silence.

"Miss Mildred? I need help! Are you here?"

Again I am answered with silence.

Hot tears are streaming down my face. I can't control them. I look back out the door, hoping to see the silhouette of my father walking toward me, but instead I see the storm, relentless and thick. There is nothing out there but dust and wind, and broken homes. If we don't get help soon there will be nothing left. I have to help. I have to get to the library.

I keep my head down as I burst through the door and out into the storm. The library is only a mile or two away. I've made the trek many times, and I know how to get there with my eyes closed. The wind stings my face as I run, but I don't stop. I can't stop. Not when the dust flies in my mouth, not when it coats my throat, not even when I am forced to cough just to be able to breathe.

THE FORGOTTEN

My eyes are locked on the ground as I run. When I finally reach the perimeter of houses, where the center of the city opens up to a long stretch of farmland, I am stopped in my tracks. The earth here, normally lush and full of life, is breaking. The dirt is dried and cracked, and a thick, jagged line of broken land stretches out as far as I can see. I feel the ground beneath my feet rumbling, and the land shifts again. I brush my hair from my eyes, and take a giant step over the crack.

There is no time to stop.

In the distance I see the dome of the library jutting out into the darkened sky. Thick clouds have nearly swallowed it whole. The rounded glass has been eroded, part of it shattered and broken, splintered inside its rusted metal frame. I run to the door as fast as I can.

"Zero. One. Four. Three," I say aloud as I punch in the code.

The door creaks open and I sprint inside. The library is almost unrecognizable. The shelves have broken, and the books lay scattered on the floor. The brick walls have begun to crumble. I look up, and see holes in the dome where the glass has been shattered. As I walk toward the third room on the left, I can feel the glass crunching beneath my feet. A strong gust of wind brings dust falling to my feet, and the library begins to shake. I close my eyes and take a deep breath.

"You can do this, Evelyn. Be strong," I whisper to myself.

I march toward the transmitter room with my head held high, and my knees quivering.

I push the door open.

I look inside the room, and let out a blood-curdling scream.

My father is in slumped over in the chair, his chin on his chest, and a metal rod rammed through his shoulder. His coat is soaked with blood. I run to his side, and lift his face to mine. "Dad? Dad, wake up!"

His eyes are wide, and his mouth is open. I shake him. I scream at him. I paw at his face. There is no more life inside of him.

He's gone. My father is gone.

I can't feel my legs. My knees buckle. I collapse onto the floor, with my head in my hands, sobbing. I think about little Noah, nestled into my mother's chest. I think about my mother, and how the few days she has left will be filled with dread knowing the storms have taken her city, stolen her husband. I think about Mister Sosa, and his house of rubble, and of Miss Mildred, whose home is filled with silence. I think of the people still left in city, and all of those we have lost to the storm.

I think about my father. I think about the sacrifice he made to bring the rest of us one tiny ounce of hope. What did he tell me when I was frozen with fear? Shutting down isn't going to fix it.

My hands are still trembling as I pull myself to my feet. I look over the control board, keeping my back to my father so I won't see those lifeless eyes of his watching me. I spot the red button to the right, just where my father said it would be. My eyes scan over the board until I spot a small, round microphone. I grab it, pull it to my lips, and slam my hand down on the button.

"Help. I repeat: We need help. My name is Evelyn Santos. My father is Alexander Santos. This is our cry for help." My voice is shaking. I take a deep breath to steady myself. "Please. If you can hear me, if there is anyone out there, we need your help. I repeat: We need your help. We don't have much time."

CHAPTER TWENTY-FIVE
Alexander Moore

Evelyn has fallen to the floor. She is convulsing. Her eyes are red, and bulging. Every so often they roll into the back of her head. A trail of blood trickles down her nose, resting at her lips. When she opens her mouth to mumble something incoherent, the blood drips inside. It's grotesque, and horrid, but I cannot look away. I think about the buildings going by me in a blur as I ran through Felicity: Ugly, broken buildings that look nothing what I imagined them to. I didn't have time to stop and wonder why a city as horrific as this is something people were willing to die over. I feel lost, betrayed.

Deep inside of me is a pain that I cannot describe, but is painted on my own mother's face as she writhes against the floor.

Char stands over Evelyn with a look of panic in her eyes. She looks at the bedroom door, and back at Evelyn, then bites her bottom lip and runs her hand through her hair. "Shit. Shit. What do we do?"

"I don't know," I mumble. My head is throbbing. It hasn't stopped since we crossed over.

"Do you think she'll be alright?"

I cross my arms over my chest, and shrug.

Evelyn's muscles contract, and she buckles forward clutching her stomach. She turns her face up to the ceiling, her eyes filled with tears. Her fingers wrap around the hem of her shirt, and she screams. It's loud, and ear piercing. Char drops to her knees, and grabs our mother's face.

"Evelyn? Evelyn, are you okay? Can you hear me?"

Evelyn's fingers drop from the hem of her shirt, and wrap themselves around Char's wrists. Her mouth is open, and she is sobbing. Whenever her cries die down, she begins to scream. Her head shakes back and forth. I hear the door handle begin to turn, and I back myself up hard against the wall with my hands high in the air. The door swings open, and Patricia walks in. Her eyes scan the room: from the music box on the bed, to her wailing friend on the floor, to Char, and then to the empty injection left on the edge of the nightstand.

"What the hell have you guys done?" Patricia asks, shouldering her way between Evelyn and Char. She grabs Evelyn by the arms and helps pull her to her feet. "What have you given her?"

"M-m-m..." Evelyn tries to speak, but her words are stuttered. Her entire body is shaking.

"It's alright, honey. Take a deep breath," Patricia says.

"I don't know. I think it's making her remember something," Char says, her eyes hard as stone. "That's what it said. I don't know what's happening."

"I... I... re-re-remem—" Evelyn sputters.

"Take a deep breath," Patricia says, brushing a strand of hair from Evelyn's eyes.

"They... I...I...tried..."

"Let's get you into the kitchen. I'll clean you up. Drink some water, and you'll feel better."

Patricia guides Evelyn out of the bedroom, holding tight to her waist as if she were a small child learning to walk for the first time. Evelyn is still shaking, and a couple of times her knees buckle out from beneath her. Every time she falls, Patricia is there to pick her back up again. She pulls a chair away from the dining table, and helps Evelyn to sit. Then she runs off into the kitchen to fetch a glass of water.

Char follows close behind Patricia, nearly clipping her heels. "What could she possibly be remembering?"

"I don't know," Patricia replies as she holds a glass under the kitchen sink.

"Whatever it is, it's destroying her," Char says. "Look at her face."

Patricia turns the faucet off, and looks Char up and down. "You look at it. You did it. Do me a favor while you're at it. Next time, come to me before you do something stupid. You two better hope she's going to be okay."

Evelyn is panting. Her chest is heaving up and down in quick succession. She is still shaking. Even though her eyes are closed, I can see them rolling around behind her lids like she is searching the room around her. Patricia thrusts the glass of water into her hand, and helps to guide it to her lips. Evelyn tries to take a sip, but chokes on it instead.

"Three days," Evelyn mutters, pushing the glass away. Her voice is hoarse, and her words hard to understand. "I was stuck in the library for three days."

"I think you need to drink," Patricia says.

Evelyn shakes her head, and squeezes her eyes shut even tighter than before. "They were dead." Her bottom lip is trembling. She takes a deep, quivering breath. "Our house... it was gone. Collapsed. I found them at the bottom of the rubble."

"It's okay," Patricia says, rubbing a hand over her back. "Take a deep breath."

I grab my stomach as the wave of nausea hits me.

Char crouches down in front of Evelyn. "Who? Who did you find?"

"M-m-my mother. Little Noah. He was so small. So small."

Evelyn rocks back and forth in her chair, crying to herself. Char looks at me, and I shake my head. I don't know what's happening. All I know is that the room is beginning to spin around me.

"It's happening again. Make it stop. Make it stop."

Evelyn is trembling, and shaking her head back and forth. Within seconds those small tremors become shakes, then become full-fledged convulsions. She throws her head back, gasping for air. It wheezes in and out of her lungs. Her nose begins to bleed again, and Patricia hurries off into the kitchen. I see her grab a cloth from the drawer and run it under the faucet for a second. While she is gone, Char rushes to my side. She puts an arm around my waist, and squeezes.

"I shouldn't have given it to her."

"You did what you had to do," I say, clutching my stomach.

"Are you okay?"

I shake my head. "I don't know."

I watch Patricia kneel down beside her friend, and stroke her hair. She smiles to herself, and I notice the dimple standing out on her cheek. Her eyes are bright brown, golden like honey. Her teeth are pristine white, and straight as an arrow. Straight, except for the bottom two teeth at the center. They are turned in the slightest bit, like Harry's.

I excuse myself to the bathroom, and bolt off down the hall back toward the bedroom. I throw open every door on my way looking for the toilet. When I find the bathroom I barge inside, and slam the door behind me. I barely make it to the toilet in time before I vomit.

Harry is still in Calloway. I don't know where he is, or if he's still in custody, or if the other patrols will even keep him alive after the stunt that Char and I pulled. I wretch, again and again. I can't control it. I can't breathe. On the other side of these walls is a world I care nothing about, and a mother I've never wanted to know.

I didn't ask to come here.

THE FORGOTTEN

I didn't ask to be freed.

The room begins to spin. I lay my head against the cold tile floor, and close my eyes. As another wave of nausea hits, I hear the screams of my mother echoing through the halls.

CHAPTER TWENTY-SIX
Evelyn Santos

A little desk on the back wall of the transponder room is the place I call my office. It's nothing but a small wooden desk with a few pencils, and a notebook I keep in the drawer. On the top right corner I've placed the wooden box that still holds my mother's medication. The lid is broken and splintered, but it is all I have left. I open the top, and glance at the five syringes still resting inside. Not a single scratch on them. I picture the rubble surrounding the box, and little Noah's hand poking up from piles of broken wood and dust, and again feel hatred inside of me. How was it that I was the only one in my family to survive? Two years later and this is all I have left of them: A broken box with useless medication, and memories of mangled bodies that make my insides hurt.

"Excuse me, Miss Evelyn? Might I have a word?"

Oliver Moore is standing in the doorway, brushing an oil-stained hand over the creases in his pants. His red hair is dampened with sweat, and stained black with oil in the places around his ears. As he waits for me to call him inside, he grabs a giant roll of paper from the hallway next to him. It must have been leaning against the wall.

"Yes, please come in."

"Thank you, Miss Evelyn," Oliver says with a smile.

"I see you've been working hard," I say, eying him up and down. "I went down to the tree line on the east border last night. The branches provide a better barrier than I imagined they would."

"Yes. They are looking quite lush, aren't they? But, I do wonder if they were absolutely necessary. Their leaves did provide a nice shade along the streets here in the city. On days like today the break from all this heat would have been welcome."

"They serve a better purpose along the perimeter."

Uprooting the trees inside the city was a controversial move to say the least, but replanting them along the outskirts of the city has helped to lessen the impact of the storms. Their tall trunks, and thick, intertwining branches make a great barrier. The idea has been working better than I imagined it would. The people may be angry at the lack of shade in their streets, but like my mother, I have done what was necessary to keep them safe.

Oliver clears this throat. "If I may." He walks over to my side, and unrolls the piece of paper over the top of the desk. "I wanted to discuss the bridge with you. I've recently been going over some calculations. As you know, we were scheduled to build an expander at the center of the bridge, in case the crack continued to grow. But it seems we've reached our distance limit for the bridge. If it's built any longer we risk it collapsing."

I sigh, and place my elbows down on the desk. With my chin resting on my hands, I glance over the blueprint of the bridge, and all the calculations, pretending to understand what they mean. I make sure to scratch the back of my head, and crease my forehead like I've seen my father do many times before. After a few minutes I lean back into my chair, and run my fingers through my hair.

"This isn't good," I say.

"We need firm direction on our next step. I can finish the bridge as it stands now, without the expander, and use whatever steel we have left to build more buildings at the back of town. Or, we can risk it and hope for the best. I would hate for us to put all of this effort into making the bridge expandable if it's going to cause all of that hard work to be destroyed."

I tap my fingers against the surface of the desk. The hole in the ground must be at least a mile wide by now. It started as a small crack, and continued to grow over time. Whenever the wind blew, the ground shook, and the earth began to shift. Most of those who were on the opposite side of the crack began to panic, and almost all of them jumped across before it became too wide for them to do so. I've never been great at math, but if the crack is still expanding at the same rate it originally was, the bridge will become pointless in a matter of months. That's the purpose of the expander: a simple crank, and extra steel added to the center of the bridge. Whenever the gap begins to grow, we turn the crank and expand the bridge.

"We need that expander. The bridge will be useless in no time if the gap keeps growing."

"If you don't mind, Miss Evelyn, I've brought someone with me today that I think can help." Oliver's long stride carries him to the door before I have the chance to respond. He peeks his head around the edge of the doorframe, and motions down the corridor. A teenage boy appears in the doorway. He has a head of shaggy blonde hair, and bright blue eyes. Oliver pats him on the back and guides him into the room. "This is my son, Charlie. He's been curious about what's been going on around the gap, and he's made some great observations that I think you'd be interested in hearing. Charlie, tell her what you told me last night."

Charlie tucks his hand inside his pants pocket, and grins. I feel my cheeks grow hot, and I tuck my hair behind my ears at least three times before I can make eye contact with him. When he clears his throat the sound startles me, and I nearly jump out of my seat.

"I've been studying the seismic activity around the gap since it first opened up," he says. "Over the past two years I have seen the tremors diminish to nothing. The chasm first started expanding at a rate of roughly ten feet per week over that initial year, and then it slowed to about twenty feet per month. Over the past year it's gone from expanding approximately two to three feet over the course of six months, to no activity whatsoever. I think it's safe to say that we no longer need to worry about expanding the bridge. The gap is now stable."

Oliver straightens his shoulders and stands up tall. The air around the room feels lighter, as if a weight has been lifted from us all. The ceiling, with its shattered glass and boarded up holes, suddenly feels brighter. I can feel the warmth of the sun shining through. The earth has stopped moving. It's over.

"How sure are you?"

"Pretty damn sure," Charlie says.

Oliver steps out in front of his son. "Like I mentioned before, without having to worry about the expander, we will have the resources to build more housing units. Our land is limited, and the population continues to grow. As it stands now we already have two, three, sometimes four families boarded together in a single home. Once my men and I complete the bridge, we should focus on building even more homes for the people to live in, on both sides of the gap."

Charlie raises a hand in the air. "Can I chime in here?"

"Chime away," I tell him with a smile.

"The biggest problem I see right now is space." He tugs on the bottom of his earlobe as he thinks, and the action looks so silly that I have to bite my lip to keep myself from laughing. "Before the chasm opened up we had people spread out evenly, but now they've all relocated to our side. That means we now have half of the land supporting the full number of residents, and the numbers will only grow from here."

"Then those that crossed will have to go back," I say.

"It's not as easy as you think. No one wants to go back to the other side of the bridge. In a few years time we won't have enough land, or supplies, to sustain everyone."

I scoff, and roll my eyes. "We can make them cross back."

"With what? Pitchforks and fire?" Charlie laughs to himself. "You can't force people to do something they don't want to do, Evelyn. That's not how it works."

Oliver nudges his son in the side, and clears his throat. "That's enough."

I clench my jaw and get to my feet, my body trembling with anger. If I told every single person in this place to march straight to the crack and jump inside, they would have to do it. No one can question me. I am the one in charge. I take a deep breath. The muscles in my arms are clenching, and my stomach is tight. Right as I am about to scream my anger at the room, there is a knock at the front door.

"What is it?" I shout.

"Miss Evelyn," a soft voice says. The door gently opens. Grace King enters with a clipboard in hand. Her wrinkled, saggy cheeks remind me of my grandmother's, long ago, when she was still around. She stares at the ground as she speaks. "I'm sorry to bother you, dear. Hank Schmidt, who was working to excavate the land in back, discovered a broken water pipe that was buried beneath the ground. It's one of three main water pipes for our side of the city that weren't destroyed when the crack opened up."

I steal a quick glance at Charlie, who is tugging on his earlobe lost in thought. I can feel the sting of a headache forming over my left eye. "What the hell does that even mean, Grace?"

"Well, it means that our water supply is diminished. I suggest we put out a bulletin warning residents that use of water must be at a minimum. Everything they use from this point on, until Mister Schmidt can seal off the broken pipe, will need to be boiled to kill off any bacteria that may have entered the supply. I'm sorry, Miss Evelyn."

My jaw is clenched so tight that I think my teeth might shatter. I turn my back on the others in the room and grip the edge of my desk. I dig my nails into the wood, feeling the pain shoot up through my fingers. We are running out of land. We are running out of water. I close my eyes. Behind the darkness of my lids, my father is clenching me by my shoulders. He is shaking me, telling me to get a grip. The only solution is to get the bridge completed as fast as possible. Then I must send people to the other side.

I take a deep breath and reach for my mother's old medicine box. I run a finger along the outer edge, feeling the splintering wood beneath my skin. A pain courses through my stomach, tightening my chest, and making it hard to breathe. Behind me I hear the soft footsteps of Grace leaving the room. When I turn around Oliver is standing rigid, with his hands in his pockets, and his eyes on the floor.

"You are going to need to finish that bridge as soon as possible. Recruit as many people as you can to help. Do whatever it takes."

"Yes, Miss Evelyn," Oliver whispers.

Charlie steps forward and clears his throat. "I recommend you put out notices now, announcing the completion of the bridge, and asking for volunteers to move to the other side. Living on the other side of the chasm might be more appealing to people once they learn about the water."

"Okay," I say softly. I don't have the energy to fight.

255

Charlie smiles and wraps an arm around my shoulder. I let myself sink into his side, the anger inside of me fading. "Things will get better, Evelyn. You'll see."

Standing close to the crack fills me with dread. Staring into nothingness, unable to see the other side, is unnerving. The wind is stronger here, thicker. Any moment now a strong gust of wind could push me over the edge. Yesterday there was another storm. That's the fifth one this year. Some of the trees along the border have begun to uproot from the strong winds.

I lean forward, and stare down into the black abyss. Charlie grabs ahold of my elbow, and pulls me back a few steps. When I look into his eyes I feel sick. I can see the toll the last few years have taken on him. He is a boy of eighteen, with eyes of a man three times his age. The exhaustion has taken a toll on us both.

"How many now?" I ask.

"Eighty-three, not including the ones that have already passed," Charlie answers.

I hang my head. "All children?"

"Yes. All children. The water seems to only affect the young. I can only assume it's because of their weakened immune systems. And it's not just those located at the back of town anymore. The disease appears to be spreading closer to the front of the city as well."

"You and I are fine."

"Yes, we are."

I pick my head up and look him in the eyes. "But why?"

Charlie shakes his head. "There seems to be no real rhyme or reason to who gets sick, and who doesn't. It could be because we're older."

"I can't even walk the streets anymore without someone shouting at me."

"Everyone is scared."

"But no one is listening!" I ball my hands into fists at my sides. "I've had one family volunteer to cross over. One single family. Once they realized no one else was going they changed their minds. We will die if we stay here. Every one of us. We will all die, because the people of this city are too stupid to leave."

"You can't blame them, you know. Have you even been to the other side since the bridge went up?"

"That's different," I snap.

"Is it? You're not the only one that lost someone they loved that day, Evelyn. Why return to those memories, when you're building new ones, better ones, right here?"

"But their children are dying! The medical ward is full. I have doctors and chemists working around the clock. They are leaving me with very little options. Either people cross, or we all die."

Charlie takes a step closer to the crack. The wind pushes the hair from his eyes, and his clothes stick to the front of his body. He places his hands on his hips, and looks back and forth over the horizon. "Your mother's box is empty, Evelyn."

My heart thumps fast against my chest. I brush a strand of hair out of my face. "I don't know what you mean."

"I went by your office last week. You weren't in. The box was sitting on your desk, empty. Thought it was kind of curious, so I went down to the med ward to talk to Doctor Edwards about it. He said you dropped it off at the lab the day before." Charlie places a hand on my shoulder. "You made a promise to me, Evie."

My cheeks grow hot, and I swat his hand away. "I've told you not to call me that." A throbbing pain echoes through my head. "I'm not standing around listening to this. I've got more important problems to worry about."

I take off towards the city, walking as fast as my legs will carry me. Charlie's footsteps follow closely behind. I hear him calling my name, telling me to stop, telling me everything will be okay, if I only gave it time. I throw my hands over my ears and keep walking. A few seconds later Charlie has me by the elbow, and he's pulling me to a stop. I whip around and push my hands into his chest.

"Stop it!"

Charlie grabs me by the wrists, holding me still. "What the hell are you doing, Evelyn? Tell me! What have you done?"

I swing my foot forward, and it hits him in the center of his shin. I wriggle my arms free. "I am doing what I have to do."

"We talked about this, Evelyn," Charlie says, rubbing the tender spot on his leg. "You can't do it. It's barbaric."

"This is my decision to make."

I turn and face the new city. The buildings have grown in size. Once they were two, three stories tall, but now they stand high amongst the clouds. From here the city is beautiful, full of hope and promise. But the land is plagued with death. Children are dying by the dozen, and the ones who aren't dead are either sick, or will fall ill before too long.

What Charlie doesn't know is that I've already sent someone over the bridge. I have been told that the land is lush, and the water is clean. There is life there. There is hope. But no one wants to listen to a sixteen-year-old girl. As far as they're concerned, I am the one that brought the plague amongst them. I am not my mother. To them, that makes me a disappointment.

"Then don't make that decision," Charlie says. "Send a team of people into the chasm. There might be water down there. Please, give it time. Don't make any decision you're going to regret, Evelyn. Think about the people. You'll have an uprising. They won't stand for it."

"That's the thing, Charlie. They won't even know it happened."

I take the small baby from her mother's arms, and gently caress her cheek. She feels warm to the touch, soft as the silk dresses my mother used to wear. The baby stares at me with her deep, blue eyes and begins to cry.

"It's okay, little one," I coo. "You'll see Momma again one day."

"I've named her Isadora," the woman states. She is lying in the hospital bed, the blanket bunched up around her stomach. "Isadora Marie Gonzalez. I think I'd like to call her Izzy, though. For short."

"That's a very nice name," I say with a smile. Then I turn to the patrol standing guard at the door, and hand the baby over. "We will let her caretaker know."

"Thank you, Miss Evelyn." The woman places a hand over her heart, and her bottom lip begins to tremble. "Thank you."

I give the woman a gentle nod, and head out the door behind the patrol. "Have her documented and checked over by the medic before you bring her over. Remember: Isadora Marie Gonzalez, nickname Izzy. Check the caregiver's documentation before handing them the baby."

"Yes, Miss," the patrol states.

He disappears down the corridor of the hospital with the baby in his arms. I smile to myself. Time changes everything. It changes fear into hope, pain into pleasure, and objection into acceptance. Of course it took time and dedication to get to this point. Some nights I still have nightmares of the day we announced. We, the severance team and I, had practiced the procedure many times. First, we establish order. Create the patrols, a group of men and women whose job it is to keep the peace, and maintain the new laws. Then, we make the announcement. All children were to leave immediately.

The women screamed and wailed. They clutched their children, who were still pale with the sickness, tight to their bodies. We had to rip them apart. The patrols dragged crying children, one after the other, over the bridge. The men tried to fight us off, but, in the end, I had done my job. Our children were safe, and on to a better life. A life free of illness.

Once we handed out the serum the fighting stopped. All was accepted as righteous, and good. I have brought them new hope, the same as my mother did long ago. In eighteen years, Isadora Marie Gonzalez will step back inside Felicity as a strong, healthy woman, ready to be reunited with her family.

This is how our city is ruled.

This is how our people will survive.

CHAPTER TWENTY-SEVEN
Char Moore

I watch my mother bring the teacup to her lips. Her hands are trembling. When she tries to take a sip, the tea spills out onto the front of her shirt. Evelyn hands the cup back to Patricia, shaking her head. I look over my shoulder at Alexander. He is leaning against a wall, his face pale, with his arms dangling lifelessly at his sides. The front of his shirt has flakes of dried vomit, and his eyes are bloodshot.

Alexander must be sick. Not the kind of sick you get when you've spent too much time outdoors in the dead of winter, but the kind of sick that comes when your world begins to unravel. My brother has taken twelve trips to the bathroom since Evelyn started relaying the information she was remembering. I don't blame him one bit. I am thankful for my iron stomach, and that my loathing turns to anger, and not illness.

"I need something stronger than tea," Evelyn says. Her voice is weak, but her fatigue has begun to resolve. Her eyes are more wide, and alert. "Do you have any whiskey? Maybe some scotch or bourbon would do. Anything, really."

Patricia wraps her fingers tight around the teacup. Her fingertips turn white. She turns on her heels, and brings the cup back into the kitchen without saying a word.

"Keep talking," I tell Evelyn. "I want to hear all of it."

Evelyn straightens out her back, and tugs at the hem of her shirt. "It was a brilliant idea at first. The children came back healthy. Seeing them well again filled me with an immense sense of pride. Even the children who were on death's door before crossing over were somehow healed. Every single one of them became healthy. Sending them away worked. It really worked."

Patricia returns with a glass, and thrusts it into Evelyn's hand. "Here. It's scotch."

"You were ripping children away from their families. I find nothing brilliant about that," Alexander says, quietly. His voice is hoarse. "Brilliance is finding a logical solution that satisfies all parties, not only your own."

"You can stand there and make judgments all you want," Evelyn says. "But you don't know how it was back then. You don't know what I had gone through."

"You're right. I don't know anything about you, or what you've been through," Alexander says. His ears are turning red, and he tries hard to keep his voice steady. "But perhaps I would have, had you not robbed me of the opportunity long before I was born."

Evelyn closes her eyes, and takes a long sip of her drink. When half of the glass has been emptied she lets her eyes flutter open. They've turned red in the short time they were closed, and tears are forming along the edges. "Any of you have a cigarette?"

Behind me I hear Alexander scoff. I don't have to turn around to know what he is doing. His jaw is tight, and his eyes are staring at the ceiling. It's what he does when he is mad. Sometimes he taps a foot, or clenches his fists. I know this because I've been there for him since the moment he was born.

"When did you know, huh?" Alex's voice is growing louder. When he takes a deep breath I can hear his lungs wheezing. "When did you realize you'd made a mistake?"

Evelyn licks her lips, and brings the glass of scotch to the front of her mouth. She inhales deep, and then finishes off the rest in one gulp. "When did I realize I'd made a mistake?" She scrunches her nose, and looks inside of her empty glass. "Not right away. The people of Felicity were compliant, of course. We only had to give the memory serum to the first generation of people, those that were there from the start. After that, the fighting stopped. The people believed what they were told: that handing over their children was something that's always happened. That was the way it was. No one questioned it. At least not those in Felicity."

"You're right about that," Patricia says. Her voice is soft, almost a whisper. She hangs her heads as she speaks. "But it was all lies. We were told there was a war, Evelyn. Why would you keep the truth from us?"

Evelyn shrugs. "Wars make for better stories. Wars are more believable. People don't question wars."

I slump myself down into an empty chair at the table, and press the palm of my hand into my forehead. All of those lies set into motion by a simple storm. I'd laugh if it weren't so depressing. I suppose that was Evelyn's point. Wars are frightening. They go against all human nature, and that's what makes them terrifying. But a storm; a storm is nature. When they come, I walk inside my house and shut the door. End of story.

"What I didn't think about was the children," Evelyn continues. "Sure, they were healthy. They were alive. But, they were... lost. That's the best way I can describe it. Deep down, the children must have felt abandoned. Some of the children rebelled, and some of them became violent. The majority of the children, however, had no interest whatsoever to return to the ones who were so willing to let them go. That was a problem I didn't know I would encounter. Can I get another drink?"

I glance at Alexander, who is still leaning against the wall, standing the way I imagined he would. As the words sink in, his stone-hard face softens. The anger in his eyes melts into sadness. Alexander understands those children the most, the ones that wished to never return. He would tell me as much on nights when he couldn't sleep. Sometimes he would wake up from the same nightmare he always had, screaming in his sleep. In those dreams he was being held up by his feet, his head dangling over a cliff, with no one coming to his rescue.

My eyes begin to sting, and I have to take a deep breath to compose myself. Alexander never wanted to cross over, and he wasn't the only one. I let Evelyn's word echo in my head: The children were lost, abandoned. Then suddenly it hits me, and it all makes sense: How Jason, the boy I've known for years, didn't recognize me when I ran into him on the street; the look on Amanda Simmons' face as she prepared to cross over.

"You ended up giving them the serum, too." I clear my throat, and sit up straight. "That's how you fixed the problem. You made them forget about their time in Calloway."

Patricia rips the empty glass from Evelyn's hand, and storms off into the kitchen. The rest of us remain silent as the sound of Patricia banging around cabinets fills the room. I hear ice dropping into a glass, and liquid being poured in after them. Patricia returns moments later with a glass filled to the brim.

"I thought there was something wrong with me," Patricia says. She slams the glass on the table next to Evelyn, and the liquor sloshes out of the top. "Why can't I remember walking over the bridge? Why don't I have any memories from my childhood? I didn't understand it then, but it all makes sense now. You stole the memories from me; from all of us." She takes a deep breath, and pushes a loose curl from her eyes. "You're my best friend, Evelyn. How could you do this to me? How could you do this to any of us? You should be ashamed!"

I stand myself up, and step a little closer to Patricia. "Let's not get sidetracked. We're all angry. Let her finish talking first."

Patricia holds her hand in the air. "Just a second. I've got one more question. Evelyn, how old were you when you first sent the children over?"

Evelyn bites her lip, and stares at nothing in particular. Her eyes are flickering back and forth, as if she is searching her new memories for an answer. "Sixteen, I believe. Maybe seventeen."

"That means I was fourteen years old when all of this went down." Her face is turning red, her entire body trembles. She raises a finger, and points it in Evelyn's face. "Fourteen years of memories gone. Wiped from existence. My father died three years after I crossed over. My mother died two years after him. Do you know what I wouldn't do to have those goddamn fourteen years back?" Patricia lunges forward and clutches the front of Evelyn's shirt, shaking her as she speaks. "You stole them from me, and I will never get them back! How dare you? How dare you?"

I wedge myself in front of Evelyn, and wrap my arms around Patricia's shoulders. As I guide her to the other side of the room she shoves her hands into my chest, and continues to scream her anger. There is nothing that I can say or do that will calm her. I grind my teeth together as she shouts in my ear. I let her slam her fists into my shoulders, my arms, my chest.

Whatever ill feelings I once had for Patricia have been dissolved in this moment. As I feel her hot tears fall on my shoulder, I can't help but feel for her. She has wasted years of energy on fake allegiance, believing lies, never once thinking to question them. I understand why Evelyn refused to tell people the truth. They would have all reacted the same as Patricia. The city would tear itself apart.

Evelyn adjusts her shirt, and then takes a long swig of her drink. She smacks her lips together, staring at her glass while waiting for Patricia to finish ranting. When Patricia's screams turn into light sobs, Evelyn places her drink down on the table and sits up straight.

"It's no coincidence that I couldn't remember who I was, and what I had done. I saw the repercussions first hand." Evelyn traces a finger along the rim of her glass. "Over one hundred children died the first two years. Most of the deaths were by suicide. Others committed horrendous acts of cruelty on others: murders, assaults, robberies. I had set in motion something that I could no longer stop. It was spiraling out of control."

"You're nothing but a coward," Alexander says, his voice shaking. "You let those children die. Whether by your hand or someone else's, it doesn't matter. Instead of fixing what you had done—"

"There was no way to fix it," Evelyn snaps. "If the children didn't cross, they would die. End of story. I decided that having one hundred children dying on the other side of the bridge was better than three hundred of them dying slow, painful, disease-ridden deaths here. There is nothing else that I could have done."

I can't help but picture Mara, lying in the dirt between two broken-down buildings, and wonder if that is what my mother had in mind when she heard about the chaos across the bridge. Is this what she knew was happening, and still turned a blind eye? Mara was my friend. She was someone's sister, someone's daughter. I can still see the way her eyes were vacant, and how the blood matted her hair to her face. I will never forget those words sprawled across her shirt: Let them forget.

I take a step closer to Evelyn, and stare into her eyes. "You chose to murder them. Maybe not directly, but it was your hand that guided them to their deaths. It was you that pulled those triggers, that slit those throats, that threw those people into The Chasm." I lean forward until I am inches from her face. "Her name was Mara Matthews, and she will never be forgotten."

CHAPTER TWENTY-EIGHT
Alexander Moore

The tears are silent as they fall. I reach my hand up and wipe my cheek, only to feel more tears streaming down just as fast. They feel hot against my cold skin. My stomach is turning, and turning. It's hard for me to hold down the waves of nausea as they roll over me, but I doubt there's anything left for me to throw up. Still, my stomach clenches. I have to wrap my arms around my waist, and steady myself against the wall to keep myself from getting sick.

Char turns her back on Evelyn, and takes a few deep breaths. Her face is red. The muscles in her jaw tighten and loosen, tighten and loosen. After a few moments, she plucks her bangs back across her forehead, and turns to face Evelyn again. "I want to know why no one stopped you."

"Because no one knew," Patricia says.

I pull my shirt up and use the fabric to blot my tears. I take a deep breath, and feel the air burning in my lungs. The room sways back and forth. My stomach dips and sways with every turn. "But the cities haven't always been ruled this way." I begin to cough violently, feeling my chest rattle. When it finally subsides my throat is hoarse, and every time I speak the words burn. "They let a child rule their city, and no one intervened. No one questioned it."

Evelyn glares at me. "Of course not. And if they did question it, what could they have done? This city belongs to my bloodline, to my name. There is no way to challenge that."

"This is messed up," Char whispers to herself. She stares at the ceiling lost in thought, running a finger through her hair. "You said Charles tried to stop you though." Her voice is still quiet as a whisper. I watch as she bites her bottom lip, raises an eyebrow, and then turns back to Evelyn. "Do you remember my first night here in Felicity? We talked about family, about my father. You said he did great things for this city. When I asked you how it was that he died you told me he was thrown into The Chasm. Do you remember telling me that?"

Evelyn takes another long sip of her drink. She narrows her eyes, and keeps the glass at her lips. After a few moments she places the drink back down on the table and sighs. "I remember."

"He was shot, Evelyn. Before he was thrown into The Chasm."

Evelyn presses the palm of her hand into her forehead, and closes her eyes. "Can you imagine what life was like for him?" She lets her hand slide down her face, covering her mouth with spread fingers. "I spared him from the serum because that's what he wanted. He didn't want to forget. Instead, he chose to carry that burden around with him everywhere. I begged for him to forget. We could have made a new life together, started over, if only he took the serum with me. He refused. He didn't want to run away."

I step forward, and point a finger in Evelyn's face. "I want to know why he was murdered. Tell me why he was shot."

Evelyn shoots out of her chair, and slams her fists down on the table. "Because I ordered it!" Her nostrils flare. Her entire body shakes. She tries to grab her glass but instead knocks it on its side. Brown liquid runs down the leg of the table and onto the floor. With a trembling hand she turns the glass back upright. "It was my duty to keep the cities safe. I did what I had to do."

Patricia presses her back up against the wall, and clutches her chest. "Oh, Evelyn. Tell me this isn't true. Not Charles."

Evelyn lowers herself back in the chair. "I didn't know it was him."

I squeeze the bridge of my nose to try to subdue the ache in my skull. "Tell me how you were able to make that decision. You should have forgotten you were in charge."

Evelyn scoffs, and crosses one leg over the other. "The medics had created a special serum for me. That was my idea, by the way."

"A special serum that does what?" I ask.

"That does what all the other serums do, only temporary. I couldn't have my memory wiped permanently. Not while I still ruled the land." Evelyn flips her hair over her shoulder, and sits up straight. "The serum would wear off twice a year. There would be maybe four hours of down time before my next dose was due. That's when I would remember enough to make whatever decisions I needed to make. Those four hours were painful. My heart ached with those lost memories, but I did it for the good of the people."

"For the good of the people," I repeat. There is no emotion in Evelyn's voice, as if she is reading her memories from a note card stored in her mind. "I think they would disagree."

Evelyn glares at me. "Anyway, that's when I met with the patrols. They helped me make whatever decisions were necessary to keep everything running smooth. Then, when it was all said and done, I would take my next dose of the serum, and everything would be forgotten."

"And one of those decisions was murdering your own husband," Char says.

"I've already told you that I didn't know it was him," Evelyn says impatiently. "The patrols found out that he was working hard to reverse everything that I had created. That's when I..." She lets her words fade into silence, and her eyes stare off into the distance. "They didn't tell me it was Charles. I never would have put the order in if I had known."

"I don't believe you," Char says, crossing her arms over her chest. "I'm a patrol. No one told me who you were, or what was going on. If you're telling the truth, why didn't I know?"

Evelyn laughs, and shakes her head. "Because I'm smarter than that. I wouldn't trust my secret with every patrol. Can you imagine the rebellion? No. Every order needs structure. There is one patrol in charge, right? The one who has been there the longest?"

"Yes," Char says softly.

"That's the patrol I trust the most. Of course that person can't do it alone, so I let them choose one or two others that they feel is the most loyal. The secret stays safe within our group until their duties end. Those that don't obey are immediately terminated."

My ears are ringing a terrible high-pitched screech. The ache in my stomach has gotten worse, and it is now in knots so tight that I can hardly breathe. It all makes sense now. Char told me about Tyler. He would have been one of the only people alive that knew about Evelyn. Except, he wasn't the only one. He must have turned to others to get his message across, and they have been shouting out for help all of this time. Now the patrols have become divided. There are those that want the cities to change, and those that want to keep things as Evelyn always wanted them to be: forgotten.

That can't be all there is to it, though. There is something that I'm missing. I chew the inside of my cheek as Evelyn and Char continue to argue. The radio. The case. The blueprints. They were all passed on to me for a reason. I tilt my head toward the ceiling as I think. The radio showed me who Evelyn really was. The briefcase showed me what really happened to my father. One blueprint showed me how to open the music box. The other blueprint…

"What's in the library?"

"Books," Evelyn croaks. "It's a library."

I look at Char and smile. "Do you still have the blueprint?"

Char stares at me for a moment before she registers what I've said. Once it hits her, she quickly reaches into the back of her pants and pulls out the flattened, rolled up papers. "It's right here."

"I told you," Evelyn says. "It's just a library."

I unroll the blueprint and lay it out over the top of the dining table. My eyes flicker side to side, scanning the drawn lines inside the library. The first time I saw this blueprint I was fascinated with the dome. It's the detail within the glass; those beautiful angles that create small prisms under sunlight. That grabbed my attention the most. Now I look over the sketch of the rooms as carefully as I can. There is the entrance, the open floor at the center, and three rooms on the left.

"What is this room here?" I tap my finger over the room at the farthest end of the library.

Evelyn glances over her shoulder to see where I'm pointing, and then scoffs. "That's the old transponder room. I used it as my office for a while. It's empty now."

I look over the paper once more, ignoring the wave of nausea rolling over me. It seems to be going in and out now. "You told us something about one of your memories that I found curious. You said that Charles suggested going into The Chasm, back before the children were sent away."

"You remind me of your father," Evelyn says. "You have the same eyes. Smart as a whip, too. I'm so sorry. You shouldn't be here."

I clear my throat. "Did Charles ever go into The Chasm?"

"There is nothing in The Chasm," Evelyn says as she slouches in her chair.

My heart is racing, and I can feel my pulse ripping through my temples. The room spins slowly, and I close my eyes and take a deep breath to steady myself. I don't know what's gotten into me.

When I open my eyes again the room is standing still, and Evelyn stares at me with eyes as hard as stone.

"That's because I believe he went into The Chasm a long time ago," I tell her.

Char steps closer to my side, and looks down at the sketch of the library. "What are you on about?"

"I need another drink," Evelyn says.

"You can get it yourself," Patricia says as she walks to my side. Our shoulders touch as we look over the paper together. I steal a quick glance at her. For a moment our eyes meet, and I am reminded of Harry. I have to clear my throat, and stare back down at the blueprint to keep myself from missing him.

"I overlooked it the first time because I was too busy studying the dome on the top. This room here," I tap my fingers on the old transponder room, "is different than the others. You see the tracing of the outside wall, like in the other rooms, but there's a second line right inside that one, sketched with thin, short dashes."

"You're going to have to explain it to me," Char says.

"I believe it represents another floor. The dashed lines seem to mean the walls are invisible, or at least hidden. Right here," I point to a smaller rectangle inside of the room, sketched out in the same short, dashed lines, "is drawn the same way. It reminds me of the thing we stood on when we arrived here. That room that lifted us up to this floor."

"An elevator," Patricia says.

"Yes. Like an elevator," I say.

Evelyn shoots out of her chair, and throws her hands in the air. "There is nothing hidden inside of the library! The transponder room was shut down years ago. I won't have talk of this nonsense around me." She rips the blueprint off the table, and crumples it up in her hands. "That's enough!"

"You can't do that!" I shout.

Evelyn shrugs as she throws the blueprint over her shoulder. At the same moment I hear two loud, chiming noises going off at once. The sound makes me jump, and it stops Char from dashing after the blueprint. Patricia pulls a small, glowing square from the counter, and presses it with her finger. She dashes further into the kitchen, and I hear her mumbling something under her breath. Evelyn reaches into her pocket and pulls out a similar square device, with a blue glowing screen, and presses a small button on the side. The sound stops. Evelyn throws the square down onto the table.

I reach forward, grab the device, and turn it over in my hands. Evelyn tries to snatch it back, but I shuffle to the side just out of her reach. She slumps forward in her chair, and nestles her chin into her chest. Her eyes are drooping. Her chest is moving up and down in a slow, methodical rhythm.

I hold the square device in front of my face, inspecting every side. "What the hell is this thing?"

"That's a phone, you idiot," Char says. "Now give it back to her so we can finish this nonsense."

"A phone? But where are the wires? The battery? How does it receive a signal?"

Char rips the phone from my hands and slams it down on the table. "Does it really fucking matter right now?"

"I...I'm sorry," I say, quietly. I feel a prickle in my chest, and I am thrown into another coughing fit. It last a little longer than the one before it.

"The signal is transmitted from the library," Evelyn says, ignoring me as I clutch my chest and wheeze. She lays her head on the table and closes her eyes. "From the old transponder room."

Char rushes to my side, and puts her arm around my shoulders. "You okay?"

I take a deep, rattling breath, and nod my head. "The air must be thinner up here. I'm not used to it."

"You two need to leave," Patricia says as she hurries back into the room. "That was my friend, Mark. The patrols have been looking for Evelyn. They know she's here."

Evelyn yawns, and nestles her head deeper into the table. "Tell them I'm going to rest first."

Patricia places her hand on my shoulder and squeezes. "I have an emergency exit in my bedroom closet. It takes you to the center of the building, and there you can find elevators that lead outside. Come on. I'll show you where it is."

She leads us down the hall, into the first room on the right. The floor is covered in dirt, and piles of dead bugs sit in the corner. Her bed is teetering in a broken wooden frame. The mattress sags in the center.

"Over here," Patricia says.

She leads us to the wall to the left of the bed, where a white wooden door sits at the center. Char places her hand on Patricia's forearm, stopping her before she opens the closet door.

"You really didn't know?" she asks.

Patricia shakes her head. "No, I didn't. And a part of me wishes I never found out. But none of that matters now. You two need to find a place to hide. Stay low for a while. It's not safe for you here."

There is a loud bang at the front of the house. Patricia pulls the closet door open, and pushes the clothes to the side with one swoop of her arm. Behind them I see the silhouette of a door hidden inside the back wall. Patricia reaches her hand up, and presses something on the wall above the doorframe. A door swings open, showcasing an empty corridor behind it.

Char takes a step forward, and pauses. "I did know your son," she says, softly. The words make my stomach turn. I can feel the bile rising in my throat. I knew she was Harry's mother from the moment I looked into her eyes. "We called him Harry. He's lived with us since he was two years old, and I've loved him like my own brother. I'm sorry I didn't tell you sooner."

There is another bang at the front door, followed by a heavy crash.

"Go," Patricia says, wiping a tear from her eye. "Before they find you."

Char grabs me by the hand and pulls me through the doorway. I turn around to face Patricia one last time, to look into those eyes that remind me so much of my best friend, but the door has already closed. I'm face to face with a rusted metal wall. With my heart racing I rush to the wall, and press my ear up against it.

I hear the sound of Patricia screaming.

The   other   side   falls   silent.

CHAPTER TWENTY-NINE
Evelyn Moore

I can hear the front door break from its hinges. It must have broken in half, and slammed against the ground. I can hear people scrambling about the room, their boots falling heavily on the tiled floor. Those people are screaming at one another. Their words are mumbled. It's as if I'm submerged in deep water, listening to them shout at me from the shore.

Someone grabs my arm. It feels like needles pricking the skin through my shirt.

Everything around me is a blur.

I think I hear Patricia calling out to me, but when I turn to face her all I see is white.

I am in a cloud, resting in the sky in the middle of the night. From below me I hear the sound of Patricia screaming.

Then there is thunder.

Everything falls silent.

CHAPTER THIRTY
Char Moore

I rip Alexander away from the wall, and together we sprint down the hall. The shiny metal walls, and crisp white floor, move around us in a blur as we run. We round a soft corner, and find the elevator in a matter of moments. I don't wait to catch my breath as I ram my thumb into the call button. The elevator groans to life; the numbers above the metal doors climbing higher and higher. Alex is panting beside me, bent over with his hands on his knees. His face is pale, his one open eye is bloodshot.

There is a ding, and the elevator doors slide open. I grab Alex by the hand, and drag him into the elevator with me. He presses his back against the inside handrail as I press the button marked G - for the ground floor. The doors slide back together, and I am forced to stare at my reflection in the metal walls. I press my hands against their cold surface, and hang my head. My stomach turns. Sweat is dripping down my face.

"Fuck," I mumble.

Alexander clears his throat. I look at his distorted reflection, at the look of pain and anger in his face, and feel bile rising in my throat. All that has happened to us echoes in the silence of this elevator. The further we descend, the more it settles in. I clench my hands into tight fists at my sides. I let my overgrown nails dig into my flesh. When I close my eyes I can feel the room spinning around me, so I let them flutter open and stare at my own face, broken and defeated. I raise my right hand, and slam my fist into the wall. I bring my hand back up, and slam it back down.

"Stop," Alex whispers.

This time I slam both fists into the metal wall, over and over again, screaming until my throat is raw; until I can feel the blood trickling on the back of my tongue. My entire body is trembling. I take a deep breath, and scream again. I grab the handrail that circles the inside of the elevator walls, grip it so tight that my fingers ache, and I scream one last time. My chest is heaving. I am gasping for air. My eyes are stinging. I clench my jaw to keep the tears from forming.

"Stop it," Alex pleads, his voice quivering. He wraps his arms around my waist, and I let him pull me away from the rail. With a strong hand, he grips my shoulder and turns me toward him. He looks like hell. "Please. Just stop. I can't watch you do that any more."

"Fuck this place," I croak.

"Yeah," Alexander replies, quietly. He drops his hands to his sides. "What are we going to do?"

I shake my head, and shrug my shoulders. I don't have an answer for him. I don't even know where we will go once we leave the building. Neither one of us has a plan, a way out, a place to lay low for a while. There is no way to know what will happen once our feet touch the manicured soil of Felicity. All Alex and I can do is stand shoulder to shoulder in silence, waiting for the elevator to reach the ground floor. Once it does, I grab a hold of Alex's wrist, heart racing, and wait for the door to open. The elevator dings, then the doors creak as they slide apart at the center.

I take a deep breath and lean my chest forward, prepared to run. Alex and I only take two steps before I see a flash of green and brown. A strong force knocks into my chest. I'm too caught off guard to struggle, and within seconds my body is being slammed into the back wall of the elevator. Alex lets out yelp as his shoulder rams into the handrail. My head is spinning as I try to catch my breath. The patrol is nothing but a blur as he turns to face the elevator doors. He drops his backpack to the ground by his feet. With his back to me, he presses a button and the doors slide to a close. The elevator begins to rattle back to life. I lunge forward, wrapping my arms around his neck, and digging my knee into the back of his thigh. The force makes him lose his footing, and he crumples to the ground.

The patrol flips over onto his back, and brings his hands up to block his face. "Char, stop! It's me!"

My forearm stops just inches from his chest. I sit back on my heels, panting. "Archer. What the hell was that?"

"I could ask the same of you," he says as he sits up.

"I'm a little on edge. You came out of nowhere!"

"There were three patrols rounding the corner behind me. I was told to check the freight elevator. Imagine my surprise when I see you two popping out." Archer looks over at Alex, who has slid himself down onto the floor, with his back resting on the wall. He clutches his shoulder with a pale, clammy hand. "Sorry about that. You look like hell. Everything okay?"

"I'm okay," Alex says.

"It was Evelyn," I say. "All of it. Things are bad, Archer."

"I know they are." Archer pushes himself to his feet. "Both of you are wanted for treason. You'll be dead if they find you. Consider yourselves lucky I found you before they did."

Alex clears his throat. "Any word of Harry? Do you know if he's okay?"

Archer shakes his head. "I'm sorry. I haven't heard anything."

I let a whoosh of air escape my lungs, and I press my hand into my forehead. I will be dead if they find me. That should hold some meaning to me, but it doesn't. Instead, all I can think about is what went down inside of Patricia's apartment. I look at Archer and my throat tightens. "Did you know about Evelyn?"

Archer's eyes dart back and forth along the wall in front of him before he finally speaks. "Yes. I knew about your mother."

"How long did you know?"

Archer's jaw tightens, and he shakes his head.

"Archer! How long?"

"Not long enough," Archer says. He presses a button by the elevator doors, and the car comes to a complete stop. "Tyler told me the morning his term ended. But he never told me what I was supposed to do with that information. I mean, fuck. Who would have thought? How could any of us have possibly known? Where the hell are we supposed to go from here?"

"I think we should try to get to the library," Alex says.

Archer frowns. "The library? That's the last place you guys should go."

"Alex thinks there's a tunnel beneath one of the rooms," I say. "He believes our father built it a long time ago, and there might be something down there to help point us in the right direction. If I'm piecing things together the right way, my guess is that Charles had been planning for this moment all along."

Archer crosses his arms over his chest. "Explain."

Alex pulls himself to his feet, and I follow suit, standing up, and watching my brother as he paces the elevator floor.

"I thought about that too," he says. "I figured that somewhere along the line the system broke; that one patrol realized how wrong it was, and it started this trickle of quiet rebellion. But if you think about it, there's more to it than that. A patrol's term is only three years. I would think there would be a time where those who believed it to be wrong would die off, mainly because thinking against the grain is always going to be the unpopular opinion. Once you come to the realization that nothing will change, and that telling anyone will only end in your death, whatever passion you had will fizzle."

"Exactly!" I pat Alex on the back. "How would Sam know about my father, if my father died when I was a young girl? How would anyone know about the radio message? The briefcase? The fucking music box! Charles has been planting the seed of doubt all along. He's the one that's kept that… what did you call it, Alex?"

"Quiet rebellion?"

"Yeah! He's the only one that kept that quiet rebellion alive. It only makes sense that we head to the library next."

I breathe a sigh of relief. At least I finally know where we will go next.

"Alright. I'm convinced. But, you'll never make it more than a few feet with him looking like that." Archer nods toward Alex. "You don't look like you belong here. You reek of Calloway."

"I could trade clothes with him," I say. "He can wear my gear."

"It doesn't matter who wears it, Char. Those clothes don't belong here." He unzips his backpack, and reaches a hand inside. "Lucky for the both of you, I keep a spare set of gear in my pack."

Archer pulls out a pair of olive green cargo pants, and the matching button-down shirt. He throws them to Alex, who doesn't react in time. The clothes smack him right in the face. He holds the clothes out in front of him, and frowns. "These are going to be too big."

"You can take my belt if you need to, but otherwise it's all I've got. It's better than the shit you've got on though. If you guys take a back way to the library, somewhere between the buildings where you're less likely to be seen, you should be fine."

Archer and I both stand with our backs turned to Alex while he gets changed. My mind is racing as we wait. There are many thin, winding streets in Felicity. They run behind and between buildings, which means there will be many places for us to duck out of sight if the need arises. I am confident that Alex and I will make it to the library. Getting inside of the library is a different story.

"Alright," Alex says. "What do I do with these old clothes?"

I can't help but smile when I look at my brother. Alex is tall, so the pants fit decent, but the shirt hangs off his thin frame like a tarp. He has rolled the sleeves up to his elbows just as mine are, but one side slouches down farther than the other. I take his hand in mine, and hold it for a second. Then I roll up the left sleeve to match the right, and straighten out the front of his shirt.

Archer holds his hand out. "Give them to me. I'll shove them in my pack and ditch them somewhere." He grabs the clothes from Alex, and starts to shove them into his bag. "Oh, and tuck your shirt in."

"You look the part," I tell Alex. "You really do."

"I feel a bit silly," he says as he tucks in his shirt.

"You look like a patrol, and that's all that matters," Archer says. He takes his gun from his belt, and tucks it into the back of his pants. The radio goes into his front pocket. Then, he unbuckles his belt, and removes it with one quick pull. "Take this to help keep the pants up. You don't want them falling around your ankles while you're running."

I nudge Archer on the shoulder. "I don't know how to thank you. I don't know what we'd do without you. I really appreciate everything you've done for us."

Archer smiles. "My reason for helping you is simple: I've seen too much shit, and it's got to end."

"You're right. I just don't know how to end it." I hang my head, and stare at the ground. "I can't see a way out of this. Not yet."

"Fucking hell, Char. There is a reason why, after all these years, no one has come forward until now." Archer presses the button for the ground floor, and the elevator creaks back to life.

"Your bloodline has ruled this city for decades. If there is anyone out there that is capable of unraveling the years and years of damage that's been done onto our cities, it is you. Want my advice?"

"Yeah," I say, my throat dry.

"Bring your mother to trial. Charge her with corruption, and let the people decide her fate. She will be removed from power, and the rest will fix itself."

"That would never work," Alex says, his voice more hoarse and weak. "As far as everyone knows, Evelyn is just another person living in Felicity. Sit all of the residents down in a room, and tell them the truth. Tell them that they've been lied to all of this time, and you will see the city destroy itself faster than Evelyn ever could."

The elevator falls silent. The air is heavy and thick, with the words still hanging in the emptiness between us. After a few moments Archer takes a step toward the door. "Enough talk. I'll go out first to make sure there's no one else out there. Then you two will run. Don't stop until you reach the library." He pulls the radio from his pocket. "Here. Take this. Keep it on at all times. It will help you keep tabs on the other patrols. That way there, if someone happens to spot you, you'll be one of the first to know."

I hesitate. "What are you going to do without it?"

"Just fucking take it. I'll find another one if I need it."

I grab the radio from him, and clip it to my belt just as the elevator comes to a halt. Archer steps out before the doors have the chance to open completely. Alex and I wait inside of the elevator, with my finger pressing the open door button. Archer jogs forward, checking between buildings as he goes, until he reaches the nearest intersection. He looks to his left, and then to his right. After looking both ways one last time he heads back toward my brother and me with a smile on his face.

"Well, this will be interesting," Archer says. "There are two patrols straight and to your right. One patrol to the left about two blocks down. The side streets looked empty as far as I can tell, but who knows how long that'll last. The library is," he thinks to himself for a moment, "about twelve blocks from here, roughly."

I look nervously over Archer's shoulder. The street is still empty. "And once I get there? How many patrols do you expect to be canvasing the outside?"

"Several. That's the best answer I can give you. You guys ready?"

I look at Alex. His eyes are swollen and puffy, and the one that hasn't already swollen shut is still bloodshot. His skin is clammy, and pale. Felicity is too much for him. He doesn't belong here. Not under these circumstances. Not with both our lives hanging in the balance.

"Yeah," I say, taking my brother's hand in mine. "We're ready."

CHAPTER THIRTY-ONE
Alexander Moore

Five blocks later, and my legs have nearly given up on me. My thigh muscles burn. My shins are aching. I can feel my lungs rattling with every gasping breath I take. We haven't stopped yet, but I know that I will throw up the moment my legs stop moving. Every inch of me feels wretched. It has taken everything inside of me to keep myself moving forward.

I trace over the blueprint of the library in my mind. I try to remember all the details hidden in the room beneath the floor. It is the only thing that keeps me going; that keeps my legs pumping. We round a corner, and Char comes to a complete stop. She throws her arm out to stop me, but I'm too slow to react. It hits me in the chest, and I fall back onto the ground.

"Get up," Char says while yanking me by the arm.

She pulls me into a small side street nestled between two buildings. There is a door to the right of us that's deeply inset into the wall. The frame leaves a few good feet of space for us to tuck ourselves away. Once we're hidden, I clutch my stomach and vomit. Char holds tight to my shoulders, and pulls me back upright. I wipe my mouth on the sleeve of my shirt.

The sound of heavy footprints rises up into the air. My heart begins to race as I hear the frantic voices of the patrols shouting out to each other. I hold my breath as their footsteps fade into the distance. Char nudges me on the shoulder, and points down the street to the right. I nod, and together we both run as fast as our legs will carry us.

Third door on the left. Third door on the left. Repeating those words dulls the pain screaming from my lungs. Old transponder room. Third door on the left. Just a little farther now. Third door on the left.

Char grabs me by my sleeve, and pulls me hard to the right. I stumble forward and nearly lose my footing. She keeps a tight grip to help keep me on my feet as we round the next corner. I've lost track of how far we've gone, but when I look at the landscape laid out before me I can see where the buildings end. I can see a stretch of open grass, and a slight prismatic hue sparkling in the distance. That must be the library.

Char slows to a steady jog, then to a slow walk, and finally she comes to a stop. She leans up against the brick of the nearest building to try and catch her breath. I stop beside her and lean forward, my hands on my knees, wheezing. I'm lightheaded, and gasping for air. Every time I take another breath I can feel my lungs rattle. A pain shoots through my temple.

"We can rest here," Char says between deep breaths. "The library is straight ahead."

"Are there…" — I put my hands behind my head, and squint — "…Patrols?"

Char shakes her head. "I don't know. We'll have to get closer."

I try to take a slow, deep breath. "Now?"

"Not yet."

I lean against the wall next to Char, and place my hands on my hips. It still hurts to breathe, but it's slowly getting better. The ache in my head is fading to a dull throb. I close my eyes and squeeze the bridge of my nose just as the radio belts out a round of static.

"No sign of them by The Chasm," a female voice states.

"Nothing here either," a male voice replies.

"Copy that."

Char smiles, and adjusts the volume on the radio. "At least we know they're not on to us."

"For now," I say.

"You're right. This has been too easy."

"Easy? I think I might throw up again."

"Then get your shit together," Char says. She looks up and down the street, making sure no one has caught wind of our trail. "It's only going to get worse the closer we get to the library. That might be where the patrols are taking Evelyn."

"Where else would they take her?"

Char shrugs. "Could be anywhere."

I think to myself for a moment. "What's in the library? Besides the transponder room, I mean. What else is there?"

Char shakes her head. "I don't know. Fuck. That's the problem isn't it? I don't know anything!"

I bite my bottom lip, and run over the blueprint in my mind one more time. "Well, we know there are three rooms inside at the very least. Evelyn could be in any one of those. If she was brought to the library, that is. We will have to find a way inside and into the transponder room without being noticed."

Char pushes herself away from the wall. "I know what the hell we have to do, Alex."

I watch as she walks, as slow and as quietly as she can, toward the direction of the library. I follow behind her trying to make as little noise as possible. She hugs her body tight to the wall. Her feet shuffle side to side as she inches forward. Once she has gotten to the next street corner, she holds her finger up in the air. I tuck myself against the wall, and hold still.

Char takes a deep breath, and peeks her head around the corner. I see her eyes darting around before she quickly snaps her head back. She leans against the wall, shaking her head. Her hands are balled in tight fists at her sides.

"There are at least five patrols out front," she says through gritted teeth.

"Is there a back entrance?"

"No."

"Then how are we going to get inside? We'll be caught," I say.

"No shit, Alex." Char runs a hand through her hair. "I don't know what I expected to find. Of course there are patrols surrounding the library. There are always patrols surrounding the library. Why would today be any different?"

"We need to distract them somehow. Get them away from the entrance."

"And how do you expect we do that?"

The radio screeches, and another voice comes through. "Just checked Hoffman's Dump. It's clear."

I take a slow, deep breath and stare at the radio as another voice replies, giving the all-clear for a different location in Calloway. I wonder, briefly, how it was that I was able to pick up Evelyn's old message with a plain radio and an electrical cord, and yet these hand radios do nothing but broadcast to one another. Different frequencies, perhaps. Different purposes. I'm still staring at the small radio clipped to Char's belt when the idea hits me.

"Can I see the radio?"

"What for?"

"Give it here," I say, reaching my hand out.

Char hesitates for a moment before handing the radio over. I hold it in my hand, and adjust the volume button up and down. I inspect the other knobs: one for the frequency, another for the power. "Have you ever experienced static over the line? Has it ever been hard to hear someone else talking?"

"It's happened once or twice. Usually when the person on the other end is close to The Chasm, or way in the back of town. Why do you ask?"

"Do you think I could pass as Archer if I were talking through static?"

"I think it's possible," Char says with a smile.

"I might be able to draw them away from the library."

Char puts a hand on my shoulder. "Okay. Whatever you do, make it sound urgent. They're not going to leave their station unless it's absolutely necessary. Tell them we're hostile. We have weapons. Make it sound like it's life or death."

"Alright," I say. "Keep a good eye on them while I do it. The last thing we need is patrols running right at us as they leave."

"I'm on it. Once you're done we're going to have to move fast, whether it's to run towards the library, or away from it. Got it?"

"I got it."

Char rubs the top of my head real quick before jogging back to the corner. She holds her hand up, waits for a few moments, and then raises her thumb in the air. My heart races as I begin to adjust the radio's knobs. I turn them one way and nothing happens. I turn them in the other direction, and after a few moments static rises over the line. I press the push-to-talk button down as light as I can, applying enough pressure to transmit a signal, but not enough to make it come through clearly.

"This is Archer. Can anyone read me?" I alternate between pressing the button hard, and pressing it soft. Hopefully it makes my voice fade in and out. "Is anyone there?"

My heart is racing as I wait for a response. A few seconds go by before a woman's voice answers. "Yes, we can read you. You're breaking up. Is everything okay?"

"I am in pursuit of the subjects." I pause for a moment to add intensity to the words. "They are armed and dangerous. Immediate backup is requested!"

"Copy that," the voice says. "What is your location?"

My location. Shit. They're only going to send the patrols closest to the area of pursuit. Of course! They're not going to send an entire squad to chase down two people. I look at the sun in the sky, and try to calculate what direction I'm standing in. Then, I bend down and grab the largest stone I can find.

"Hello? Are you still there? We need a location," the voice says.

"I am three quarters of a mile to the east of the library," I say, pressing the button hard and then light again. I pull the radio away from my lips and hold it against the brick wall in front of me. Raising the rock up high, I bring it down as hard as I can next to speaker, while making sure the button isn't pressed too hard. I slam the rock down three more times. "Shots fired! Shots fired!"

I run as fast as I can to Char's side, and peek around the corner with her. Three of the patrols run east like I was hoping they would. The two remaining patrols are talking to each other. One of them pats the other on the back, and then runs to the east. The last patrol hangs his head for a moment, and then straightens back up.

"We have to move fast," I say. "I had to give them a location that wasn't far from here to make sure they'd be the ones leaving. It won't take them long to find out we're not there."

The remaining patrol is pacing back and forth in the front lawn of the library, pausing only when he faces east, as if he's looking for any sign of his colleagues to return.

"There. Right there," Char says. "Wait for him to walk back this way. Once he turns we'll run."

"He'll hear us as we approach. We can't sneak in the front door with his back turned. That'll never work."

"Don't worry about that. Follow me. Quick."

The patrol turns his back on us. Char steps out from the corner, her eyes hard as stone. She takes a deep breath, and then leans her chest forward. Before I know it she is running to the library. I stumble forward, and then begin to run after her as fast as my legs will carry me. I can feel the blood rushing to my ears, pounding out through my temples. My stomach flops, filled with another wave of nausea. I concentrate on the back of Char's head, several yards in front of me now, running faster than I've ever seen her run.

The patrol reaches the end of his march, and he pauses for a few moments, looking off between the buildings as Char predicted he would. A few seconds later he turns around. The patrol's eyes grow wide as he spots us. He pulls the radio from his belt with one hand, and the other hand drops to his gun. Before he gets the chance to put the radio to his lips Char lunges forward, tackling the patrol to the ground. She crawls on top of him and presses her knees into his shoulders.

"Grab the radio!"

I run to the patrol and pry the radio from his fingers. He screams out for help while shaking his head back and forth. His legs are flailing and kicking.

Char leans forward, and presses her hand into the patrol's mouth. "Shut up!"

The patrol paws at her hand and tries to pull her away. When that doesn't work, he wedges his arm in front of his chest and tries to shove her away. She presses her body down harder, refusing to move. The patrol pulls his arm back, and swings a fist into the side of my sister's jaw. She closes her eye and winces, but her hand remains pressed into his mouth.

The patrol's fist lands one more time against the side of Char's face. This time the pain makes her yelp. She adjusts her weight, and brings a knee up higher, trapping the patrol's arm beneath it. They continue to struggle against each other until finally the patrol is able to shift his body enough to free the gun trapped beneath his hip. He jerks his hand free, and it shoots down to his side. His fingers fumble with the clasp as he tries to free the gun.

"Char! He's got a gun!"

I'm paralyzed. All I can do is scream. The patrol frees his gun as Char sits up. I plead for him to let us go. I shout at him about Evelyn, and about the library. The words are falling so fast from my lips that even I can't understand them. The patrol turns his head and stares at me. For a moment I feel like he hesitates, like he wants to give in, wants to let us go.

He pulls back the hammer of his gun. That distinctive click echoes through the air. The patrol raises the gun and points it at my chest. I trip over my own feet as I stumble back. While I am falling I see Char lunge forward. She rams her forearm against the patrol's throat. She raises herself up into the air, and uses the momentum of her body to ram into his throat even harder.

The patrol's eyes grow wide. He tries to gasp for air, but manages nothing more than a labored breath. The world begins to spin. I turn to my side, and dry heave into the grass. Nothing comes up, and after a few moments the clenching in my stomach subsides enough for me to see Char prying the gun from the patrol's limp fingertips. She rolls into the grass and onto her back. Next to her, the patrol takes his last wheezing breath.

"We have to go," I say. My voice is shaking. "They'll be back before long."

Char pushes herself to her feet without saying a word. She turns her back on the lifeless patrol and fixes her shirt, tucking the bottom back into her pants, and adjusting the rolls of her sleeves. Her head falls to her chest for a moment, and I see her take a deep breath before she walks to the entrance of the library.

"You'd better take his gun," she says, holding it out in the air. "I don't need two of them."

The gun feels heavier than I imagined it would. I hold it awkwardly at my side, not sure what to do with it. After a few moments I decide to tuck it into the back of my pants in the same way that Archer did.

Char pulls the library doors open, and steps inside with her hand resting on her holstered gun. She glances back and forth across the expansive, open floor. Once she determines it empty she waves for me to follow. The inside of the library is breathtaking. The dome shimmers above us. The sun glistens through the thick glass with a soft prismatic hue.

"Third door on the left," I say.

We keep ourselves tucked against the book-lined walls to the left, counting the hidden doors as we walk past them. The third door on the left is hidden amongst the mathematics section. I try to wedge my fingers into the thin outline framed in the wall. I can't get a good enough grip. I push the shelves with my hands but the door doesn't move. Char takes a step back, and heaves her shoulder into it. The shelves rattle. Several books tumble to the floor. The door doesn't budge.

I run my fingers along the empty spaces on the shelves. My fingers brush over a small lump. I stand on the tips of my toes, and pry over the edge. There is a small, red button hiding in the back. I press it and nothing happens. I press it again, and again. Frustrated, I ram my thumb down into the button and hold it there until my nail turns white. The joints creak, the shelves begin to vibrate, and after a few moments the door swings open.

Once the door is fully opened the joints begin to creak again. The shelves are vibrating, and the door begins to crawl to a close. Char grabs me by the arm and pulls me through the opening. As soon as we are on the other side, the door slams shut behind us.

There is a large unit against the far wall. It's covered in buttons, and metal levers. Thick wires run up from the back, over the wall, across the ceiling, and then back down again. Above us hangs gears that have been rusted, but somehow they still turn. They make short, sharp movements as they click together. Around me the sound of a whirring motor blends together with a soft hissing noise. Beneath the ground, a small vibration tickles the soles of my feet.

This is it.

This is the room we've been looking for.

CHAPTER THIRTY-TWO
Evelyn Moore

My head is heavy. The air around me is dense, and everything is black. I can feel the weight of the universe pressing down on my chest. My head is still throbbing. I don't know where I am, or what I am doing here. I only know that I am sitting in a chair. There are voices around me speaking in hushed tones. I can hear footsteps creeping closer. Something touches the top of my head, and when it jerks away I can suddenly see again.

A patrol is standing before me, holding a black canvas bag in his hands. A strand of my hair dangles from the seam. He throws the bag to the ground and crosses his arms over his chest. I frantically look around me, trying to gather clues as to why I am here, but nothing makes sense.

My chair is placed at the center of the room, on a floor that's warped and riddled with mud. The wall to my left has molding wallpaper that's somehow been shredded, and the wall to my right has nothing but wooden bones. The door is in front of me, shut, but hanging at an angle that lets the sun peak in through the cracks. Two patrols stand on either side of it. I recognize one as

Alma, the girl that tore my house apart. The other has fiery red hair, and freckles covering her face.

"Where am I?" I look back at the patrol in front of me. "What am I doing here?"

"Emergency protocol," he says.

I close my eyes and take a deep breath. My head is throbbing, and my throat aches. My eyelids feel heavy. I remember sitting at Patricia's table when I fell asleep. After that, I have a vague memory of the patrols bursting in and taking me away. I was too tired to fight them off. But where is Alexander? Where is Char?

I press my fingers into my forehead. "Did you kill them?"

The patrol crouches down in front of me, and stares straight into my eyes. "Who else was with you, Evelyn?"

I shake my head and press my lips together.

"Listen, Evelyn. This is an emergency, which means that the emergency protocol must be followed. I'm going to need you to be honest with me so I can do my job correctly. We already know about Patricia. She's been dealt with. Who else was with you?"

"Only her. It was only Patricia. Did you kill her?"

The patrol stands back up and adjusts his belt. "She has been dealt with, yes."

"Enough talking, Shawn," says the red-haired girl. "Let's get on with it."

"Alright, alright," Shawn says. He runs a hand through his dark hair. "Give me the injection."

I squirm in my seat as the girl walks toward me. When she reaches my side, she puts a hand on my shoulder and I jump. The girl laughs a soft, gentle laugh. "It's alright, Miss Evelyn. We aren't going to hurt you. This is protocol."

"I know the damn protocol," I snap. "I wrote it."

The red-haired patrol disappears behind me for a moment, and when she returns she is holding a syringe with a long needle attached to the end. Shawn rips it from her fingers, and holds it up in the air to inspect the tip.

"I am supposed to tell you that this memory serum is five times your normal dosage," he says. "When your memory leaves, you will be unable to remember even the most basic things. For example, you may have a difficult time remembering your name for a short period of time. The worst of it will be over in a few days, but in the meantime you're going to be scared. Lauren here is assigned to keep an eye on you until you return to your normal, unaware self. Is that understood?"

"This is for the greater good," Lauren says with a smile.

I smile back at her, anticipating the moment I will no longer remember the high-pitched screams of the children as they were ripped from their mother's arms. I don't want to remember the worn, tired looks on the patrol's faces while they read me their violence reports from Calloway. Whatever was inside of that injection this morning was different than anything else I've taken. It was strong, more severe than normal. I shouldn't be able to remember the pain. I shouldn't be able to remember the shame that I felt. I have to forget again.

"Let's get this over with," I say.

Shawn leans down until he is inches in front of my face. He gives me a quick pat on the back, and then tilts his head until his mouth is inches from my ear. I can feel his hot breath on my skin. "I know that you were lying to me," he whispers. "I know that your children were there with you, too. I want you to know that I'm going to find them for you."

I jerk my head back. As I do, I feel the prick of the needle entering my neck. The serum is cold, and I can feel my veins turning to ice as the liquid spreads. My lids begin to droop. My pulse lightens, and I take long, heavy breaths. I dip my head and close my eyes, waiting for the sleep to come.

"Is it working?" Lauren asks. Her voice is distant, muffled.

"I don't know," Shawn mumbles. "Check her pulse."

There is a presence beside me now. I cannot see them, but their shadow casts a darker hue beneath my eyelids. A finger is jabbed into the side of my neck. I can feel it pressing against my veins.

"Well, she's still alive." Lauren's voice sounds louder, clearer. "But how do I know if it's working?"

The tips of my fingers grow warm, and that warmth begins to spread up my arms, my shoulders, across my chest. Soon the heat of blood replaces the chill in my veins. My pulse rises, my chest heaves up and down with new breath, and my eyes flutter open. I shake my head back and forth to clear my mind.

"Shit," Shawn says. "Evelyn? Can you hear me?"

"I can hear you," I croak.

"Fuck." He crouches down before me, and places a hand on my shoulder. "Tell me what you remember."

I swat Shawn's hand from my shoulder, and stand up with enough force to knock my chair on its side. Lauren tries to grab me by the arm, but I jab my elbow into her chest to keep her away. I glance at the door and notice Alma talking into her radio. I try to lunge at her, but Shawn wraps his arms around my waist and pulls me back.

"That's enough. Calm down," he says.

I struggle against him, throwing my elbows behind me, kicking my legs. Shawn grunts in my ear. He lifts me up in the air, and slams me down against the floor with enough force to make my ears ring. I wrap a hand around my ribs and cough.

"I remember," I choke out. "I remember everything."

"That's impossible," Lauren whispers.

Shawn grabs me by my shirt collar, and lifts me to my feet. I shove my hands into his chest, and push him back. "Get your hands off of me."

"This isn't right. This wasn't in the book," Shawn says.

Lauren marches over to Shawn and crosses her arms over her chest. "You didn't give it to her right."

"I read the instructions three times, Lauren. Don't give me that shit. One injection in the neck, that's what it said. It should have worked instantly."

"Maybe it was expired," Lauren says with a sigh.

"It wasn't expired." I close my eyes to try and rid myself from the dull ache at the front of my skull, but every time my lids fall shut the memories rush over me like a hurricane. In the storm of the past, I can hear my husband's warning to me the night he went away. Once you find it, you can never go back. When I open my eyes again, the three patrols are staring down at me. "It was Charles."

Alma steps forward with her radio clutched tight in her hands. Her cheeks are glowing a bright shade of red. "A patrol was found dead at the library. They believe that the subjects are inside looking for something."

"Those pricks," Shawn says through gritted teeth. "I don't need this right now. Has anyone gone in after them? Have they been apprehended?"

"No, sir. They are considered armed and dangerous. The other patrols are waiting for further instruction from you."

Shawn glares at me, and his lip curls into a smirk. "Tell the others to guard the outside of the library, and make sure the subjects stay inside. I'm going to put an end to this nonsense."

I push a strand of hair from my eyes. "What are you going to do?"

"Don't you worry about it," Shawn says as he pats me on the shoulder. "This will be over with soon enough." He turns to Alma, and smiles. "Head to the library and help the others guard the door. Make sure no one goes in or out. We're going to make them cooperate."

"Yes, sir," she says, before turning on her heels and leaving.

Shawn wrings his hands together as he nods his head. "Okay. Okay, we can do this. Let's go put a stop this bullshit. Lauren, you grab Evelyn. Make sure she doesn't run."

I shoot him a look. "Where the hell would I go?"

Lauren interlocks her arm in mine, and gently pulls me into her side. "Don't worry about him, Miss Evelyn. He's having a hard time dealing with the stress."

"Come on. Time to get going," Shawn says.

He removes the gun from his belt, and motions for Lauren and I to follow him out the door. The first thing that hits me once we are outside is the smell. It reminds me of gasoline, and the low burning embers of a fire. There is a faint hint of garbage lingering in the air. This can't be Felicity.

I look around me, with my heart dancing wildly in my chest. We are at The Chasm, and the land that stretches out before me is as dead as it is in Felicity, but it's the houses in the distance that catch my eye. Dilapidated, crumbling homes. From here I can see their collapsed roofs, and boarded up windows.

Lauren tries to pull me along, but I keep my body rigid. I dig my heels hard into the ground. I have to look a little longer. I have to know where I am. This can't be Calloway. It can't be. I turn and face The Chasm. I place my hand across my forehead, shielding the sun from my eyes. Way out on the horizon I see the lights of the buildings jutting high into the sky. Beside me Lauren groans, and I hear the soft sound of footsteps approaching.

"I thought we had people guarding the edge," Shawn mumbles.

When I turn myself around I see a little girl closing in on us fast. She wears a smile wide on her face, accentuated by two thick, brown braids on either side of her head. Her pale blue dress blows with the wind as she runs. The bottom hem of her dress is frayed so bad that it has begun to tear up the front. I try to take a step back but Lauren keeps me tightly in place. A lump is forming in my throat, making it hard to breathe.

The girl runs up to me, and twirls back and forth. Her dress puffs up into the air, and sways around her body. I can see the ripped, dirt-stained tights covering her legs. She wears only one shoe. It has a giant hole at the front where her big toe pokes through. The girl stops twirling, and lets out a high-pitched giggle. She wipes her nose off on the back of her filthy hand, and looks at me with wide eyes.

"You's my momma?"

"No," Shawn snaps. "Now off you go."

"Then you turn go?" The girl points toward the bridge. "Felicity?"

"I, um... I—"

Lauren bends down, and pats the girl on her head. "Where's your caretaker? They must be worried about you."

The girl shrugs. "He go Chasm."

Lauren clears her throat, and takes a deep breath. "You'd better be off then. You're not allowed this far out on your own."

The girl smiles wide, showing off her yellow-stained teeth. She turns on her heels, and begins skipping off toward the broken city she calls home. The tears forming in my eyes turn Calloway into a distant blur. A pain explodes through my chest, ripping my breath away. I can't breathe. My knees grow week, and my legs begin to tremble. Lauren pulls on my arm, trying to move me forward, but I can no longer feel my feet.

I collapse to my knees. My palms dig into the dirt, scraping their tender flesh.

This is not how things were supposed to be. This is not the Calloway I created.

What have I done?

Through the blur of tears I see Shawn standing before me. He reaches down, grabs me by my shoulders, and pulls me to my feet. His fingers wrap around the front of my shirt, and he snarls as he speaks. "Pull your shit together."

Shawn lets go of my shirt with a forward motion that causes me to stumble back. I trip over my feet and fall hard onto the ground. Now I am nothing but an empty shell sitting on a bed of cracked dirt, and forgotten memories. I close my eyes and imagine myself melting into the ground beneath me. Anything to get me away from the world I have created.

Lauren wraps her arm around my waist, and I let her pull me to my feet. She pats me on the shoulder, and smiles. "It's alright, Miss Evelyn. We're going to help you. Soon you'll forget everything again."

CHAPTER THIRTY-THREE
Char Moore

I look over the switchboard on the top of the transponder, too afraid to touch anything. Everything looks old, like the entire board would crack with the slightest pressure. There are red buttons, blue buttons, black buttons. There are switches and levers, and glowing red and green lights. I run my hand on the underside of the board, hoping to find a book of instructions taped somewhere within reach. My search leaves me empty handed.

"I'm going to need some help figuring this out," I say.

I turn around to see my brother still standing near the door. His hands are on his knees. Sweat is dripping from his pale, almost translucent skin. He tries to take a deep breath, but his lungs rattle, and he is left gasping for air. I run to his side, and put my arm around his shoulders.

"Alex? Alex, what's going on? Are you okay?"

Alex shakes his head and stands upright as he begins to cough. His eyes are wide, almost panicked, as he tries to regain his composure. I don't know what to do to help him, so I pat him on the back. It takes a few moments for him to calm down. He leans into my side, and exhales deeply.

"The air here," he croaks. "Is it thinner?"

I shake my head. "Not in the city, but it is dangerously thin as you cross over The Chasm. You must be having a harder time recovering. All this running isn't helping either."

"I'll be alright. Let me look at the board."

He stumbles to the switchboard, and leans his body against it. He runs a finger over the top with a light touch. I see his eyes flickering over the lights. He presses a small red button and waits, but nothing happens.

"What was that supposed to do?" I ask.

"I don't know. I was testing it," Alex says.

"We don't have much time."

"Well, it's not exactly labeled. I'd have to take it all apart and stare at the wiring before I could figure it out, and we don't have time for that."

I groan, and hang my head. "What do we do?"

"I really don't know, Char. What's your instinct telling you?"

"To press all the damn buttons until something happens."

Alex shrugs his shoulders with a smile on his face. "Sounds reasonable."

He starts at the top left, pressing the button tucked away in the corner. After a few seconds of silence, he pushes his finger into the next button, but again nothing happens. He makes his way through the control panel, pressing a button, waiting, pressing another. In the end nothing happens except some loud buzzing noises, and a harder vibration beneath the floor.

"That was useless," Alex says. "Let's try something else. This time you should press the buttons, and I'll work on moving around these levers. It's likely a combination that'll work, like an entry code or something."

I look back over my shoulder and see the door still closed tight. It won't be long before someone finds us in here. Swallowing my nerves, I begin to press the buttons in the same order Alex did moments ago. At the same time, my brother works on shifting the levers back and forth. Nothing we do seems to work. I slam my fist down on the control board, and groan through gritted teeth. When I lift my hand up I notice one of the buttons has cracked in half.

"Shit," I say.

"Hold on a second," Alex says. "Something weird happened. Try that again."

"You want me to hit it?"

"I heard something shift beneath the floor when you hit it. This control board looks ancient. The wires could be crossed beneath it, or something could be loose. I don't know. Just hit it."

I ball my hand into a fist, and slam it down in the center of the panel. When I look at Alex for reassurance, he is standing with his arms crossed, smiling. He sees me staring, and nods his head as if to tell me it's okay to try again. I lift my fist up a little higher this time, and bring it down on the far right side of the panel. I hear the distinct sound of grinding gears. Metal on metal. I hit the panel one more time and the floor begins to shake.

"Step back," Alex says.

I grab Alex by the arm as we stand against the far wall together. The floor groans and shakes beneath our feet. I can feel Alex's muscle tighten beneath my fingers as a small hatch opens up at the center of the room. Next to me I hear Alex laugh under his breath, which turns into a violent coughing fit. Any excitement is temporarily swayed as my brother collapses into my side. I wrap my arms around his shoulders and hold him tight.

"It's alright," I tell him. "Try to take slower breaths."

Alex shoves his hand into my chest. I stumble back right at the same moment he turns to the side, and begins to vomit. I don't think the pressure change is causing him to be like this. It's almost as if he's been poisoned, but he hasn't eaten since we've crossed over, and he hasn't drank anything either. I wonder if the patrols gave him something when he was arrested to help him comply. It doesn't make sense though. That was hours ago. He's not complacent, he's sick.

"I'm okay," Alex says, wiping his face on the back on his arm. "I must have caught a bug or something."

"That's not a bug, Alex."

"I think I'm starting to feel better," he says. "I'm sure it'll be gone soon. In the meantime, we need to move. There's no way that someone hasn't stumbled on that patrol out front yet."

"I don't know, Alex. You don't look so good."

"Stop worrying. I'm fine," Alex says, shaking his head.

I swallow hard, feeling the lump in my throat. With my fists clenched tight, I walk to the open hatch at the center of the room, and stare down into the darkness. Not knowing what's inside, I decide to sit on the edge of the opening with my feet dangling over the edge. I place my hands on each side of the hole, and lower myself down slow. The walls around me are metal, and there is a glowing panel directly behind me that acts as my only source of light. It has two buttons: One marked G, the other marked S.

"There isn't much room," I say. "Lower yourself down carefully."

I back up against the wall as tight as I can as Alex drops down haphazardly next to me. He lands with a thud. I rush over to him, and help him get to his feet. He winces as he stands, and he hobbles to the panel.

I raise an eyebrow. "You alright?"

"Twisted my ankle when I fell," Alex says as he looks over the panel. "Seems right on par with the kind of luck I'm having, doesn't it?"

I let out a small laugh, and rub the top of his head. "Looks like you were right about the elevator."

"Let's see where it takes us," Alex says with a smile.

If there is one thing I learned by being inside of the elevators in Evelyn and Patricia's places, it is that the main floor is always marked with a star. In this case, it's next to the button labeled G. I squeeze in beside Alex, and ram my finger into the S. The top hatch we dropped down through swings to a close. The walls begin to groan, and suddenly the elevator jerks to the side. I hold on to Alex's arm as we begin to descend. It's not a long ride. It only takes a moment for the elevator to come to a stop. A small door slides open next to the panel. I have to turn to the side in order to slide myself through.

If Alex is right I will be standing inside of a tunnel that leads to The Chasm, a place that no one except the dead has visited. I'm not sure what lies ahead. A wave of cold air rushes over me, and my throat tightens. I hold my breath as I step off of the elevator. My heart drops as I look at the room around me.

"Move," Alex says as he pushes past me. "Let me see."

"I'm so sorry," I whisper.

Alex takes two giant steps, and then stops. He whispers something under his breath, so soft that I can barely hear him. I don't know what it is that he says, but I suppose it doesn't matter. I can read the disappointment on his face. We are not inside of The Chasm. We are inside a simple room with withering red brick walls. They look as though they will crumble at any moment from the weight of the library above.

The room is dark and musty. An old lamp shines dimly in the corner. It's our only source of light. The left side of the room is covered with bookshelves, but only a few books still remain. On the other end of the room there is a small, wooden desk. A warped cardboard box sits on the top.

"This can't be right," Alex says.

"It's okay. This… this makes more sense, right? I mean, did we honestly think we'd end up inside of The Chasm?"

"I did."

I put a hand on his shoulder, and can feel the chill of his skin beneath his shirt. Cold, yet moist with sweat. "There must be something important down here. It wouldn't be marked on the blueprint otherwise."

Alex shakes his head. "Or maybe the blueprint is just that: A blueprint. They don't need to have a special meaning. They don't need to have hidden agendas. Their purpose is to map out a building before it is constructed." He droops his shoulders. "How naive of me to think otherwise."

"Maybe you're right. But, why would Charles bother building a hidden room beneath the library if it didn't house something important?"

"I don't know."

"Then we're going to find out," I say with a smile. "I'll check out the bookshelf. You look through that box over there. We're bound to come across something."

Alex brings his hands in front of his mouth, and coughs. His eyes are squeezed shut, like he is wincing with pain as the air shoots through his lungs. When he pulls his hands away I notice a splatter of red on his chin. I walk over to him, and tilt his head toward the light to get a better look.

"I'm fine," Alex says.

The bit of red on his chin looks like blood. I grab his wrists, and turn his hands over so his palms are facing up. "You're not fine, Alex. You're coughing up blood."

Alex pulls his hands away, and rubs them down the front of his pants. "It's nothing. The air is too dry. I've been coughing too much."

"We need to get you out of here. Find you a doctor. They won't refuse treating you if I force them to."

"Stop," Alex says. He turns his back on me, and opens the lid of the box. "We don't have time for that right now. I feel fine. I promise."

"I'm giving it ten minutes," I say through clenched teeth. "Then I am dragging you out of here kicking and screaming if I have to."

Alex rolls his eyes. "You're wasting time then. Those books aren't going to read themselves."

I take a deep breath with my fists clenched at my sides. I march over to the bookcase, and begin pulling the books off the shelves, one by one, reading the titles as I go. They mostly seem like old, educational books. There are some about algebra and geometry. Some about the English language. I find a book marked HISTORY, and hold it in my hands a moment before flipping through the pages. One quick glance and I know there's nothing useful written inside. I toss it behind me, and grab a large, leather-bound book. The spine is made of knotted yarn. The cover of the book is blank. I hurry and flip it open. On the center of the front page, in huge handwriting, are the words Quality Report.

"I think I found something," I say.

"Yeah," Alex whispers. "Me too."

With the book still open in my hands I dash to Alex's side. "This seems to have written reports of the water quality in Felicity." I turn a few pages at a time. "See? This one here talks about the toxicity levels being high, and even lists the amount of children that were ill over the years. Three hundred and ninety-four. That's insane."

"But—"

I flip through a few more pages. "Look. This must be around the time the children crossed over. You see? The water is still tainted, but the amount of ill children total zero." I flip to the very last page in the book, and quickly read over the words. "Oh holy shit. No. No fucking way. Absolutely impossible."

Alex peers over my shoulder. "What?"

I point to the words on the page with a trembling finger. "This."

"Let me see," Alex moves a little closer to my side, and squints his eyes as he reads. "As of this day, October Eight, there are zero traces of elements inside of the water. Toxicity level—" he clears his throat, and lowers his voice, "—is non-existent."

CHAPTER THIRTY-FOUR
Alexander Moore

Char is gripping the leather-bound book so tight in her hand that her fingertips are turning purple. Her nostrils are flaring. She throws the book across the room, clenches her fists, and screams. No words. Only anger. The sound of her voice cuts through my skull, and my ears are ringing. My temples are throbbing. My vision in blurred again. I try to blink the fuzziness away, but it doesn't seem to help.

I found a paper inside of the box. Well, I found several papers, but one stood out to me as more important than the others. I don't know what it means yet, and I will never find out if this damn eyesight doesn't straighten itself back out. I lean my back against the desk and close my eyes. I take a few slow, deep breaths. Char is still angry. The sound of ripping paper fills the room. She is tearing the pages from the books, as if somehow she could erase history.

Evelyn sent the children over the bridge because the water was tainted with poison. They were sick, and they were dying, and she decided to send them away. But now we know the water has been clear for some time, yet the children still remain on the other side. No one has any idea. No one knows that Evelyn had the opportunity to bring the children back, and she chose not to.

"Shit, not again," Char says. "Alex, are you okay?"

I open my eyes to see Char standing in front of me. A look of worry is spread across her face. I am abruptly aware of the warmth trickling down my face. I wipe my nose on the back of my hand, and when I pull away I see blood.

"Yeah, I'm fine," I say. "I found something that I wanted you to take a look at."

I hold the paper out in front of me, slightly wrinkled from being gripped so tight in my fist. Char keeps her eyes locked on mine as she grabs the paper from me. It takes her a few moments to turn her attention to the document. When she finally looks it over, and I see her eyes settled on the last words at the bottom of the paper, her face falls.

"I don't know what this is," Char says. "Where did you find it?"

"On the desk," I say. "The box is in awful shape. There's mold all over it, and the lid pretty much crumbled in my hand when I lifted it. But, someone had written MEDICAL WARD on the side of the box. It was faded, but I could still make out what it said."

"So, like doctor's notes?"

"Kind of. Look at this," I say, pulling a thick folder out of the box. "In here it talks about the memory serum, or whatever it's called. It took them several tries to be able to duplicate the medication Evelyn's mother was taking, and then it took a couple of years after that for them to get the dose right. It was all easy to understand. The dates, and results are listed together, like the book you found."

Char puts her hand up, and makes a face. "I don't want to read it."

"Well, there are folders and folders of evidence about medical testing, how well the serum worked, anything you can think of, right in that box. Turns out they have a mist they can send out, that causes temporary memory loss in the event of an emergency. But that paper you're holding right there is different. It talks about The Chasm, and wind direction. There are dimensions to some sort of square box written down as well."

Char frowns as she reads over the document again. My vision grows blurry as she does. I lean against the desk and close my eyes once more. This time I rub my temples in a slow, methodical rhythm. I can feel my insides twisting and turning. My ears are ringing, my head throbbing. I keep my breathing steady, and press my temples a little harder. After a few moments the ringing in my ears subsides. The pain in my head hurts slightly less, and when I open my eyes I can see straight.

"Hey! I asked if you knew what the hell any of this meant."

I chew my bottom lip, and rub the back of my neck. "What?"

"Do you know what any of this means? I've asked you four times already."

"Oh, sorry." I clear my throat. "I was thinking. I didn't hear you."

Char shakes her head, and thrusts the paper back into my hand. "Enough of this. I'm getting you out of here."

"Stop it. I'm fine," I say as I place the paper down on the desk, and smooth it over with my hand. "Would you let me take you out of here if the roles were reversed? We're not going anywhere until we figure out why we're down here."

Char sighs, and crosses her arms over her chest. "Then we need to figure it out quick."

"Okay. Okay. Let me try to break this down. Here is what I've figured out so far." I run a hand over my hair, and take a deep breath. "For some reason this square box, which I assume is a device of some sort, is down inside of The Chasm. Otherwise, why else would they have what look like the exact dimensions of the gap?"

"Where do you see that?"

"It's right here." I point to the center of the page, where a thick, jagged line is drawn vertically on the paper. On the bottom is a scale key, which I recognize from old geography books I found at the dump. "It indicates width, and length, that seem to match dimensions of The Chasm. Of course I can't be certain, but there's nothing else around here with those kinds of dimensions. It has to be The Chasm. They talk about lowering it down with a crane. It all fits."

"Right," Char says. "So you're saying there's a box inside of The Chasm? What's it there for?"

I shake my head. It sends a pain shooting through my temple. "I don't know. Whatever it does, these marks here," I point to the thin curving lines drawn swirling around one another. They run over the dimensions of The Chasm. Between these curving lines are small arrows drawn one after the other, their tips all pointing west, "They seem to indicate wind direction. Whenever there is a storm Calloway gets it first, right? Every time. Our weather patterns always travel from east to west. These arrows are flowing from east to west. Whatever that contraption is, it seems to be directed toward Felicity."

"But it was found in the box with other medical documents," Char says.

"Yes," I say.

"Maybe that's what stores the memory serum. You said they have the ability to mist the memory serum into the air. It could be where it comes from."

"No. I don't think that's it. The names don't match up."

"What names?"

"Here. It's scribbled on the side here, next to the box. It says—" I squint my eyes, and tilt my head, reading the word slow. "Dimeth… dimeth-something-amine. I can't read it."

Char grabs the paper from the table. "Give that to me." Her eyes flicker back and forth as she reads over the word. "I've seen that word. I think it was in one of the books."

"In one of the books you were looking over?"

Char stays silent as she drops to her knees. She begins scooping up pieces of ripped, discarded paper. After she quickly looks at one, she tosses it over her shoulder, and then hurries to read another. "I know I saw it. Where the hell is it?"

As she frantically searches through the torn pages on the ground, my stomach begins to clench. My insides are swaying back and forth, dipping, bobbing, like a ship at sea. I grab the side of the desk, and clutch my stomach. A stabbing pain shoots through me. I keep my lips pressed tight together, not wanting to make a sound. We are too close to the end.

I turn my face to the side, and swallow down the bile I feel rising up in my throat. My chest rattles. I take a short, wheezing breath, which sends me into a coughing fit. I throw my hands over my mouth to cover the sound. When it's finally over, I see Char still digging through papers on the ground. Thankfully, she seems oblivious.

"Yes! I found it. Right here," Char says as she pushes herself to her feet. She is holding three wadded up pieces of paper in her hand, torn haphazardly from a book. I can still see a bit of the binding along the edges.

She hands me the paper, and my eyes quickly search for the word. It stands out at the top of the page in bold letters, impossible to miss: Dimethyltryptamine. I silently mouth the word as I read it, still unsure of how it's pronounced. It doesn't take me long to realize that this drug, which has been thankfully abbreviated to DMT, isn't a memory serum as I suspected. The very first paragraph describes what the drug does, how it can cause states of euphoria or hallucinations, and how those effects can alter a person's consciousness.

A knot grows in my stomach as my eyes drink in every word: How they tested different doses, experimented with the best way to administer it. I learn quickly that ingesting the drug does nothing, because the metabolism can burn it off quick, and that injecting it, or even inhaling it, works best. I am reading so fast that sometimes my eyes skip a few words, and I have to go back and reread a second, or sometimes third time.

Char shuffles closer to my side. I can feel her presence hovering near me, staring over my shoulder. "What? What does it say?"

I turn the first page over in my hand, and start reading the back. Different doses. Different concentrations. They tested this drug for years, using their own residents as guinea pigs. My throat tightens as I realize that most of those that had been experimented on had no idea. They weren't volunteers. Not by choice. Over the course of two years dozens of people died by heart attacks, strokes, brain hemorrhages.

I let the first page drop out of my hand and it flutters softly to the ground. It took them three years total. That's what this page says. Three years after the testing started they found the perfect dose, and they discovered the best way to administer it. My eyes fall to the bottom of the paper, to the final paragraph: the beginning of our end. My body grows cold. I wad the paper up in my fist and throw it across the room.

My pulse is pounding in my ears, loud and chaotic. It's hard to think, to comprehend what it is I read. Inside of my aching chest my heart beats fast, but weak. It is tired. I am tired. It could be the chill that is spreading through me, numbing my skin. The tears in my eyes blur the room around me, turning everything a strange shade of gray.

"Talk to me Alex." Char's voice is distant, and it echoes in my head. "What the hell is going on?"

I place my head in my hands and I let myself cry. How could I have known? How could any of us have known? The reason the children are still on the other side is because they would all end up like me. There is a fire burning through my veins. It is scorching me from the inside out.

I take a deep wheezing breath that throws me into another coughing tantrum. Every gasp of breath sends an agonizing pain shooting through my chest. Char grabs my arms and rips them away from my face. She gives me a hard punch to my chest, which somehow clears my airway. The next breath I take is a little less labored.

"Tell me what is going on," Char says, her voice shaking. "What did it say?"

I clear my throat, and swallow the pain back down. "What do you see when you look at Felicity?"

"We don't have time for this."

I lightly touch her elbow, and give it a soft squeeze. "I need you to answer me."

"I don't know, Alex. It's a city."

"Yeah, I know." I steady myself against the wall. "But is it beautiful?"

Char takes a step back, and shakes her head. "Are you kidding me right now? What the hell kind of question is that?"

"Shut the hell up for a second and answer me," I say. My head is spinning. I bite my lip, and ignore the pain in my head. "Is it beautiful? What do the buildings look like? What color is the grass? What about the streets?"

Char sighs, and looks deep into my eyes. I hope I'm wrong. For her sake, I hope this has been nothing more than a misunderstanding.

"Yes, of course Felicity is beautiful." She tries to tuck a strand of short hair behind her ear, but it falls right back out. "The buildings are tall and smooth. Most of them are bright white, like clean snow. The grass here is a brighter shade of green than I thought possible. And, what else did you ask? The streets? Those are thin. Smooth like the buildings. Now that it's warmer out most of the streets are lined with flowers. Is that good enough?"

I take a deep, rattling breath, and close my eyes. "I couldn't figure out what all the fuss was about." My voice is shaking, and my bottom lip is trembling. "Why would anyone want to leave the ruins of Calloway for the ruins of Felicity?"

Char places her hand on my shoulder. "What are you talking about?"

"It's not real, Char. None of it is real."

Her hands are grasping both of my shoulders now, her nails digging into my bones. "Stop it."

"The buildings right outside this library have been reduced to almost nothing. That's what I see. They're tall, yeah, but I see them as decaying, withered skeletons. They've been eroded in spots, and some of the white have been stained red. I assume that's from the dust storms." I have to stop a moment to catch my breath. "I see brown, dying grass. I see broken streets, with weeds shooting up beneath the cracks."

"You're not feeling well. You need to see a doc—"

"You can't see the fog rising up from the vents in the streets, but I do." The pain is my head is growing, aching, screaming. "It's exactly like the fog that surrounded the bridge when we crossed over The Chasm."

Char's fingers are digging so hard into my skin that I'm sure she's drawn blood. "That's enough."

"Look at what happens to Calloway during a storm," I say, wiping the tears from my cheeks. "There are shattered windows, broken doors, collapsed roofs. There is no way that Evelyn could maintain the same beautiful infrastructure that everyone was used to seeing. The storms are too bad for that. Don't you see? Everything in Felicity is a lie."

I am thrown into another coughing fit. It's a little shorter than the last time, but twice as painful. When it's over I can feel the air scratching at my lungs.

"How is it possible, Alex? How can she fake an entire city?"

The sound of my heartbeat floods into my ears. I bend over, clasping my stomach. I dry heave again and again. Nothing comes up, because there is nothing left inside of me anymore. Char still clutches me tight, keeping me upright as my knees begin to buckle.

"Drugs," I say, wheezing. "They're in the air, all over Felicity. The fog around the bridge isn't fog at all. That's the drug being fed to you before you even lay eyes on the city. That's what the device is in The Chasm. "

Char shakes her head. "That's not it. It can't be." She chews her top lip and stares off to the side, thinking to herself. "You've

329

got it backward. Yes. Yes, that makes more sense. The drug is there for you, for the people in Calloway, to keep you from wanting to stay. Right? You wouldn't want to come back once you saw how awful it was. That has to be it. It's the only thing that makes sense."

My throat stings as I laugh. "Is it really so hard to believe? Evelyn had already drugged people into forgetting. Is altering their reality any different? I'm sorry, Char. I shouldn't laugh. It's funny when you think about it, though. Calloway may be a shit hole, but at least it's real."

I feel a warm trickle of blood running down my lip. Char takes my head into her hands and stares into my eyes. "What's happening to you?"

"Evelyn could have fixed everything if she had waited for the water to clear. Instead, she replaced the toxins in the water with poison in the air. I'd like to think that she had no idea what would happen, but she knew. It's all written down. The children can't come over, Char. Their bodies metabolize the drug too quick. They see everything as it really is, but not without consequence." I sigh, and hang my head. "The air is poison to them. If the children come over they will die."

Char digs her nails into my cheeks. I clasp my hands over hers, and she pulls my face so close that our foreheads touch. "Don't say that, Alex. You don't know what you're talking about. You're going to be fine. You're going to be okay."

I try to swallow, but the pain makes me wince. "Everything hurts, Char."

Her hands slide down my neck, and she presses her lips into my forehead. "We're getting you out of here," she whispers. "I'm taking you back to Calloway. If I can get ahold of Archer, he can bring a doctor to you in a couple of hours."

I smile and nod, but deep down I know the truth.

My story ended the moment I crossed that bridge.

It's too late for me now.

CHAPTER THIRTY-FIVE
Evelyn Moore

I stumble across the jagged, cracked dirt toward another house as run down as the last. The air around me is thick, and heavy. It's hard to see, hard to feel anything other than death. Lauren is pulling me forward, making sure I don't hold us up any longer. I want to break free. I want to go back to Felicity and forget any of this ever happened. But I can't. Charles made sure of that. He knew what would happen to me, and he didn't care. Not one little bit.

Lauren gives my arm a gentle squeeze as we approach the front of the house. "We'll wait here while Shawn goes inside."

Shawn walks to the front door, and raps his knuckles against the splintered wood. A patrol emerges, and motions for Shawn to follow him inside. They both retreat back into the house making sure to slam the door behind them.

"This won't take long," Lauren says with a smile.

I close my eyes, and tilt my head up to the sky. A loud thud fills the air. Shawn beings to shout, telling someone to follow him outside. There is another loud thud that sounds like a heavy book being thrown into the wall. I let my eyes flutter open and I see Shawn bursting through the doors with his gun clenched angrily in his fist. He shoves it back into its holster, and buckles the clip. He straightens out his shirt, and then reaches an arm out behind him. A few seconds later, he drags a young boy out of the house by the collar of his shirt. His dark skin is bruised a deep shade of purple around his eyes, and on his arms and neck. Dried blood is caked around his mouth.

I try to pull away from Lauren, but she keeps her grip tight. "Who is that?"

"He's a bargaining tool," Shawn says.

Lauren squeezes me a little tighter as I try to pull away again. "What have you done to him?"

"You have to stop trying to pull away from me, Miss Evelyn," Lauren says. "You're going to end up hurting us both."

"He's fine. There's nothing wrong with him," Shawn says. "Let's go."

Shawn walks towards the bridge, dragging the boy along with him. The thin, fog-laced air causes the boy to cough. Every breath he takes is laced with a wheezing sound. Shawn pulls him forward hard, and he stumbles to the ground.

"You can't bring him into Felicity," I say. "He's not old enough to be here."

"There are exceptions to every rule," Shawn says. He grabs the boy by his collar and yanks him back to his feet. "He is more needed in Felicity than he is in Calloway."

I press my hand into my forehead, trying to clear my head. "Does that mean he knows Alexander?"

"Alex didn't do it." The boy cranes his body to the left, twisting Shawn's wrist. "Alex didn't kill Mara! He didn't do it! She was our friend!"

Shawn opens his hand and lets the boy fall hard to the ground. With one swift motion, he swings his fist down across his face. "Shut the hell up."

Blood shoots from the boy's nose. The sight of it makes my stomach turn. I turn my face away, and look out over The Chasm.

"Don't worry, Miss Evelyn," Lauren says. "This will all be over soon."

Shawn pulls the boy back to his feet and glares at him. But the boy, whoever he is, doesn't pay attention to Shawn any longer. He is staring at me with eyes that have almost swollen shut.

"You have to stop this," I say. "You have to bring him back to Calloway."

"I'm sorry," Shawn says as he keeps marching forward. "These decisions are no longer yours to make. Not while you're in the state that you're in.

"It's simply protocol," Lauren says. "You'll be back in control soon enough. You should know that, Miss Evelyn. You wrote the rules."

When we finally reach the library there are four patrols waiting for us out front. Alma is guarding the front door alongside another patrol. Both of their guns are drawn. The other two patrols stand around a body lying dead in the grass. I see pale blue skin peeking out from the pant leg of his dark green uniform. When I stand on my tiptoes I can see the bruises on his neck, framing his collapsed windpipe.

Shawn nudges the body with his foot, and makes a face. "Did they get his gun?"

"Yes, sir," the patrol on the right replies.

" Of course," Shawn says. "Status?"

"The subjects are still inside."

"Obviously."

"I also have three patrols on their way here now." The patrol unclips the radio from his belt. "They should be here any moment to accompany you. The rest of us will stay out here to keep watch in case one of them should escape."

Shawn holds his hand up. "That won't be necessary."

"The subjects are armed," the patrol says. "They've already killed one of us. What makes you think they won't do it again?"

"Because this time we have collateral," Shawn says, tugging on the front of the boy's shirt. "This isn't going to end well for them. One way or the other."

The patrol brings the radio to his lips. "Cancel backup at the library. I repeat: Cancel backup at the library."

"Alright." Shawn turns to me, and smiles. "This is what's going to happen — the four of us will stand right inside the library doors. We can't risk them hearing us walking through the library, and it'll catch them off guard when they see us. It'll be a fun little waiting game."

Shawn pulls the boy forward, and then shoves him back with one quick motion. The boy stumbles to the ground at my feet. I

335

take a step back, and turn my face away, waiting for him to regain his footing. Once he does, Lauren grabs her gun and aims it at his chest. Shawn opens the library doors as quietly as he can, and steps inside with his gun held out in front of him. He turns left, and then right, inspecting the room around him.

"All clear," he whispers. "Come on."

Lauren shoves the boy in the back, making him walk in before us. Once we're all inside, she clutches my arm in hers, and pulls me into her side.

"Whatever it is that you want me to do, I refuse," the boy says.

Shawn sighs, and rolls his eyes. "I'm the one with the gun, you idiot. It doesn't matter if you refuse or not."

A creak echoes through the halls of the library. Shawn smiles, and he turns to face the sound. A wave of nausea rushes over me, turning my skin cold. I squeeze my eyes shut, as the footsteps grow closer.

"It's time," Lauren whispers, squeezing my arm. "Are you ready?"

CHAPTER THIRTY-SIX
Alexander Moore

Char's hand is wrapped around mine as she pulls me to the elevator doors. It's hard to feel my legs as we walk. Every inch of me is on fire, every muscle, every bone. Once we are inside of the elevator I have to lean against the wall to keep myself upright. When Char looks at me I shift my eyes toward the ground, because I do not want the worry in her eyes to be the last thing that I see. Any moment now and I will be gone. I can feel the poison overpowering me.

The elevator groans to life. Char wraps an arm around my waist as we ascend back up into the library. The elevator dings, and then the hatch slides open. Char uses the small elevator rails to steady herself as she exits. Once she's out, she lies on her stomach and extends her hand down to me. I use the rails to raise myself closer to the hatch, and then I let my sister pull me through the opening.

Once we're back on our feet, Char keeps me clutched tight to her side as we walk back through the transponder room. I can feel the floor vibrating beneath my feet, and can't help but wonder if that is the machine buzzing, working hard to emit the poisonous fog into the city.

Once we reach the door leading back out into the library, Char brings us to a halt, and places her free hand on my shoulder. "Can you run?"

I shake my head. "No. I don't think so."

She takes a deep breath, and pulls the gun from her belt. "That's alright. Everything is going to be fine. We'll make it."

I smile and nod, my eyes still focused on the ground. It takes a lot of concentration to make sure my feet are placed one after the other. One wrong step and I will fall. I don't think I'd have the energy to get back up again. The door clicks open. Char pulls me tighter against her side, and she whispers in my ear as we move. She tells me that everything is going to be okay. She assures me that she loves me, and that this will all be over soon. I shift my shoulders enough to bury my face into her neck. I take a deep breath, trying to burn her scent into my memory. Maybe, just maybe, I'll carry it with me when I leave.

We take a few steps into the library. I can feel the warmth of the sun shining down on us from that beautiful dome. Before I have the chance to savor the moment Char's body stiffens. She comes to a sudden halt, and pushes me upright. I'm still trying to blink away the blurriness in my eyes when I see her whip her gun out in front of her. I stumble forward, my head spinning. There are two patrols blocking our exit, and... No. It couldn't be.

"Harry?"

"Alex! Don't listen to them. They're going to—"

His words are cut off by a swift punch to the side of his head. Harry winces, and cradles his head in his hands. The front of his clothes are caked in both blood and dirt, and his skin is so bruised it's turned a deep shade of purple and blue.

"Stop!" I take a step forward, but fall to my knees.

"It's okay," Harry whimpers.

Another patrol, a red-haired girl, has her arms intertwined with Evelyn's. She laughs a horrific, high-pitched laugh, and shakes her head. Her laughter makes the other patrol begin to laugh as well. He pretends to wipe a tear from his eye as he raises his gun and points it at my sister's chest.

"Isn't it beautiful?"

"Let us go," Char commands.

I struggle to get to my feet. Once I do, I begin to cough until I taste the blood trickling down the back of my throat. When it's over, it's hard to breathe. "He needs... he needs to go to Calloway. He... he can't be here."

"Listen to me, Shawn," Char says. Her voice is calm, and soothing. "We need to get Harry and Alex back into Calloway. Alex is sick, and Harry will be sick too if we don't work fast. There isn't much time. If you—"

Shawn laughs. "That's not how this works. Either you surrender and come with me to The Chasm, or your friend dies. It's that simple."

"No," Char says, shaking her head. "You can't take us in without charging us with something. We've done nothing wrong."

"Nothing wrong," Shawn says with a laugh. "Your brother and his friend are wanted for murder. And you, Char, are now wanted for being an accomplice. You also brought a minor into Felicity. That's its own crime, punishable by death."

I clench my fists at my sides, and dig my nails into the flesh of my palms. "We didn't kill Mara. Mara was our friend!"

"Innocent people don't run," the red-haired patrol says. "Why did you run?"

"Because you gave us no other choice," Char says. "You killed Mara, didn't you Shawn? You wanted to pin it on Alex so that you'd have a reason to take him out of the equation. You wanted him gone, because he was too close to figuring it all out and that scared you."

"I have no idea what you're talking about," Shawn says.

My pulse pounds in my ears, blocking out the sound of their voices as they continue to argue. In the end it doesn't matter who killed Mara. She is gone. There is nothing anyone can say or do, no amount of truth that will bring her back. Whether it was Shawn, or another patrol, or even a random stranger on the street makes no difference. It was Evelyn who really killed her. At the core of it all, at the center of everything, there is only Evelyn.

"Okay," I say, and the room falls silent. It's hot in here. Too hot. I wipe a line of sweat from my forehead. "If we surrender will you take us back to Calloway?"

Shawn tilts his head to the side. "Is that what you'd like?"

"No," Char says. "We're not agreeing to anything until you promise both Harry and Alex will be safe."

"Yes. That's what we'd like," I say, ignoring my sister. "Take us to Calloway and I won't put up a fight. You can do what you want once we get there."

"Then no," Shawn says. "You will not be taken back into Calloway. You will meet your fate here, in Felicity. There is no immunity for your actions."

Char shifts her stance, and adjusts her grip on her gun. "Evelyn, you have to do something. Tell them to listen to me. Tell them to take the boys back into Calloway. You know the air here is killing them."

"I'm sorry," Evelyn whispers.

"Look at him!" Char shouts. A tear breaks free and trails down her cheek. "Look at your son! If we don't get him into Calloway he's going to die. I know you don't care about anyone else, but you have to at least care about him."

Harry's face falls. "What do you mean? What's happening?"

"Don't worry," I tell him. "I'm going to be okay."

Evelyn clasps her hands in front of her, and hangs her head. "You're not going to be okay. I'm sorry, Alexander. You weren't supposed to be here."

Char pulls back the hammer of her gun, and, using her left hand for support, aims it at the center of Shawn's chest. "That's it. Let them go, or I'll shoot you."

"Go ahead," Shawn says with a smile. "You shoot me, then Lauren shoots you, she shoots your brother, she shoots your friend, and then finally this bullshit can end."

"Dammit, Evelyn!" Char shouts. Her voice is shaking with anger. "Do something! Tell them to let us unto Calloway!"

"If you talk to her one more time I'm going to put a bullet in your head," Shawn says.

The room around me begins to spin. Everything is a blur. There is a light humming fading in and out of my ears. My head is buzzing, and my heart skips every other beat. I know it won't be long now. Getting into Calloway will make no difference when it comes to me. But Harry? Harry still has a chance.

"Okay," I say. My own voice sounds distant, like I am shouting at myself from the top of a cliff. "We'll surrender."

Char's body stiffens. "Alex, what are you doing?"

"It's alright, Char. It's going to be okay." I turn to Shawn, and raise my hands into the air. "Let me say goodbye to my mother first."

"Don't do it, Alex," Harry cries. "Don't let them take you."

Evelyn smiles, and nods her head at Shawn. He takes a deep breath, and sighs. "Fine. Go ahead. But one wrong move, and I'll kill you."

My eyes are stinging, burning like they've been staring too long at the sun. When I blink, I can feel the heat of my tears trailing down my skin. I approach Evelyn, and stand only inches in front of her. The red-haired patrol, the one that had her arm, gently lets it go and steps to the side with a warm smile on her face.

"I have lived for fifteen years without knowing you," I say. Evelyn's face has grown blurry, turning her hard, dead eyes, soft.

"I've always wanted to meet you, to tell you how much you mean to me, and it looks like this is the last chance I'll get."

Behind me I hear Char clearing her throat. I think she speaks, although the blood pounding through my ears makes it impossible to hear. I try to take a deep breath, but only end up coughing violently. It takes a few moments for me to regain my composure. When I do, I have to ignore Shawn's glare, and the barrel of his gun pointing at my head, as I smile at Evelyn. I stare into her cold, hazel eyes. They are dead. Lifeless.

It's funny to think back to how I got to this moment. A few short days ago I was sitting in my front yard, trying hard to get that damn bike tire to spin correctly. It kept me distracted, because I was too worried about my sister to do much else. It was her death that scared me the most; knowing that in three years time her life with me would be over. Now, it's my life that is ending. It is her that I leave behind. I wonder if she will resent my decision as much as I resented hers.

Evelyn gently caresses my cheek. "I'm sorry, son. Your father would have been very proud of you."

"That's okay." I place my hand over hers, and smile. "Will you hug me? I want to know what it feels like."

Evelyn spreads her arms, and I tuck myself inside of them. I place my cheek on her forehead, and wrap my arms around her neck. There is a calmness spreading through me. For a moment, I feel free. I know what I am about to do is right. Because of this, I am not afraid. No one questioned Evelyn's right to rule because

343

these cities belong to her bloodline. My bloodline. I know what I have to do.

In one quick motion I reach my left hand behind me. I wrap my fingers around the gun still tucked into the back of my pants. Being careful not to draw attention to myself, I swing the gun forward and press the muzzle into Evelyn's chest. I keep my right arm secure around her neck, letting our bodies be the shield that keeps the others from seeing.

I tilt my head back enough to stare into her eyes. "Char will be a better leader than you ever were."

For a moment, as my fingers begin to squeeze down on the trigger, I think I see Evelyn's face soften. She closes her eyes and smiles as the gun goes off. The force of the shot knocks me back. As I stumble to the ground I see Evelyn collapsing, clutching the hole in her chest as blood oozes out from between her fingers. I fall hard onto my back, and smile. There are screams filling the room, and between those screams I hear another gun roar.

A flash of white rips through my vision.

CHAPTER THIRTY-SEVEN
Char Moore

My mouth is dry. The room around me seems to grow darker and darker as I stand with my gun aimed at Shawn. I can see Alex from the corner of my eye. He is pale and sweaty, and every time he blinks his eyes take a little longer to reopen. His muscles take turns trembling. First it's his arms, then his legs, and then both of them together. I've tried to convince Alex that this isn't the way to go; that giving in and surrendering isn't going to fix anything, but he isn't paying attention. He made up his mind the moment he saw Harry.

I can't let him do this. We have to get out of here.

"Evelyn, you have to do something," I say. "Tell them to listen to me. Tell them to take the boys back into Calloway. You know the air here is killing them."

"I'm sorry," Evelyn whispers.

"Look at him! Look at your son! If we don't get him into Calloway he's going to die. I know you don't care about anyone else, but you have to at least care about him."

I stare at Evelyn, trying to block out the pained screams of Harry as he tries to make sense of his friend's fate. I can't help but wince when Alex lies and tells him that he's going to be okay. There isn't enough time to argue.

Evelyn clasps her hands in front of her, and hangs her head. "You're not going to be okay. I'm sorry, Alexander. You weren't supposed to be here."

I take a deep breath and pull back the hammer of my gun. I shift to the right, making sure the barrel is pointed right in the center of Shawn's chest. "That's it. Let them go, or I'll shoot you."

Shawn smiles with his yellow teeth. "Go ahead. You shoot me, then Lauren shoots you, she shoots your brother, she shoots your friend, and then finally this bullshit can end."

My heart is pounding against my ribs. I swallow the hard lump forming in my throat. I try to keep my body still as I tremble with anger. "Dammit, Evelyn! Do something! Tell them to let us into Calloway!"

"If you talk to her one more time I'm going to put a bullet in your head," Shawn says.

My eyes dart around the room, looking for another way out. I can't run because there is nowhere else to go, and Alex wouldn't make it more than a few steps. Lauren is gripping Evelyn's arm tight with one hand. A gun is in her other hand, but it hangs haphazardly at her side as if she's already come to the conclusion that she won't need to use it. If I shoot Shawn, I may have enough time to shoot Lauren before she can react. But how many other patrols are waiting for us on the other side of the door? I doubt I have enough bullets to get rid of all of them.

"Okay," I hear Alex say. His voice is small, and weak. "We'll surrender."

My muscles stiffen. "Alex, what are you doing?"

"It's alright, Char. It's going to be okay." He raises his hands in the air. "Let me say goodbye to my mother first."

I keep my eyes on Shawn as Alex trudges over to Evelyn. Seeing him sends a shiver of dread down my spine. The hairs on the back of my neck stand up on end, and my insides are empty and hollow. I can't figure it out. I can't figure out what Alex is doing. My ears grow hot, and every breath I take is cut short by the pain in my chest.

I clench my jaw tight. It sends a pain shooting through my temple. Shawn has his gun focused on Alex. I can't see what my brother is doing without risking his life. I need to watch Shawn. I'm too afraid to even blink.

I clear my throat, hoping to draw my brother's attention. "Think about what you're doing, Alex. We can still make it out of here. Please. Please, don't give up. Come with me. I'll find a way out of this. You have to trust me."

I am like a ghost: unseen, unheard, as I watch my brother tuck himself into Evelyn's arms from the corner of my eye. The sight of his frail, limp body pressing into his mother's chest makes my heart hurt. My head is humming; my mind is spinning. This isn't like Alex. My brother wanted nothing to do with our mother. What is he doing? Why this? Why now?

The longer I hold my gun in the air the heavier it feels. The weight of this moment is pressing down, down, down on my arms, telling me to give in. But I won't. I can't. It takes everything in me to keep my hands steady, to keep the gun aimed at Shawn. Sweat drips down my forehead. I can feel it resting on the tip of my nose. I bite my bottom lip and steal a quick glance at Alex. He is still buried deep inside of Evelyn's embrace.

"Okay, Alex. That's enough," I say. "Come on. It's time to get out of here."

No one is listening.

"Alex! That's enough!"

A knot is forming in my chest, and it grows bigger with each passing moment. My heart is beating so hard, and so loud, that I have to swallow in order breathe. Shawn is growing angrier, his face reddening. He shakes his head, and his nostrils flare in and out. Lauren places a hand on his shoulder, and whispers something into his ear. For a moment I think he will finally relax, but then I see a flash of green.

A gunshot echoes inside the library walls.

I catch Shawn pulling the hammer back on his gun. The shot didn't come from him. He wasn't the one that fired. My skin grows cold. I tilt my head enough to see Evelyn stumbling back. She falls hard to the ground with a hand clasped over her chest. Blood is oozing out from between her fingers.

I scream my brother's name as Shawn fires his gun. I am still screaming as I aim at his chest, and pull the trigger. He stumbles back. I fire two more shots. The gun falls from his limp fingers, and it thuds against the floor. I gasp for air, unable to breathe, unable to think. I shake my head, trying to clear my mind.

"Char!" Harry screams.

Harry lunges forward, wrapping his arms around Lauren as she fires her gun. Three loud, echoing shots pierce the air around us. A sharp pain radiates from my shoulder. I fall to my knees, clutching my chest. Harry is still trying to wrestle the gun away from Lauren. I shout for him to move, and he dives onto the ground. The pain screams through my shoulder as I raise my arm, and fire two shots. I wait for the sound of Lauren's body to thud against the ground before I let my gun fall from my hand. I crawl my way to Alex. My shoulder is throbbing. My head is pounding. I can feel the tips of my fingers growing cold.

I scoop him into my arms, and cradle his head.

"No. No. No," is the only word I can mumble.

Blood is trickling from a small hole at the center of his temple. It's drenching my shirt, and pooling on the ground around my knees. I press my hand against his wound to try to stop the blood. I can't see. Everything is going white. My skin grows cold. Cold, except the palm of my hand, kept warm by my brother's blood.

"He's gone," Harry cries. "He's gone, Char. He's gone. Why is he gone?"

My throat tightens. I can no longer breathe. The smell of his blood fills my nostrils. I let Alex's body fall from my arms. Harry tries to grab ahold of me but I twist myself around, and begin to crawl away. The room is spinning. It's spinning, and spinning, and I cannot stop it. Someone has stolen my air. I can't breathe. I can't breathe.

I press my face into the cold, hard floor and I scream. He is gone. My brother is gone. Harry grabs my shoulders, and tries to pull me up. I squeeze my eyes shut and clench every muscle as I scream. I scream until my throat is raw, until my body trembles. Beside me I feel Harry pressing into my side. He wedges himself in front of me, grabs my face, and holds it in his hands.

"I... I can't breathe," he chokes out.

I push my hair from my eyes, and wipe the vomit from my lip. My shoulder is throbbing with pain. As I am still shaking, and trembling, Harry has grown pale. His eyes roll into the back of his head, and he falls onto his side.

I grab his shoulders, and shake him hard. "Harry? Harry!"

I lift his chest to my ear, and listen. He is still breathing. He might still have time. My right hand falls to the side as I try to think, and something hard and small brushes against my palm.

That's it. That has to be it.

With trembling fingers I reach into my pocket, and pull out the breather.

I shove the tip of it inside of Harry's mouth and slam my thumb on the button.

I collapse onto my back and hear him take a clear, deep breath.

Then I close my eyes, and let the world go black.

CHAPTER THIRTY-EIGHT
Char Moore

I fold up the last pair of my pants and shove them into my patrol pack. It is strong, and durable. It'll last longer than these cities ever will. I zip up the pack, and slump it to the ground at my feet. I sit down on the edge of my bed, and take a look around my old bedroom. This room reminds of things as they used to be; how they should still be. I put a hand over my heart, and dig my nails into the skin. The pain from my wound radiates down through my arm.

There is a soft knock at the door.

I drop my hand to my side, and sit up straight. "Yeah?"

The door creaks open, and Harry pokes his head inside. "Archer is here to see you. Can we come in?"

"Yes, of course," I say.

Archer and Harry stand shoulder to shoulder in front of me, both in patrol green. Establishing a new set of patrols in Calloway was the first thing I did. Putting Harry in charge of them was the second. His lungs will never be fully healed, and he can't run or exert himself anymore, but he's the person I trust the most for the job.

After those orders were put in place I made sure to change the way the patrols are run. Now those who enlist are given a five-year term, and after that term is up they are free to live as they choose. There are no more of Evelyn's secrets for them to keep, no more reason for their terms to end in death. It's a small start, but it's one that I hope will change our city for the better.

"Hey newbie," Archer says with a smile. "I have a status report for you."

I clear my throat. "Okay."

"Felicity's held up well since Evelyn's departure. The people there had no idea what had happened. It's been two months now, and no one's talked about it. No one even misses her. Turns out she didn't have many friends, and those that do remember her have no idea who she really was."

"Good," I say, then turn my attention to Harry. "What about Calloway?"

Harry straightens his back and stands up tall. "Doctor Mitchell has set up an office at the front of town. He's only been set up for two weeks and he's already got a good stream of visitors. Um... what else? Oh, setting up the garden was a great idea. It looks like we've already got some lettuce popping up."

I smile. "Is that so?"

"Yeah! Maybe a few more months and we'll be able to start harvesting."

"That's great," I say, plucking a stray piece of lint from my pants.

"You should see it out there, Char. Things are going to change. People are happier. You can feel their energy when you walk through the streets."

That is because I have given them a purpose. I have given them opportunity here, hoping they will no longer be obsessed with what lies on the other side of the bridge. Now the residents can choose a job to keep them busy. They can become gardeners, carpenters, housemaids, or patrols. Some of the older ones have chosen to take on the roll of educator, or care taker.

Whether I've truly given them purpose, or if this is only a temporary distraction, the people do seem to be adjusting well to the change. It's too soon to tell how stable things will become in the future, but if Harry says that the people are happier now, I'm going to trust him. I only wish there were more that I could do.

Archer plops himself down on the bed next to me. "How have you been holding up?"

I shrug my shoulders. "I'm fine."

"Things are good," he says.

"Not as good as they could be."

"Turn the machine off, Char. Let the people know the truth."

I shake my head, slowly. "You know I can't do that."

"Why can't you? They'll adjust. People are more resilient than you give them credit for."

"No, Archer," I say. "People are selfish. They take pride in the things they own. Those things – their homes, their possessions – make them happy. You can't give them paradise, and then rip it away from their unsuspecting hands."

Archer runs his fingers through his hair, and stares at the ground for a minute as he thinks. "Okay." He runs his tongue over his teeth, and then perks up. "Well, what if you do it gradually? It won't be so sudden."

"I've thought of that already. That would only make things worse."

"I don't see how that's possible."

"Do something for me." I turn to Archer, and grab his hands. "Imagine the most beautiful thing you've ever seen. Now imagine that thing is sitting here in the palm of your hand. You can feel it. You can hold it. It's yours to keep forever, and the simple thought of owning it makes you happier than you've ever been. Are you imagining it?"

"I don't understand what you're doing," Archer says.

"Now, imagine that beautiful thing turning to dust in your hands," I say. "This thing that you loved, that you thought you had forever, has become sand falling through the cracks of your fingers. You watched it slowly wither and decay and there was not a damn thing you could do to save it. You are left feeling helpless, and lost. That is what would happen to Felicity."

Archer pushes my hands away from his, and scrambles to his feet. His eyes shift between me, and the backpack slouched on the ground. "You're going to walk away, and forget it all, the same way she did. You've given up before you've even started."

I press my lips together, and stare at the wall beside me. "I'm nothing like her."

Harry clears his throat, and fidgets with the hem of his shirt. "Look, Char. I know how you're feeling. I lost a brother, too. But you can't run away. Not when we need you the most."

"I'm not running away," I say.

Those words are dripping with lies, and it's hard for me to hide it. They're right. I am running away. I am running because I can no longer look at Felicity without feeling sick. The city fills me with disgust. There is a part of me that wishes I had never learned the truth. The people of Felicity go about their lives, laughing, smiling, oblivious. To them it is real. To them, nothing has changed. Nothing ever happened. They will never know what Alexander did for them. The thought makes me sick.

Everyone in Calloway knows the name Alexander Moore. Even the patrols know who my brother was. The stories I've heard of him over the last few weeks have made my heart ache for him. I learned that he helped someone fix a broken sink after he overheard them talking about it at the General Store. He once shared his last roll of bread with a girl he found clutching her stomach with hunger. Alexander didn't even know her name, but she never forgot his. It's stories like those that make me miss him the most.

Three days after word spread of my brother's sacrifice, I found his bike on the front lawn. The person who stole it had a change of heart. The front tire was fixed, and it even had a new set of handlebars installed. When I gave the bike to Harry he couldn't stop crying.

Every single person here in Calloway knows of Alexander Moore.

Those in Felicity would never understand.

Archer crosses his arms over his chest, and clenches his teeth together. "What do you call it then? If it's not running away, what is it?"

"I'm searching," I say.

"Searching for what?"

My eyes scan the floor of the room, and I take a deep breath. "Life. Other cities. Anything. There is a world beyond those trees that we have all been conditioned to ignore. Back when Evelyn was still a child, when that storm destroyed her home, she was told that help would come. That's what she said. Her whole reason for going to the library was to send a signal for help. That means there are people out there, Archer. There could be land better than this. We could rebuild somewhere else."

"Don't be stupid, Char. There isn't anything left out there," Harry says.

"He might be right," Archer says. "What if there's nothing left? You don't know how dangerous it could be. You don't know anything about it."

I snatch the backpack from the ground, and swing it over my shoulder, wincing at the pain. It is a sharp reminder of what I've been through to get to this point. The wound is always throbbing, like an old heartbeat. "I suppose I won't know until I look."

"You can't do this," Harry says. His eyes are glistening, but he keeps his chin high.

I place my hands on the sides of his heads, and smile. "You'll be fine without me. I promise."

I turn toward the bedroom door, but before I get the chance to take a step forward, Archer grabs me by my arm. He whips me around until I am facing him. "This is where you belong. Running away isn't going to fix anything. You are our leader now."

"Yes," I say, shrugging out from under his grasp, "and as your leader, it is my job to make sure the people are safe. I can only fix so much, Archer. The truth still stands: The children can't keep living on their own, and they still can't cross the bridge. If we are going to survive, we're going to have to do so somewhere else. There is no life for us here anymore."

I don't wait for either of them to respond before I march out the door. My feet carry me through the run-down kitchen, through the dust-covered living room, and out the splintered front door. I stand on the front stair, and look out over the city. It's a beautiful day. The sun is shining bright, warming everything it touches. A few sprigs of green grass are poking through the weeds.

I hear the laughter of children rising up through the air. When I turn to look behind me I see two little girls skipping arm in arm down the street, smiling. One is wearing a pale yellow dress, and the other is wearing a small button down shirt with a pair of light blue jeans.

They smile at me as they skip past, then a few seconds later the girl in the yellow dress pulls her friend to a stop. She turns and stares at me, wide-eyed. "This is Alexander's house."

The other girl gasps. "That must mean you're Char."

357

I nod. "That's right. Where are you two headed? Off somewhere fun?"

The girl in the dress does a little dance with her feet, and squeezes her friend's arm a little tighter. "We're going to The Chasm!"

"Yeah!" the other girl says excitedly. "We want to see if we can get a little closer than we did last time."

I laugh, and shake my head. "Why would you want to do something like that?"

"Because," the girl in the dress says, shrugging.

"Because we want to see Felicity," the other girl says. "Have you been there? Is it as beautiful as they say?"

"I heard that you can see the lights at night, but I'm too scared to go there when it's dark."

"She's too scared. I'm not."

My throat grows tight. "But—"

"Do you know Billy Thompson?" the girl in the dress asks.

I shake my head. Everything feels numb.

"Billy Thompson said he's going to try to cross over on his own next week," the girl continues. "He said at nighttime the guards are too tired to pay attention. He said he's going to make it."

The other girl nudges her friend in the side. "You weren't supposed to say anything!"

"What? She has the right to know," the girl in the dress says.

"But... but there's nothing in Felicity," I say weakly. "No. He can't cross over. He can't."

"Okay, well... don't arrest us," the girl says, as she tugs her friend in the yellow dress back down the road. "It was only a rumor."

I stand there and stare at them as they begin to shuffle off. My heart is racing, my head spinning. I stumble forward, and cup my hands over my mouth. "Tell Billy not to cross!"

The girl in the dress waves her hand in the air, and then tucks her head close to her friend's ear. She whispers something, which makes them both laugh hysterically. I can still hear the echo of their voices as they turn the corner, and disappear behind a boarded up blue house. I take a deep breath, and let the air fill my lungs. My fingers clutch the straps of my backpack as I swallow down the lump that had built up in my throat.

Everything is going to be okay.

I turn on my heels, and begin to walk to the back of Calloway. I can see the faint silhouette of the trees clustered over the horizon. There is nothing to worry about. Everything will be fine without me.

Things are going to change.

They have to change.

THE FORGOTTEN

ABOUT THE AUTHOR

M. Stringfield is a writer by day, and a reader by night. She is a lover of action-packed stories, whether they are thriller, horror, or science fiction. She is naturally drawn to everything weird, and a little bit crazy. She lives in a suburb of Chicago, Illinois with her husband, two children, and goofy looking dog.

You can learn more about her by visiting her website, mstringfield.com.